TO UNITE A REALM

Mary Beesley

Boroughs
Publishing Group

www.BOROUGHSPUBLISHINGGROUP.com

TO UNITE A REALM
Copyright © 2020 Mary Beesley

ISBN 978-1-953810-19-9

To my courageous Grandpa and Grandma Robert and June Matheson, and to all my Scottish ancestors from the Clans: Matheson, Gray, Stuart, Campbell, Robertson, Stewart, Ross, Bain, Sinclair, Wilson, and Taylor.

In Fac Et Spera (Do and Hope)

4

ACKNOWLEDGMENTS

Thank you to Boroughs Publishing Group. To Michelle and the entire team for believing in my book and for bringing my story into the light.

Thank you to my family, especially my mom and sister, Katherine, for reading my early drafts and giving me much needed encouragement.

Thank you for my husband and kids for all the times you let me lock myself in the office to write.

Thank you to Rebekah Romney for not only critiquing my manuscript, but answering the phone when I call. Thank you for sharing your expertise as an attorney and a writer.

Thank you to my Texas writer's group: Jen Looft, Jen Johnson, Lisa Lewis, Debbie Ochoa, Stacy Wells, Priya Ardis, and Nuha Said. Thank you to my California writer's group: Jen White, Autumn McAlpin, and Cara Cragun. You've all spent hours poring over my words. I wouldn't be here without you.

Most importantly, thanks to God for inspiring me to start writing fiction seven years ago, for gifting me the perseverance to keep going, and the creativity to spin a compelling story.

TO UNITE A REALM

CHAPTER 1

Rebel

The blood in my veins froze at the glint of steel Chief Bear Gray angled against Trista's throat. I stood in front of the crowd at the East Tower, watching the horror unfold in the middle of the courtyard. At my side, my sister Lanie tucked her shaking arms against her ribs.

"Vera," Lanie whispered my name like a plea, but I could do nothing to save Trista from the Grays. The tyrants had killed my friends before.

"It was an accident." My father, the chamberlain of our small conquered country of Campbell, stood before Bear Gray. Father's expression was grim, the irises of his eyes blue pinholes in a sea of white.

A three-foot-tall eun perched on Father's shoulders, the bird's deadly claws dangerously close to his throat. The Grays cultivated the horrid birds in secret. They took our precious innovations but didn't share their treasures.

Standing behind Trista, Bear's son Angus held a pistol at the ready, its muzzle pointed at the ground. His eyes were the color of frosted sky and his angled jaw was set in hard lines. Despite the acidic hatred burning in my lungs, I knew before I could rest I would have to draw his beautiful murderous face in aching detail.

Bear's blade stayed perilously close to Trista's windpipe, but he rotated his shoulders to look at my father, who stood a few feet to his right. "When was the last time you had an accident at one of yer labs?" His growling voice rumbled across the crowded courtyard.

Father paled. His shoulders curled in against the threatening bird and the chief's accusations.

"When was the last time you lost an entire batch of red velvet vaccine?" Bear spoke with the uncivilized accent of Alta Glenn, all slurred words and round edges. Dark hair covered the back of his hand holding the knife at Trista's throat.

My vision blinked in and out as dread roared through me. They were never supposed to have found out Trista destroyed the precious red velvet vaccine they'd come to steal. How had it gone so terribly wrong?

I turned to Lanie, but she only had eyes for the cruel chief. She worked in the red velvet labs. She wouldn't have answers. She wasn't a rebel. Lanie would rather marry Angus than kill him.

"Unfortunately, even with all our safeguards," Father answered, "mistakes are made."

"Aye," Bear said. "They are." His words were stones around my neck, condemning us. We were going to die, join the long list of people destroyed by the Grays.

Trista yelped as Bear reached out with his left hand and grabbed her arm.

"You were the last person in the lab last night?" Bear's nose buckled in the middle and bent slightly right. He'd broken it two years ago fighting Ian Wallace, and he'd never had it set properly—a warning to would-be rebels.

She nodded miserably. "I'm sure the refrigeration was on and working properly when I left."

"Then what happened?"

She looked like a toy doll in Bear's ferocious clamp. Her lip quivered.

Fear turned my body to ice.

"Any number of things could have cut power to the lab," Father said. "With the influx of people using electricity in the West Tower—" He sent a meaningful glance around the courtyard of the Cromarty Institute, especially at the fifty armed men and women from Alta Glenn who'd accompanied Bear and Angus on this annual visit to Campbell.

Saddled horses twitched and stomped on the manure-smeared cobblestones. The Grays didn't usually bring an army. I should have discouraged Trista, but we'd agreed the "rulers" didn't deserve the difficult-to-make vaccine. This batch was promised to the people of

Hogg, the marshy domain to the east. They'd suffered a serious outbreak. Children were dying by the dozen.

Bear's eyes widened. "Yer blaming *us*?"

Father shrugged, the bird on his shoulders ruffling. Those creatures sensed far too much. "It explains the timing. The circuit breakers could have easily tripped and shut down. The cooling machine for the serum must be manually reset when the electricity surges or disrupts. It happens all the time."

I bit my lip, hope a desperate swelling in my heart. Father had delivered that line perfectly. My eyes flickered over Bear's face. *Believe him. Believe it was an accident.*

Bear's knuckles went white as he tightened his grip on Trista's bicep. "Is he telling the truth?"

To my horror, she hesitated. Her gaze flashed to Father. "Yes."

Bear's eyes narrowed. "York."

With a rustle of feathers, a silver-winged eun perched on a woman's forearm spread its wings. I flinched. The wingspan, longer than a man was tall, spread a shadow like ragged teeth over the ground. It flapped slowly, and landed next to Trista. My pulse tripled.

The birds could detect lies.

Bear released her arm and lowered the blade from her throat. "Kneel."

She whimpered as she obeyed. It hurt to watch, but I couldn't look away. I didn't blink.

"Hold out yer arms, palms up on the ground," Bear ordered.

Trista splayed her limbs over the cobblestones. Tears streaked her face. She looked to Father, but his face was impassive. What could he do? What could any of us do? I chewed on the inside of my cheek as I failed at finding a way out of this.

The eun's curved talons clamped her wrists.

"Tell me what happened to our vaccines," Bear said. "Look at York when you answer."

Trista's body shook, but her words came out stiff, as if reciting them. "The vaccine should be kept at forty degrees at all times. If it gets above fifty, the serum will spoil and the vaccines are no longer effective. Last night, the refrigeration failed. This morning the doses had reached sixty-one degrees."

The bird watched her in silence.

"Has this happened before?" Bear asked.

"Yes," Trista said.

"Lie." The bird's voice was fingernails on slate—a shock every time an eun spoke. Chilling prickles skittered down my nerves at the raspy accusation.

Bear's jaw worked. "What happened with the refrigeration?"

"I don't know," Trista said.

"Lie," York said.

I gnawed my knuckles, willing the bird to be quiet.

Bear crouched at her side, the leather of his boots creaking. His knife slid forward, resting against her throat again. "Did you turn off the refrigeration?"

She shook her head, but stopped when her skin split against the blade. Her eyes popped wide and rolled down, trying to see the weapon. I took an involuntary step forward, but Lanie clamped her hand on my arm, stopping me.

"Answer the question." Bear's voice was low and chilling.

"Yes."

Tears built behind my eyes. *No.*

"Why?" Bear asked.

Her eyes flashed with defiance. "Those vaccines should have gone to Hogg. To the outbreak centers. You don't deserve our protection."

"That's treason." His pronouncement landed like boulders.

She spit in his face.

My entire body lit on fire.

The glistening glob slicked down Bear's cheekbone and into his beard. "Any last words?" His voice was too calm.

"No." The cry tore from my chest. Father's warning gaze cut to me as Lanie's hand clamped over my mouth, smothering my scream.

Bear ignored me, but Angus's stunning gray eyes, shimmering with anger, settled on me. Searing white flame burned up my belly. I latched onto Lanie's forearm, my nails digging into her sweater as I pressed her palm tighter against my lips.

"This is only the beginning." Trista's eyes had turned to coal chips. She lifted her chin.

"No." Bear's shoulders drooped. "This is the end."

It happened so fast. One heartbeat Trista was kneeling, proud and vibrant. The next, red poured down her neck, her face ashen and gasping. Wet gurgles bubbled up her broken throat.

Bear lay her on the ground, and his murderous hand turned almost gentle as he rested it on her hair.

His face was dark, his eyes hooded as he watched her until she no longer moved—her life dripping off the blade at his side. My legs turned to wet noodles.

Though Trista lay there, I kept seeing Emilia. Another friend. Killed. Terror sliced through my body. It could've been me.

Lanie's fingers on my face went limp and fell. I sucked in a ragged wheeze.

A woman in the crowd screamed. The pack of Glenns took a step closer to their chief. Angus's jaw was tight and his expression unreadable as he stared at my friend's fallen form.

Monster.

I grit my teeth to stop myself from yelling the string of vile curses building on my tongue.

"The punishment for treason is death." Bear's voice was eerily calm as his gaze raked over the stone-faced Campbells. "You do not help yourselves by destroying the strength and integrity of our United Realm. Divided we cannot stand." Bear turned his burning gaze on my father's blank stare. "How quickly can you have another batch of vaccines ready?"

"I haven't had a chance to assess the state of the serums, but I expect it will be months."

Bear's nostrils flared, and his mustache quivered. "Make it weeks."

Father lifted his hands up, palms open. "We will do our best, but science is not an unruly child to be pummeled into submission."

By the uptick of Bear's brow, it seemed the chief understood Father's words were an insult to their crude ways. Bear whistled, and the eun on Father's shoulders launched into the air so roughly it left a dripping red line on Father's collar.

"Put your house in order. I don't want to return here after the gathering to do it for you." Bear paused, and I heard his final unspoken threat in my heart: *After I've killed you too.*

Father swallowed and bowed. "That won't be necessary." He wrapped a thin hand around his neck, as if imagining it severed from his body. His fingers came away bloody.

Bear's gaze locked on me like a predator finding prey. My tongue turned to sand. "Good." Terrors of all creeping demons, he smiled at me. "We'll look forward to Lanie and Vera joining us at the gathering." He turned to my father. "May it not be yer last." His threat hung in the air like poisoned fog.

Why must *I* go to the gathering? Lanie was going to become chamberlain of Campbell after my father. She should be the only one they required at the gathering.

Angus watched me, a crease between his brows. At twenty-four, he stood a palm taller than his father and had the same thick brown hair, although his was cropped short about his ears.

I forced my expression into an emotionless mask, but my stomach twisted into painful knots.

Traitors were killed at the gathering.

The Grays retreated to their waiting horses and mounted. Without a backwards glance, they trotted out of the courtyard. A stampede of men, women, and horses raced south out of Campbell, toward the coastal domain of Porto.

I hoped they would all get red velvet disease.

CHAPTER 2

Belle Borg

Father, Mother, Lanie, and I boarded the Ormond Fort Train, a black hunk of steam- and smoke-smeared metal. Wolfton, the Grays' regent to Campbell, two of Father's advisors, and four personal guards accompanied us. Wolfton's coat had the Grays' twin pine tree insignia embroidered on the breast. As if I'd ever doubt his loyalty to them.

I sat next to the window, tucked my tweed skirt around my legs, and stuck my nose to the glass. Outside, steam danced around workers loading boxes into the belly of the waiting train—boxes filled with tools, toys, and technologies from our many factories. All going to the Grays. All in exchange for the privilege of being their subjects. I buried the worry that we rode to our death and let curiosity take over.

I'd never been to Alta Glenn. I'd been to visit Emilia and Ian Wallace in Hogg, and Father had promised me a trip to Porto this summer. He wanted Fitzgerald Marsh to court me. I wanted to see the ocean and harbors.

"Good morning, Lady Vera."

I tilted toward the voice. A guard sat across from me, his knees nearly touching mine. I stared, first because I wondered what he wanted, and then because he was nice to look at. He had light brown skin, amber eyes, and dark hair tied up in a knot on top of his head.

"I'm Koda." He smiled.

I couldn't stop my lips from mirroring his. He glanced down at my smile. "How old are you?"

"Twenty-one," he said.

A year younger than I. "Young for a guard."

"I've completed my training and this is my first position."

"I'm glad to hear my safety is in such experienced hands." My voice was flat as water.

Koda winked.

I blinked. *Flirt.*

He revealed a handsome smile.

I turned back to the window to hide my blush.

The train gave a screech and lurched into motion. Lanie scurried over and took the seat next to me. We sped through the industrial sector and into cultivated fields. I meant to draw skeletal sketches of the changing landscape, but my traitorous pencil kept drawing Koda. I sketched him with romantic eyes and a stronger jaw than was strictly accurate. I tilted my book up in embarrassment. Lanie got a peek, and she nodded in appreciation. I chuckled, and Koda turned his golden eyes on us. He raised his brows in question. My lower lip curled between my teeth as I drew him again.

Two hours later we crossed the border, leaving Campbell and the life I knew. I held my breath over the bridge crossing the Stuart River and remained tense after that. The train barreled up a hill and as we crested, Belle Borg came into view.

The sprawling acropolis had been built a hundred years ago on the backs of the defeated soldiers from Campbell, Porto, Perth, and Hogg. Great-Great-Grandfather Gray had come out of his mountain cave and conquered every southern land between him and the sea, as well as the Perths to the east.

Belle Borg, the symbol of bondage and bloodshed, was beautiful. The white stone castle capped the mountaintop like glittering snow. Long glass windows winked in the sunlight. Flags waved their sinister welcome.

I'd heard the Grays only lived at Belle Borg during the annual gathering each spring. I couldn't imagine why they would choose tents in the high mountains over this splendor. The train dashed down the neighboring slope, and the castle disappeared behind a high wall. The train track ended outside the western gate. We lurched to a stop.

"Koda, you shadow Vera," Father said as he walked through the cabin. "Milo, don't let Lanie out of your sight."

Milo was a veteran guard we knew well. Lanie's shoulders dropped. I would've been happy to trade her my young pup, but I wasn't the heir to Campbell. Koda stood—my same height. He strapped a baldric with four knives to his chest and checked the pistol at his hip before shrugging on a jacket. His presence at my side provided zero reassurance as I stepped out onto Alta Glenn soil.

Cold wind bit my face. I shrugged my shawl closer, grateful for the high neck on my sweater. An eun with wings like coal tracked our progress from its station on the wall. With mounting trepidation, I ascended the path to Belle Borg. The open portcullis glinted like teeth waiting to devour me.

The grand entry crawled with people. The floors were hewn from precious wood. Thick drapes and oil paintings decorated the walls. I marveled at the beauty, but also the waste. The stone and plaster buildings in Campbell did not greet me with this kind of warmth and welcome.

A woman strode forward, addressed us by name, and led us up a polished wood staircase and down a long wooden floored hallway and into a suite with wood walls and heavy timber beams on the ceiling. I ran my hand over the warm wall panels, my mouth ajar.

"It's not such a commodity here," Mother said. "Alta Glenn is immensely forested."

Lanie darted off to explore the suite, and Father left with his guard and advisors. Our other three guards fanned out to check the security of our rooms. As if they could possibly keep us safe. If Bear wanted us dead, we hadn't the slimmest hope. Ian and his brothers had all been strong and trained to fight. Little good it did them.

Before their deaths, Father had a close relationship with Chamberlain Wallace from Hogg. The Wallace family would visit Campbell often. Emilia Wallace was like another sister to me. We took all our lessons together when she came to Cromarty Institute. Her older brother, Ian, spent hours convincing me of the many reasons Hogg and Campbell would be better off on our own without Alta Glenn and the tyrannical Grays. I wiped leaking eyes and swallowed back my emotions.

Glenn porters brought in our trunks and handed over a letter. Mother read the note before passing it to me.

Welcome Hugo and Margaret Wilson and the lovely ladies, Lanie and Vera.

Please join us in the Emerald Dining Room for dinner at sunset. Please feel free to dress down.

I jerked my head. "Are they mocking us?"

Mother chuckled. "Someone is poking fun."

"They expect us to go to a formal dinner in nothing but a shirt and pants."

"I assure you, they do not expect that from us."

"Vera." Lanie's excited voice filtered over from another room. "You need to see this."

Mother and I traipsed into the sitting room. It wasn't the deep couch or watercolor paintings that held my attention: it was the wall of glass.

Lanie shifted back and forth, nearly dancing, in front of a living mural. I staggered at the size of the distant northern mountains frosted with white. A dense forest blotted the east in darkness. Sheep dotted verdant pastures in the valley below. Besides the smattering of barns, no buildings marred the overwhelming expanse of wilderness.

I clutched the solid chair next to me to stop the feeling of free fall. Hand firmly around wood, I was still safe and warm and firmly inside. The city of McAndrew, my home, with its polished streets and mini manicured gardens, felt a world away.

"Thrilling, isn't it," Mother said, her pale eyes bright.

"Dizzying," I said.

"Shall we get ready for dinner?"

"Yes." Lanie brought a hand to her tightly bound waist. "I'm half starved."

Lanie and I each had our own bedroom, a treat since we shared at home. I flung onto the bed, thinking how fun it would be to sprawl out during the night. The bed looked softer than it was. I landed with an abrupt *thud*.

Koda's worried face appeared at the door. "You okay?"

I propped on my elbows. "You going to jump at every bump?"

"Yes."

"Knock first." I waved him away, but his attentiveness sent a secret flush through me.

Lanie came in. "Did you see your shower has a window?" She darted across the room and into the lavvy before jumping back like an overexcited child. "It must be the strangest sensation to be looking outside while naked." Her eyes danced as if imagining the brazen thrill. "What are we wearing tonight? I don't want to wear my best dress, but I want to make a good first impression. The Marshes are going to be there," she squealed in delight.

I flopped back on the bed. I hadn't seen the Marsh twins since they graduated last year from Cromarty and returned to Porto. A week before he'd left, I'd given Fitzgerald my first kiss.

I'd taken him down to the river to show him the mural I'd helped create. Only the two of us, in our private world of under the bridge. He'd held my hand, our fingers twining together. He'd brushed a loose piece of hair behind my ear and cupped a warm palm around my neck.

"Your painting is beautiful, Vera." Fitz wasn't looking at the bridge's colorful underbelly. Freckled lips leaned closer.

I stopped breathing entirely.

Fingers worked into my hair, sending chills down my spine. "But it doesn't compare to this view."

Our lips met. He wrapped my waist and scooted me closer. I'm not sure we were all that good at the kissing, but we had fun practicing. When I finally pulled away, he held my hand all the way to dinner. Fitz graduated the next week and returned home to Porto. He hadn't written.

Not to be cowed by the Gray's rude invitation, I picked out a pink dress with puffed sleeves and a heavy petticoat. Mother plaited my hair and wrapped the braid around my crown twice.

Koda waited near the door. A black dinner jacket hid his weapons. Father hadn't returned. With our guards in tow, we set out for the emerald dining room.

"You look beautiful," Koda whisper as I walked past.

I smiled, but didn't let him see it. We rounded a corner, and I jerked backwards, ramming squarely into his chest. His arms flew protectively around me as his eyes scanned the hall.

Flustered by the unexpected warmth of his hands, I shifted away. "Sorry." I brushed out invisible wrinkles in my skirt. "That surprised me." I waved a hand at the kyoto head suspended on the wall. Yellow canines curled over a hairy jaw. Horns shadowed beady eyes.

Koda's shoulders loosened, and he laughed lightly.

"There are many more of those around here," Mother said.

I straightened my back and glared at the gaping maw and dead eyes above me. "Let's go."

In the dining room, green marble fireplaces roared at either end of the rectangular space. Strangers conversed next to a long table. Bear and Angus stood together near the far end. They didn't wear dinner jackets. Thin cotton clung to Angus's broad chest. I hated myself for noticing his remarkable body. None of the models in my artist's anatomy class had ever looked like Angus. I forced my focus away as my fingers twitched for a pencil.

The Perth contingent wore swaths of bright fabric wrapped around their heads and bodies. Bead-embroidered jackets distinguished the new ruling family from Hogg. I couldn't look at them. They were the Wallaces' replacements.

"Lanie." Misty Marsh strutted over, high-heeled boots clinking. Lips and eyes popped with heavy makeup.

Porto had always been the hub of new fashions. Her shining black pants looked painted on, revealing the shape of her curvy legs. Lanie pursed her lips in annoyance, and Mother politely didn't look down. I felt like an overstuffed armchair.

"You're here," Misty said.

Forced to be here.

Misty clasped Lanie's arm, her eyes full of mischief. "Let's go talk to Angus."

I didn't follow.

"You're going to miss the Younger," she called back over her shoulder.

I turned at the teasing voice. "I haven't missed him yet."

Fitzgerald Marsh approached. His gaze roamed down the length of me, and he crinkled his auburn brows. "You're looking quite dressed." His blue eyes glittered.

"You missed a button."

His focus dropped to where his open collar revealed freckled collarbones. He chuckled. "Tell me you have pants for the hunt at least."

"I don't need pants," I said coldly. "I don't hunt."

He shook his head. "Of course not. What will we be doing whilst the others prance around in a sadistic display of their physical prowess and brutality?" He mocked me, but he did it with such a look of interest that my defenses failed, and I had no barbed retort. Fitz leaned closer. "Possibly a game of tressel in the library?"

"You wish to lose again?"

"I won't let you win this time."

"I'd like to see what that looks like." Damn him. I'd meant to be cold and disinterested, but instead I was flirting like a simpering schoolgirl.

Doors opened and a string of servers entered with steaming trays. Bear's voice silenced the crowd. "Welcome to the gathering. Please take yer seats."

Fitz put a hand on the small of my back. "I can't even feel you through all these layers." His whisper tickled my neck.

"Good."

He let out a hardy infectious laugh, drawing attention. I glanced toward the chief and found Angus's appraising gaze lingering on me. I smothered my smile. I should say hello to the heir. But, nope. His gaze locked on mine and a chill crept up my spine at the amused tilt of his lip.

They'd killed Trista eight days ago, and he smiled like nothing happened.

Stomach tight, I let Fitz guide me to the seat at his side. I politely declined the roast pheasants and pig stomach, but the side dishes took me by surprise. Pointing my fork at the sliced potatoes and melted cheese on my plate, I leaned close to Fitz. "Do you think I could get this recipe?"

"Then what would you do with it?"

"Give it to a cook."

"You don't know any of their names."

"You do?"

"Of course I do. How do you think I got all those extra tarts?"

After Fitz graduated, I'd missed his remarkable ability to make food appear at all hours of the day. I'd seek him out during study hours for the snacks. "I thought you stole them."

He cocked his head in mock offense. "The only thing I stole was Tasha's heart."

"Tasha? Is she the old lady who whacks people with her cane?"

"She never whacked me."

As we spent the meal in easy banter and reminiscing about Cromarty, I relaxed. I would enjoy spending time with my old friend and exploring this pretty place. All would be well, I told myself. If I wanted it enough, I would make it true.

I hoped.

Heavy doors opened and Father entered, his face white as milk. "Excuse my tardiness."

"Welcome, Chamberlain Wilson." Bear's voice carried an amused undertone.

They took pleasure in our servitude. In our suffering.

With a grim nod, Father slid in next to Mother near the head of the table. He didn't eat.

The chamberlain from Perth stood and half bowed to the chief. "We've brought a gift from our lands. With your permission, we wish to bring it out."

Bear sent the woman a genuine smile. "Please, Hazeal. What do we have the pleasure of enjoying tonight?"

She motioned to the waiting servants. "Gratsafruits, highness."

It was like they *wanted* to be subjected to the Grays.

A man presented me a small bowl with gratsafruits and slivers of honeyed mint. I spooned the first segment, and sweet citrus burst over my tongue. I groaned loud enough for Fitz to look at me sidelong.

After the meal, the Glenns directed us toward a grand ballroom where bagpipe music beckoned. I walked down the hall at Fitz's side, surprising myself by anticipating a dance. His fingers slipped around my palm. I halted at the touch and turned away from the golden light spilling from the open doors ahead.

He brushed a piece of red hair off his forehead. "We're not going in there." Excitement bubbled in his blue eyes. "We're going outside."

Lanie loitered in the shadows of a darkened hallway, clearly anticipating the adventure.

Outside? Trepidation blipped through my belly. Light, warmth, and music beckoned from down the hall.

"Away from nosy parents and hovering Glenns," he said.

"All right."

Fitz's lips carved up, and he tugged me toward Lanie. "Can you ladies lose your tails?"

Koda and Milo waited for us by the ballroom entrance. Lanie glided over, her wide skirts rustling, and spoke too quietly for me to hear. Koda's eyes jerked to me in concern. Lanie laid a doctorly hand on his arm. The two guards nodded and ducked into the concert ahead of us. Lanie returned with a victorious smirk.

"What did you say?"

"I told them you have severe diarrhea. I'm taking you back to the room, and we'd like a couple hours' privacy."

"They believed you?" Mortification rose.

She nodded. She'd inherited some of Father's gloss.

Fitz trembled as silent laughter wracked his body. I elbowed him in the ribs, and he fell against the wall.

"Let's go," Lanie said.

I would have harbored guilt at ditching Koda if I had felt any confidence in his protection, but now I was embarrassed and wanted to disappear.

"Where's Misty?" Fitz looked behind us.

Lanie shrugged. "She said she'd catch up."

We followed Fitz as he weaved through deserted hallways.

"You know this place well," I said.

"Seven years of boring gatherings when you refused to come. I took to exploring." He opened a thick door.

Cool night rushed to greet us. Lanie and I accepted the elbows he offered. Hiding my unease, I stepped into the wild. The door closed behind us with a final ominous *thunk*.

This outside was nothing like outdoors in McAndrew. At home, streetlights brightened clean roads, painted buildings, and metal benches. Here, stars failed to illuminate the murky ground and untamed nature. Exhilaration and fright filled me. My thin shoes sank into spongy ground, and the chill crept through my bodice.

An eun, all shadows and gleaming claws, flapped down to investigate. I clung to Fitz's wiry arm.

"It's all right," he said. "It's only patrolling. We won't try to leave the gates." He put his arm around my waist and held me against his side. If this was a ploy to touch me, it was working. I wanted to be closer.

The door opened behind us. I whirled. Misty and Angus stepped outside.

Fitz groaned and put his face against my ear. "Why must she ogle him? He was *not* invited."

I liked Fitz.

Misty and Angus stopped in front of us.

My hands went protectively around my corset. I swallowed down the venom at the back of my throat. "Good evening, Younger." My voice came out low and raspy.

One side of Angus's lip lifted at my use of his formal title as heir to the United Realm. His direct gaze scanned my face and the braid wrapped around my head to look like a crown. "Lovely to see ye, Vera." His accent was as thick as his father's. Good. If he spoke like an untamed Glenn, it would be easier to forget the three years he spent as a student at Cromarty.

When he'd lived in Campbell, he'd adapted his diction with ease. He'd masked his ruthlessness with articulate speech and proper clothing. Back then we'd been friendly. Back then my smiles hadn't been forced and stiff.

He held out his hand to me. I stared at it in horror, a memory surfacing.

Emilia and I had been walking down the road from Cromarty to McAndrew. Angus had been coming toward us. As we drew abreast, I'd slipped on the loose gravel and skipped desperately sideways. Angus's steel arm had gone around my waist, steadying me. He'd pulled me against his chest with one smooth tug. His big hand curled over my ribs. His warmth seeped into me. My insides had twisted when he'd looked down. His strength, the smell of wood, shocked me to the core as he held me close. I'd thrust myself away.

"Pardon me," he'd said with perfect diction. "I thought you were about to fall."

"You thought wrong." I *had* nearly hit the ground, but it was the zing of attraction that had me spitting spice. I hadn't wanted to feel anything for this man. Ian had been convincing me and Emilia that the Grays didn't belong in Campbell. They took and took and didn't give back.

Recalling that day, it took me a long time to realize I'd been staring stupidly at Angus's hand, nicked with scars and callouses. It hung awkwardly between us. My knuckles itched at the thought of his lips brushing them. Had those brutal hands been the ones to administer the poison that had taken Emilia and Ian from me?

A flash of danger bloomed in his eyes. He lowered his hand.

I'd made a mistake. *Be charming.* I coerced pleasantries out of my mouth. "It's nice to see you. Belle Borg is beautiful." The words left bitterness on my tongue.

"I'm glad you like it."

Misty looked from me to Angus. Her forehead creased but her voice came out high and excited. "What's the plan?"

"I want to show Vera the reflecting pond." Fitz looked to Angus for approval.

Angus didn't say anything. He put his hands in his pockets and looked at Fitz expectantly. Fitz seemed momentarily caught off guard, but he rallied with a cry, "We're off." Fitz took one of Lanie's hands and one of mine as he set out—captain of this mission.

I glanced over my shoulder. Angus kept his hands in his pockets, and Misty looked put out. Twice she tripped on her heels, forcing him to steady her.

We passed a ghostly clump of trees, and a howl punctured the air. I froze, and my gaze leapt traitorously to Angus. He was the only real protection I had against the wild. Belle Borg loomed like a giant haven behind us. I wanted back into its widespread arms. I forced my breathing to calm at Angus's relaxed. stance. He caught me looking and held my gaze an unnervingly long moment.

What was he thinking?

I turned away. Never mind. I didn't care.

Ahead, stars glittered over a flat surface. Fitz stopped us at the edge of the ring of stones surrounding the small pond.

"Pretty," Lanie said.

Dreamily beautiful. The watery darkness intensified the brilliant cosmos. Stars flickered in and out of existence on the rippling mirror. Mesmerizing. I leaned closer, feeling the lake had something to show me. My shadow blotted out the reflection of lights, and I hoped the inky swirl was not a dark omen. A patter of paws and a rustle of leaves above my head sent me flinging up and into Fitz's chest. My heart clamored to escape its cage.

"It's okay." He held me tightly, running a soothing hand over my back.

"What was that?" I hated the weakness in my voice.

Angus glanced into the tree. "Looks like a raccoon."

"Is that bad?"

He chuckled, and my spine straightened. "It's more 'feart of us."

Not likely.

Misty sidled up to Angus and wrapped her palm around his bicep. "Because you're here."

Gag.

Fitz lifted my chin with soft fingers. "You okay now?"

My eyes widened at his face a breath from mine. He was going to kiss me. Not here. Please not in front of everyone—in front of Angus. I could feel the Younger watching. It irked me that I cared what he thought.

I stepped back, forcing Fitz to release his hold. "I'm fine, thank you. A little startled, that's all."

Moonlight glinted off Angus's gray eyes as he scrutinized me.

What was that look? It had been bothering me all night. Father's ashen face popped into my mind. I marched forward, stopping an arm's length away from Angus. Eyes narrowed, I tried to interpret his expression and failed. "What?" I demanded, my tone hot.

Thick brows shot up.

"You know why my father is upset?"

"I've had interesting conversations with Hugo recently." His voice was annoyingly calm and pleasant.

Mine was anything but. "About what?"

His jaw hardened at the bite in my voice, and he seemed less inclined to answer.

Fear roared in my ears. Were my parents being murdered in the castle at this moment? Had Angus agreed to come with us tonight to make sure we were out of the way? I inched toward Belle Borg, my dress strangling me.

"Is everything all right?" Fitz asked.

No. "Yes." I forced a smile. "Thank you for showing me the pond. It's lovely. Please excuse me. I need to return."

Fitz looked taken back by my formal cold words. Angus's expression was a grim mask.

"See you later," Misty said, clearly happy to improve the male to female ratio.

"Do you want me to come with you?" Lanie asked. "Do you really have bowel troubles now?"

"No." I hoped Angus knew she jested. Then I hated myself for caring. My insides weren't right, but it wasn't from sickness. "Stay and have fun."

Nerves on fire, I scooped up heavy skirts and sprinted over the mangy gardens. I burst into the castle and followed the blare of pipes and piano—the sounds of Hogg. The Grays pretended interest in the domains, served food and music from each country, but it was all a disgusting façade.

On the threshold of the ballroom, I scanned the seats and the dancing faces. No Mother or Father. An usher stood near the door, and I bumped into his side in my hasty retreat. I tore down the hall.

"Vera." Koda was at my heels. "What's happened? Are you still sick?"

"I need to find my parents."

Koda fell into step at my side as I held my skirts and ran. The animals on the walls seem to come alive, chasing me through the halls. My lungs strained against my bodice. Light leaked under the door of our suite.

"I'll go in first." His breathing remained calm and quiet.

I gulped down air and flung inside after him. "Mother. Father."

Guards jumped from the couch in surprise.

Father came out of their bedroom. "What is it?"

Mother followed him into the sitting room, looking green.

Gushing relief, I dashed forward and throw my arms around them both. "I was worried about you. You seemed upset at dinner. And…" My words died. I didn't admit that Angus had looked at me funny, and I kept thinking about the Wallaces and Trista, and I'd panicked.

Father asked the guards to wait outside. Koda looked at me with concern before he obeyed, trailing the other two into the hall. I didn't want him to go.

Father patted my arm as he drew me around the low table and motioned me to sit. My anxiety grew with the deepening creases on his face. Mother and Father flanked me on the couch.

He looked out the dark window as he spoke. "I hate to upset you, but I guess that can't be helped. We have an unpleasant decision to make."

Frost skittered down my nerves as I sensed unpleasant was an understatement.

He opened his mouth. Closed it. He inhaled and spoke in a rush. "You have the opportunity to marry Angus and become the future chieftess of the United Realm."

I reeled back as if I'd been slapped. "I beg your pardon?"

"If you deny the proposal—"

"Of course, I do." My trembling hand came to my throat. "I could never marry that swine." Angus's knowing smirk was all I could see. What a monster. The depths of the Grays' vileness truly knew no bounds.

Father held up a forestalling hand. "In that case, we'll be removed."

Mother squeezed my palm. The floor felt like it fell away, and I dove into icy darkness. "Wha—" I couldn't form words over the block in my brain.

Marry Angus or my parents die.

The Grays would kill them without hesitation. I pressed a fist against the sharpness in my breast. "I'm having a heart attack."

"I'm sorry," he said. "I've tried reasoning with them, but…"

"How long have you known?" My voice sounded odd, like a faraway echo of its former strength. "Since their visit to Campbell? Your closed meetings with only Bear and Angus? You and Mother in your bedroom—you were talking about me marrying Angus." My temperature rose as betrayal hit me square in the heart. Father had led me to believe they were discussing a politically advantageous match for Lanie, not me. "You lied to me." Anger heated my words.

He nodded, his expression unapologetic. "I was trying to protect you."

"You made me an ignorant fool." All evening Angus had watched me flirt with Fitz, knowing he'd have me soon enough. I rubbed a knuckle into my wounded chest.

"You're not a fool. I am. I thought I could fix it. Talk them out of it. Make this dilemma disappear." His forlorn face focused my thoughts and quieted my fury.

"It's not your fault." I inhaled, forcing composure. "What happened?"

"They believe they've uncovered evidence of rebellion in Campbell. This is their punishment."

"Killing you."

His face crumpled.

"Go on. What's the evidence?"

"It doesn't matter."

"What are the accusations?" I was proud of the sharp edge to my tone.

He studied me. "Watt's Laboratory invented a new explosive. The Grays wanted to know about it sooner, before it was proven and tested. Ridiculous. Apparently, we have a hidden stockpile of explosives and weapons. It's all false claims and hearsay. Nothing worth substantiating. Nothing worth getting your hopes up over."

I knew about all of this. I'd helped orchestrate it. My thoughts snagged on the strangest part. "Why would Angus offer to marry me? Why are they even giving us this option?"

"You're beautiful," Father said. "With magical eyes." He'd always said my green-rimmed pale blue eyes would eclipse a man. "You're brilliant and funny."

"You're kindhearted," Mother said. "Good and creative."

"You might think that, but Angus certainly doesn't."

Father sighed. "I really don't know why this is the choice they gave us."

"What about Lanie?" I selfishly clutched at any way out of this. "She seems to actually like him."

Mother shook her head.

"He wants you." Father's soft voice was a sharp contrast to the cutting reality.

What perverse pleasure did Angus find in demanding me? I tried to imagine being married to him, those rough hands on me, moving into the wild, leaving my family, having his babies. I gagged in my mouth, bringing a hand up to swallow the nastiness back down.

"Forget it," Father said. "I shouldn't have mentioned it. We won't give you to them. I have a backup plan."

Hope burst to life in my chest.

"It'll be risky, but I think I can sneak us out. I have a poison that isn't deadly, but it'll make someone quite sick." Father had poison— on his person. He didn't stop talking, cutting off my chance to question that tidbit. "If I take a dose, you three will have an excuse to take me home immediately for treatments. We can travel to Porto and catch a merchant ship to Taylors."

"Out of the United Realm?" I jerked in shock, my elbow spearing Mother. She wrapped thin fingers around my arm.

He nodded, features solemn. "It's the only way we can escape them, but we will. We have gold and jewels enough to set up nicely in Taylors."

"You would leave it all to spare me an unfortunate marriage?"

"Of course. Your life, your happiness, is everything to us."

Mother smiled sweetly and nodded her agreement. "We will build a new life in Taylors. I heard they have a great love of art there."

Temptation tugged at my heart, stronger than any worldly force. The thought of freedom from the Grays nearly overwhelmed me. But in truth, that wasn't freedom. That was letting them win. Surrender. I refused to be a coward.

I swallowed a mouthful of acid and rammed to my feet. "No." My voice was steady and crisp. "I will marry Angus Gray. You will keep your home, your title, your heads. Everything that belongs to our family."

The whites of Mother's eyes gleamed in surprise.

"But know this. I will get my revenge."

"Vera." Father's voice was so soft it drew my tears dangerously close to the surface.

"I've made my decision." Focusing on revenge would get me through this. Strike at the heart of the beast and slay it.

Father's expression was grave as he studied me. Then, ever so slowly, he nodded. He stood and kissed my brow. "You're the strongest person I know. I'm proud of you."

My family was worth any cost.

Mother hugged me. "I love you."

I bit my tongue lest I backed out before I'd even begun. Coppery blood mixed with bitterness in my mouth.

"We have a meeting with them in the morning," Father said. "You don't have to come."

"I'm coming." I would greet my bleak future face-to-face. "Good night." I darted to my room before I crumbled.

Numbly I climbed onto the hard bed. I stared at the ceiling in horrified shock. My life had blown up in a single moment.

No more Cromarty.

No more Campbell.

No more friends and festivities.

No more hope of love.

I heard Lanie come in hours later and go to her room. We'd shared a bed all my life, yet she didn't check on me. I hugged my ribs as if I could smooth the emotions churning inside me.

The world went quiet, but I didn't sleep.

I was going to be chieftess.

CHAPTER 3

Engaged

I emerged from my room the next morning to find a red-eyed Lanie staring blankly at the rainy landscape.

"Father told you."

She nodded and turned her pleading expression to me. "You're so brave."

I pursed my lips. I didn't feel brave. I felt like a cotton ball. "Thanks." The polite word sounded as tired as I felt.

"Misty will be jealous."

"That doesn't make me feel better at all."

"I'm sorry."

"Me too."

She burst into tears and mine rose to greet them. I crumpled on the couch at her side. She wrapped an arm around my hunched back. I let myself be honest for a moment. I let myself be young and afraid. "Angus is going to put his big grimy hands on me."

"It might not be so bad."

Of course she would think that. He'd fooled her with his chiseled muscles and angular face. "I'll have to live in a tent and eat meat every meal."

Lanie didn't respond to that one.

I sobbed until I had a pounding headache to add to my fatigue. Sniffling, I sat up and moved out of her comforting touch. I couldn't lean on her anymore.

Standing on wobbly legs, I stumbled to the shower and turned on the water as hot as it would go. I tried to burn every thought and feeling away. I willed myself to be like the statues at Cromarty, cold and unbreakable.

I dressed in red—the color of death. A simple braid hung forlornly behind me, the ends brushing my waist. We left the guards behind. They were truly useless.

With Mother and Father, I trudged to my doom. I would bring down the Grays, but it would cost me my life.

We entered a room with dark furniture and bookshelves lining the walls. Bear and Angus sat in armchairs near a cold fire. The head of an unfamiliar animal stared down at me from the mantel, another victim of the Grays' bloodlust.

I felt like that poor creature with my head disconnected from my body. Father bowed and opened his mouth.

I spoke first. "I will marry you."

Angus's eyes popped out like bubbles. He looked from me to Bear in total disbelief.

They thought I'd let them kill my parents. They were so heartless they couldn't understand selfless love or sacrifice.

"She will marry me," Angus said, dazed, and to no one in particular.

The chief studied us. His eyes narrowed suspiciously. Silence stretched.

"I expect she will be safe and well cared for." As if Father saying it made it true.

Bear snorted. "Of course. She'll be family." My knees weakened in horror as the reality settled around me like iron chains. "I expect she will produce plenty of strong heirs." His brown eyes raked over my curves. "She has the hips for it."

I bristled. "I am not an animal for breeding."

"None of yer birth-preventing potions." Bear's voice held a solemn command.

I was a sparrow joining vultures. I could do this. I *must* do this. I nodded.

Bear tilted a hairy jaw toward his son, looking as if he'd been given a bag of candies, and he wasn't sure if they'd been poisoned. "What will yer mother say?"

Panic passed over Angus's face.

Because she wouldn't approve of me? The thought insulted and discomforted but, dammit, I didn't approve of him.

Chieftess Naira Gray didn't travel the domains, and from the rumors, I never wanted to meet the shrew. Another delight to look forward to in my bleak future.

A low thundering laugh started with Angus and spread to Bear. I watched in dismay as the two brutes' deep rumbles mocked our plight. Mother and Father were stone statues.

Bear hiccupped and wiped watery eyes with his sleeve. "Well congratulations, son."

"I guess we're really doing this." Angus's face was a portrait of bewilderment and disbelief as he looked at his father. "You did want me to marry strategically—and soon."

Bear rolled with deep laughter.

My blood boiled. "It's not funny."

The laughter stopped abruptly. Angus studied me. His gaze burned up and down my body.

"I'm sorry, lassie," Bear said. "Don't be offended at my surprise. Ye appear to want to murder him more than marry him."

I clenched my teeth, and my lips curled into what I hoped was a smile.

"But ye shall be have yer wish of being chieftess."

My hands trembled with rage. How dare he attribute my sacrifice to power grabbing.

He threatened my family. He killed my friends. I'd never actually *wish* to have anything to do with him. I opened my mouth to let the chief know how horrible this deal was, but fingers around my fist stopped me. Father's warning look silenced my temper. I was not to upset the Grays and bring us all under greater punishment.

The deal was struck, however unpleasantly, and my family would be spared. I would get revenge soon enough.

"We'll have the ceremony on Friday," Bear said.

Invisible chains squeezed the air from my lungs. *Two days.*

"Angus can head north as planned the day after." Bear sent me a baffled look. "With his new wife."

I turned my attention to my soon-to-be-husband.

Angus's brow furrowed deeper than usual, as if looking into the harsh sun.

I intended to burn.

CHAPTER 4

Waiting

Word of my engagement spread, and I didn't have to feign sickness that evening. I cowed in bed feeling like death, refusing all visitors except Koda. He didn't look at me with jealousy like all the women at Belle Borg, or with guilt like my family. He sat near my bed, knife and whetstone in hand.

"Vera?" Lanie's voice filtered through the door as she knocked.

"Have her give Fitzgerald my regrets," I said to Koda.

"I can hear you."

I didn't reply.

"Please come," she begged. "How will it look to have you hiding in here?"

I slunk out of bed in my wrinkled nightgown and opened the door. "It would be worse for me to go looking like this."

Koda grunted out a quiet laugh.

She looked me over, and the fight left her. "Love you, V."

"Have fun." I closed the door a little too hard, whirled, and caught Koda staring up at me with honeyed eyes. Why couldn't it have been someone like him? I fought back tears and lost.

He shifted uncomfortably. I turned my face away and tried to scoot past his chair, but he caught my arm. My strength failed, and I crumpled into his lap. His strong arms engulfed me. He smelled of cotton and soap. His warmth soothed me.

"I hate him," I said quietly.

His hand stroked my back. Vaguely I thought this was highly inappropriate, and I should get up. Instead, I relaxed against his chest. I imagined I heard him whisper, "He'll pay."

I fell asleep listening to his rapid pulse. I awoke disoriented and hoping I'd had a terrible nightmare. In darkness, I fumbled around a strange bed. The door opened, and the hall light silhouetted Koda's body. Reality punched me in the face, and I hid under my blanket.

He set a plate on the nightstand. "Dinner."

"No thanks."

"Dinner."

"Go away."

His weight landed on the bed, and I peeked my face out of the sheet. He put a hand on my back. "Sit up."

I obeyed, leaving the bedding covering my legs. He'd taken off his jacket and weapons. He wore only a shirt and pants. His hair hung unbound to his shoulders. He looked younger, sweeter—except for the new bossiness.

"Open." He held a fork full of mashed yams near my mouth.

I giggled at the ridiculousness. He popped the food between my teeth. The salty sweetness unlocked my hunger, and I reached for the fork. He pulled it out of reach. He speared a giant bean and held it up.

"I can do that." I held out my hand.

He leveled his playful golden eyes at me. I opened my mouth and giggled again when he spoon-fed me—easier to think of it as goofy instead of oddly intimate. I tore the fork out of his hand and pulled the plate onto my lap. He retreated to the chair by the window with a hint of reluctance in his step. I ate, then set the empty plate on the tray.

He stood and moved to pick it up.

"Not yet." I wasn't ready to face the darkness alone.

He froze.

"Play triple rings with me?"

He hesitated. I slipped out of bed, suddenly aware of my thin nightgown and bare ankles. I rummaged in my pack for the marbles, rings, and cards. I settled against the pillows on the bed and patted the space at my side.

He sat across from me instead. I dealt. Koda won the first hand, and with his victory smile, tension seemed to slide off his shoulders. He won the second and third. I only had two marbles left. When he won the fourth hand, suspicion bloomed.

"You cheater."

He cracked up. I lunged, sending marbles and rings flying. I shoved his shaking shoulders. He flopped onto his back. He grabbed my waist, taking me with him. My false anger whooshed out when I landed on his chest. His laughter died. We froze. His gaze drifted to my lips, a breath away from his.

I would marry Angus in two days.

Dropping my head, I buried my hot face in the blanket next to his ear. Frantic heartbeats clashed against our tense bodies. My last nights of freedom. I would never see Koda again, and so I relaxed, melting against his warmth for one breath. Two. Three.

That was all the affection I'd get to enjoy. Forever.

I shifted up and scrambled back. Clutching my knees to my chest, I tried to hold in the comfort he offered, but his warmth slipped away like a dream upon waking.

Face flushed and movements stilted, he stood. "Good night, Lady Vera." He darted out, forgetting the dinner tray.

When I fell asleep, nightmares plagued me. In a red-tinged world, I ate raw meat and walked barefoot. I birthed dozens of children, each an exact copy of Angus, exquisite figures with cruel hearts. The children fought, pushing each other off cliffs and drowning the babies in rivers. A raging Angus stood above me, a pistol in his bloodstained hand.

Lanie shook my shoulder, rescuing me. Sunlight sliced through my eyelids to my brain. Tomorrow I would marry Angus. Lanie couldn't save me from that dark fate.

I sat up with a jolt. She'd brought pregnancy-preventing pills for Misty. I was entering the dragon's lair, but at least I didn't have to have his spawn.

"Lanie."

She startled as I cried out her name.

"I need your Preprep."

Already dressed and fresh-eyed, she dropped on the bed at my side.

Feeling like a madwoman, I clutched her arm. "Please, Lanie. I can't have a child right now."

"What if you get caught?"

"I won't. I'll hide it. I'll say it's to strengthen my weak bones."

She raised a skeptical eye.

"Something better then, but please help me. Did you already give them to Misty?"

"No, not yet, but I told her I have it for her."

"We'll make up an excuse, no one can know that I'm taking it."

"All right. But she'll be mad."

"I'm mad. I'm to marry a savage."

"Shh. I'm sorry. I know. I'll go get them."

I exhaled as she left. My first subversive act of this marriage. Strengthened and reassured, I spent my last day of freedom—who was I kidding, I'd never been truly free—writing letters to friends at home, arranging my things, and trying not to think about *him*.

That became impossible when I looked out the window and saw the hunt pass into the open fields beyond the castle wall. Like when Lanie gave me the red velvet vaccine injection or stitched the cut on my ankle, I couldn't look away.

A boar shot out of the trees. Eyes wide and snout steaming, it tore up the dirt as it ran in a frantic line. Six hunters emerged after the terrified creature. Fitz and Father were the last of the delegates to the scene. Fitz had gone hunting after all—now that I'd been trapped by another.

The chief bore down on the pig, but with a desperate dive, the boar evaded Bear's spear and doubled back for the protection of the trees.

"Go, little buddy," I whispered encouragement as it neared the undergrowth. It might make it. Besides Bear, the other hunters appeared to be more worried about staying on their horses than using the weapons they held. I knew Father wasn't about to aim his spear at anything breathing—at least not on purpose. I could see why guns were banned on this hunt.

The pig chewed up the ground as it pounded toward freedom. Angus appeared at the edge of the tree line. On foot, he popped out from behind a thick trunk like he'd been lying in wait. The pig ran full tilt onto Angus's upheld sword.

It never had a chance. Blood splattered over Angus's shirt and cheek. When he stood, his arm dripped red.

It was his smile of triumph and pride that sent me running from the window.

Shaking, I vomited until there was nothing left to wring out.

I felt like that little pig with nowhere to hide and no escape to be found.

Tomorrow Angus's sword would spear me.

CHAPTER 5

Married

Bear made the formal wedding announcement that night at dinner. Wearing a funeral red gown, I stood at Angus's side. I didn't speak and didn't smile. Neither did Angus. I sat next to him. The whole roasted pig blocked my view of my parents' faces across the table. Angus held a serving knife out to me.

I shook my head. "I saw it running earlier."

"Ye would have its life wasted?"

"I would have its life spared." Mine too.

"It died quickly and humanely in an event fostering camaraderie and unity. Its death nourishes our people. Where is the wrong in this?"

I hated that I didn't have a good answer. Lifting my chin, I looked away. We ate in silence. I tried not to spend too much time pining for the chattering group down the table. Lanie, Misty, and Fitz didn't spend any time pining for me.

After the meal, Angus bowed politely. "I'll see you in the morning, Vera. I hope you sleep well."

He hesitated, waiting for the reply that didn't come. Frowning, he strode away.

Fitzgerald sidled up to me. "I guess I can't complain that you set your sights a little higher than me."

My face flamed.

"But it doesn't have to feel good."

"I'm sorry." I said it automatically, not sorry at all for the man who would go home in a few days, free as the wind.

"Congratulations, future chieftess."

"Thanks." I cringed, detesting that he imagined me as cloying and strategic as Misty. We were both hunting down princes, but for different reasons. I intended to bury mine.

"Where's Koda?" I asked Father when we'd gathered around our sitting room for our last night together as a family.

"He's with the Glenn guards."

A blimp of panic pressed into my chest. "Why?"

"I got him a position headed north. I convinced the head of the guard to take him on as a trainee. Koda's smart and capable, and he'll be an asset to them."

I relaxed. "Only you could persuade a Glenn to hire a Campbell soldier."

He grinned. "I wanted someone from home with you. He will look out for you when I can't."

When I was far away and gone. My chest pinched. I shouldn't have gotten so close to Koda last night. I wished I were marrying him instead. "Thanks, Father."

"I'm sorry it's not more. It all happened so quickly. I don't even have a proper gift."

"Koda is the perfect gift." Although I wasn't sure I wanted a constant reminder of what would never be mine.

Mother unclasped the necklace she always wore and held it out. A polished oval pebble hung from a gold chain. "This granite reminds me of you. Never forget, you are strong, unbreakable, and beautiful."

"Thanks." Sadness washed over me.

"Thank you, my brave girl," Mother said. "Now we have a future chieftess on our side." She wrapped her thin arms around my shoulders, and I hugged her back, letting myself be held as I hadn't since I was a small child.

***

We didn't have time to get a decent wedding dress, and I was glad. I wore my nicest gown, a pale blue skirt with a lace overlay and a cream bodice that revealed my collarbones and neck. The corset dug into my ribs as Mother cinched the silk ties. A little tighter and it might dull the throbbing pain in my heart.

Today was my wedding day.

In an hour, I would marry Younger Angus Gray, heir of The United Realm.

"I forgot the hair ribbon." Mother hurried out, her red-rimmed eyes down.

Lanie picked through the leather bag a porter had given me for my things. The duffle was all Angus had allowed me to take to my new home. I swayed—maybe the corset was too tight after all. My remaining luggage was now in Lanie's room. Hers now.

Lanie brought over a tiny vial. She hid it in my bodice, wedged between my breasts. I fancied for a moment it was poison instead of lubricant for my unpleasant future. She held up cream pills. The Preprep jar was labeled *For Constipation.*

"Really?"

She grinned. "They won't even look twice."

"They might begin to wonder when I don't get pregnant."

"Maybe they'll send you back."

"Or they'll kill me and find a new chieftess."

Mother walked into the room. "Don't joke about that. This is hard enough already."

"You're not the one about to marry a tyrant," I said.

"We're all soldiers with our part to play," Mother said.

Calling the people of Campbell soldiers was a serious mislabeling. We were scholars, quick with a pen and slow with a sword. But I strengthened at her words. I would play my part well.

Mother weaved the ribbon through the top pieces of my hair, letting the rest lay over my back.

Father peered in from the door. "Ready?"

Not even a little bit. "Yes."

I took his arm and started to sweat long before we reached the ballroom. Delegates and Glenns flanked the center aisle leading to my doom. Bagpipes played. Chandeliers cast golden light. Fire licked my spine and burned across my face as I glided before the gathered group. I couldn't meet Fitzgerald's eyes. Koda gave me an encouraging smile from where he stood against the far wall with a group of Glenn guards. Misty dabbed her eyes with a handkerchief and sniffed back tears.

Angus waited for me at the front of the room. If I didn't know he hid a rotten core, I could've admitted he looked appropriately handsome and regal. Panic struck me like lightning. Any bravery I might have felt in accepting this marriage fled. All plans of future retribution shriveled to raisins, clogging my arteries. I couldn't breathe. Fear stretched and clawed, multiplying with every painful step closer to Angus Gray.

Marriage.

Hatred sloshed in my stomach. Blood rushed to my cheeks, heat searing my brow and carving through my nerves. I faltered. Father's grip tightened on my arm, reminding me—for him, Emilia, Ian, Trista, and Campbell, my home, I *must* do this. Strength silenced my alarm. I took a deep breath. Chin up, teeth tight, I marched forward.

Angus wore a black suit and a solemn expression on his freshly shaven face. Father passed me over to the villain with only a kiss on my brow. I set my hand in Angus's thick palm. His fingers burned hotter than my face. I let go, clasping my hands together over my fluttering belly.

"It's a momentous occasion," Bear said, standing next to Angus and me. A feathered headdress crowned his brow and trailed to the floor. "We are honored to join the Gray line with the esteemed Wilsons."

I bit my tongue and tasted blood.

"Join hands," Bear commanded.

Angus and I faced each other. I stood as tall as his jawline. This felt like a bad dream as I held out shaking hands, and we interlocked fingers on both hands. I turned to stone in an effort not to rip free of his predatory hold. Thick lips turned down, and his gray eyes forecasted a blizzard. I didn't break his stare. Sweat trickled down my spine.

Bear's voice boomed. "Angus Gray, do ye give of yerself to Vera Wilson completely?"

"Aye," he said, hard, flat, steady.

"Vera Wilson, do ye give yerself to Angus Gray completely?"

I opened my mouth and choked. I coughed and tried again. "Yes," I whispered, weak, wavering, and soft.

Disappointment flashed over Angus's face. *The nerve.* I wasn't the disappointment here. Ire strengthened me. My jaw rose.

"Unfortunately, Naira isn't here to do this part," Bear said. He added in a quieter voice, "She won't be happy about it either." The chief handed me a headband made from rare white eun feathers.

Angus bent down, and I quickly placed it on his brow, trying not to touch his brown wavy hair. He set a matching feathered band gently on my head.

"It is done," Bear said.

With jarring abruptness, like the people performing it, the ceremony ended.

I was married.

To my enemy.

CHAPTER 6

Consummated

Angus turned me to face the cheering crowd. Mother wiped tears from her eyes. Lanie broke formation and ran to embrace me. I used it as an excuse to let go of his hand.

"Try to at least fake a smile," Lanie said into my ear.

"Bye, Lanie."

"See you soon, V." She retreated to stand by Mother and Father.

I forced up the sides of my mouth and waved good-bye as Angus paraded me toward the door. Seeking another friendly boost, I sought Koda. He wasn't looking at me. His eyes, burning with hatred, were fixed on Angus. It wasn't a friendly boost, but it strengthened me nonetheless. Koda would come with me, and together we would bring down the Grays.

Bear had told me that the wedding celebration would take place in Pinehearth, with Angus's mother and people. After today's ceremony, there would be no special party for us. We would be free to leave to complete the marriage union. Bear had made it seem like he was doing us a favor.

Angus and I left the safety of the ballroom and entered the empty hall.

Alone.

Dread breeched my carefully constructed mind blocks. "Aren't you hungry?" I asked as we strode down an unfamiliar corridor. "Shouldn't we go eat with the others?"

"We have some scran in our room."

Our room.

Bleeding skies.

Two guards stood at the mouth of a short hall.

"Congratulations, chief," the woman said.

"Thanks, Ona." His voice was low and good-natured. He truly had no shame.

The male winked at me as we passed. I swallowed, feeling smaller with each step. Angus held a door open for me. My wide dress caught on the metal flower decoration near the handle. Even my clothing rebelled against going inside the bedroom.

Angus tugged on the skirt. It didn't budge. Strong fingers grasped a chunk of fabric and jerked. Anger swelled as the sound of ripping lace rent the air. I lost balance as I came free. He caught me with a long arm around my tightly bound waist.

"My dress." I tore away from his warm touch.

"You were going to wear it again?"

"Well, no." It wouldn't fit it my tiny luggage allotment. I folded my arms. "But still, you ruined it with your brute impatience." Like he was going to ruin me. Terror rose in my gut as I imagined myself like that sad strip of lace by morning.

He closed the door and turned the lock. Even if I screamed bloody murder loud enough, the guards down the hall couldn't do much. Not that I expected anyone to rush in and save me from my new husband. It would've been nice to know they could have gotten inside the room.

I stood like a statue, and Angus treated me like one. He poured himself wine from the decanter on the table. He crunched on an apple as he took off leather boots. They hit the ground with a thud. He shrugged off his formal jacket. His loose white shirt joined the mounting pile of clothes. His olive skin clung to defined stomach muscles. A few hairs grew over his heavy pectorals.

I stared in awe and fright. No one at Cromarty looked like that—hardened by manual labor and tanned from the sun. With a stiff inhale, I turned away from the half-naked ogre only to face the bed. The sheets were already pulled down. A towel lay folded over the top. For when he made me bleed.

Horrors.

My arms tightened protectively around my middle. I jerked when I felt fingers on the back of my dress. Whipping around, I faced a stern mouth and cold steel eyes.

"I'd like to wait. I'm not ready for this." I did my best to sound reasonable.

"Why?" He looked down his straight nose at me.

I balked. How was it not completely obvious? He put his hands in his pant pockets and waited. He had no heart. It shouldn't have come as a surprise.

Chills ran over my arms. When I didn't speak, he put his hands on my shoulders and spun me around.

"Wait."

He sighed in frustration as I whipped to face him again. Fear was a living monster in my chest. "Please give me a little time. To talk."

"You may ask me anything."

Every thought abandoned me. I felt his patience wane. His hand lifted from his side to reach for me again.

"Have you done this before?" I blurted the random question.

"No."

I thought that would make me feel better, but it didn't.

"My mother found me kissing a girl when I was sixteen." Angus turned and pointed to one long sliver of a scar across his broad back. "This was my education. My own pleasures do not come before the Realm. With my position comes responsibility." He twisted his voice into an almost comical imitation of a female tone, but I found no humor in realizing I'd soon meet the woman who'd given him that stripe. He spoke again in his low baritone. "My mother is not interested in a bastard heir." A ghost of a smile softened his wide mouth. "I'm sick of waiting."

"But..." The plea went unfinished as my thoughts sputtered to blackness.

"You married me."

"I'm not ready."

"Tomorrow we will be sleeping in tents." He picked up his half-empty wineglass and put it in my trembling hands. His face had regained its grim determination.

I guzzled the drink and handed the red-tinged glass back.

"You can get what you apparently consider the worst behind you and move on. We're doing this whether you maintain that injured attitude or not."

"You would force me?"

His nostrils flared as he took a deep breath. "You agreed to this marriage. What did you think you were agreeing to? What do they teach at Cromarty these days—how to suck the fun out of life?"

I huffed, insulted and outmaneuvered. Sweat slicked the vial between my breasts. I'd come prepared for this, but clearly not actually prepared. My shoulders slumped in defeat.

"We are not married until we consummate the union. You are free to walk out that door right now and the marriage will be like it never happened." He marched to the spread of food, picked up his apple, and ripped off a bite.

I closed my eyes, slowly inhaled, and thought of Emilia, Ian, and Trista. I pictured Angus dead. "Forgive my nerves. I'm ready."

He had his back turned and with each breath, his muscles relaxed, his shoulders lowering. "Would you prefer I didn't watch you undress?"

I preferred to leave all fifteen layers on. I swallowed the ball of ice in my throat. "I can't untie my corset."

He faced me with incredulous eyes. "That's the dumbest thing I've ever heard. Can't undress yourself."

I bared my teeth.

"Literally like a caged animal." He bit his lip, as if holding back amusement.

An animal without claws, I thought with regret. Tears prickled behind my lids. I didn't fight when he padded over and turned me around. My retribution would come later. He poked at the tight laces. I peeked over my shoulder when he stepped away and dug around his jacket. Light gleamed off the dagger he picked up.

My heart lurched. He wasn't going to kill me, was he? Fear lashed at my ribs like a barbed whip.

"You'll have new clothes tomorrow anyway," he said.

Glenn clothes. I pinched my eyes shut. His palm gripped my thin shoulder, and his knife slashed through all my layers of protection. The heavy weight of my clothes fell to the floor. The knife handle thumped against the carpet.

My hair tickled my backside. I jolted when warm fingers wrapped around my waist. Slowly, he spun me to face him. I kept my eyes sealed, as if that would make me disappear. When nothing happened, I peeked through my lashes.

Angus's eyes were nearly black as he scanned my body. With a strong arm around my ribs, he drew me against his chest. Smooth skin slid against mine. He smelled of trees and salt. His face lowered. I turned my head, and his mouth found my jaw. The skin beneath his lips tingled.

"No kissing." Kissing was for lovers. He didn't have to kiss me to make an heir. Of course, I didn't plan to give him one of those either.

He drew back as if slapped. His voice was hoarse and deep. "Why not, dear wife?" He cupped my jaw and planted his mouth firmly on mine. His tongue tasted of apples and wine and male. He took his time, as if proving his ownership.

Fury raged through my blood.

With me tight in his arms, Angus took a step toward the bed. The vial skidded across the floor and dinged into the bed leg. He eyed the ground, looking for the sound. He dropped me and strode over to the vial. Anger rolled off him in waves.

"You were going to poison me?"

I covered myself with my hands. "No."

His face hardened.

"No." I lowered my voice. "That was for me. For my protection."

"What does that mean?" His lethal tone demanded an answer.

I focused on the piece of torn lace on the floor. "So it doesn't hurt me so much."

"Must you insist on hating this? If you relaxed and tried, you might actually enjoy it."

"How could I possibly be expected to enjoy this?"

Emotions churned over his face: disbelief, hurt, sadness. Maybe I was interpreting those wrong, because he glanced at the ceiling and exhaled pure exasperation. With a tight jaw, he took off the lid and sniffed. He touched the jelly with his finger. Handing the vial to me, he said, "Go on then."

The glass shook in my hand. Angus folded his arms, his pink nipples staring at me. I trembled as I scooted to the bed and slipped beneath the sheet. Curled in the fetal position, I'd prepared myself as well as I could by the time my large naked *husband* insisted on joining me.

He threw back the blanket, the breeze spreading chills over my skin. The dim light etched his body in chiseled detail. I closed my eyes. Darkness was worse. Squinting, I watched him climb onto the bed, the mattress groaning under the weight of his muscular frame.

With a palm on my shoulder, he rolled me onto my back. His arms bracketed my body like a cage. His rough hand turned almost soft as his fingers moved over my neck and down. Despite the despair rolling through my heart, my skin warmed at his touch.

"You're beautiful, Vera."

His words made a mockery of what this should be. There was nothing beautiful in what he was about to do to me. Though I'd never forget the stunning image of fire in his eyes or the shape of his looming body, all strength and pure male. That torso turned heavy as marble as he settled on top of me, and pinned me like prey.

His earthy scent of the woods after rain rolled over me. His hair itched my cheek and tangled with my eyelashes. My arms lay at my side, my hands fisted in the bedclothes in anticipation, then pain shot up my core. I inhaled a sharp breath as my fingers clawed the sheets, enduring his motion and his heavy weight. He groaned, his face buried in my neck, oblivious to how I reacted and my gasps. A few rushed thrusts, and it was over.

Eyes drooping in pleasure, Angus rolled off me. One hand on his chest, the other flung over his head, he stretched out in apparent bliss. More painful than what he had taken moments before was the crushing knowledge I would never melt into a puddle of satisfaction or know the enjoyment that might come from love. He'd stolen that from me, along with everything else being his wife would take from me forever.

At least it was done, and he'd hadn't dragged the ordeal out. That's what I told myself.

Lying there, contented, he had a smooth young face. It would be so easy to kill him—easy for someone who used weapons for more than scraping paint—or someone who smiled after killing a wild pig. It would have been easy for Angus.

I turned away from him and curled up like a newborn, my blood seeping into the towel. I'd come here to destroy Angus, but he would kill me, piece by piece. Lanie had told me different ways people could die from internal bleeding. She could add this to the list. He stirred. *Not again. Not again.*

He peeled off the bed, and I heard water running in the lavvy. Two tears squeezed out of my eyes before gingerly I stood and wrapped the towel around my torso. Red trickled down my thighs. I stopped on the threshold of the bathing room. Angus didn't look up from where he bent over the sink. He was so much bigger and stronger than I.

How weak I must seem, and I hated that.

Inside my chest something snapped, like crystal breaking. Angus was right. The worst was over. I was no longer innocent. I would not be afraid. No more would I cower to this man. I whipped the towel away from my body. His head snapped up. I flung the cloth on the counter. His gaze drifted to the bright stains.

You did that to me.

Head high, I cranked on the shower. His eyes narrowed as I began to wash, unconcerned with my body on display.

I may be yours, but you are mine—and so is your Realm.

CHAPTER 7

Good-bye

Angus didn't touch me the rest of the night. I clung to my side of the mattress and slept poorly, made worse by his deep steady breathing. I considered waking him out of spite, but preferred him unconscious. I awoke to a woman bustling about my room. He was gone.

"Oh good. Yer up."

Not hardly. I felt like the stone hanging from my necklace.

"They're saddling the horses now. You're to be at the gate within the hour." She set a stack of clothes on the bed. "I'll bring you something to eat."

I waited for the door to close before I slipped out of the sheets. The pants were soft, but shockingly form-fitting, and the shirt ended a bit past my waist. It was much too loose over my unbound chest and didn't cover my bum in the least. I had no complaints about the warm, comfortable leather boots. I braided my hair and wrapped it in a low knot. I didn't have much of an appetite, but I forced down the bread, cheese, and olives, then the woman led me through quiet halls.

Beyond the closed doors, my family slept in warm beds. *Good-bye.* Tears marshalled behind my eyes, and my legs screamed at me to run. I ignored the temptations. Overlooking all I'd lost, I focused on the things I'd gained: access to the Grays and protection for my family. If I fled, I wouldn't be able to kill Angus.

Outside, bitter wind jerked me to attention. Dull gray skies signaled the predawn hour. Koda appeared at my side. I stopped, and the woman guiding me walked away.

He spoke quietly. "You all right?"

I was married to Angus and leaving civilization for a life of dirt and misery. "Fine, thank you." I knew he meant well, but I didn't appreciate the question. What I really wanted was a hug and a loaded pistol. Not necessarily in that order.

"Where are your clothes?" He glanced down at my thin shirt and tight pants and quickly glanced away. His cheeks reddened.

Embarrassed, I folded my arms.

From across the yard, Angus saw us. He left his conversation and strode over.

"I'm here if you need me," Koda said in a rush.

I needed him.

He traipsed over to a cluster of travelers, leaving me alone to face my *husband*. Skies, I loathed that word.

Angus stopped too close, invading my personal space. I flinched. *Don't kiss me.*

"Riding pants look well tidy on you."

"Oh." The unexpected compliment hit like a healing tonic. I unfolded my arms. "Thanks."

A red lip slid up, and I could almost still feel his heavy eager mouth on mine. Unbelievably, the memory wasn't as vile as I expected. The soft dawn light flattered his well-formed face.

"Ready to ride?"

Um. No. The horse attached to the string in his hand looked like a monstrous fiend out to kill me.

"This bonnie is Pearl." He stroked the horse's long white nose affectionately. "She's my wedding gift to you."

Last night would be my gift to him.

He drew Pearl's head closer, and I took a step back. Was I supposed to touch it?

"Thank you." Was it too late to run back inside to my family? "I've never ridden a horse before." I had no desire to start now.

He groaned in annoyance. "Of course not. Such a skill is beneath you."

I bristled. It was certainly an unnecessary skill in Campbell.

The woman reappeared and handed me a fur-lined coat. This time my thank you was deep with feeling. I nearly jumped into the warmth.

"Have Gent tie Pearl with a lead rope," Angus said to the woman.

Good riddance, Pearl.

"You'll start with me," he said. "Then we'll need to shift your weight around to spare the horses." He motioned me to the side of a black beast much taller than Pearl.

I could do this. I got through last night. I could do anything.

"Put your foot in the stirrup."

I looked around dumbly.

"Never mind." He crouched. Strong hands gripped my hips. My teeth jammed against his presumptuous touch. I left the ground. "Leg over."

I landed on the saddle, a painful throb rolling through my tender parts. The horse shifted, and I swayed. I clutched the saddle in fright. Solid earth seemed dangerously far below. Tension pinched my shoulder blades together. Angus held the bridle and walked.

I lurched forward. "Ho. Whoa."

He averted his gaze, but not fast enough for me to miss the laughter in his expression. My nostrils flared and rising resentment chased my fears away. He led me to the front of our group of fourteen riders and four packhorses. Koda sat nervously on his horse near the back. He caught my gaze, and I relaxed. At least I wasn't totally alone.

"Hold this." Angus handed me the reins.

"I don't... I can't."

He let go, and I scrambled to grab the leather. For a heart-stopping moment, nothing prevented the beast from galloping off, but he stayed still. Kicking off a mounting block, Angus swung up behind me. His arms encircled my waist, and he picked up the reins. I exhaled, annoyed that he made me feel safer.

He clucked his tongue. "Aye, Coal."

Horseflesh rumbled beneath me. I leaned forward, trying not to touch the man behind me, but the effort was exhausting and utterly futile. I gave up and leaned against his solid warmth. The sun rose, illuminating sprawling green valley. I unbuttoned my coat and let the wind cool my core. We followed a wide road north. Too soon, Belle Borg disappeared behind us.

"Why didn't you want to marry Lanie?" I asked, turning to see him.

He hesitated before answering. "For one thing, she's currently set to become the next chamberlain of Campbell. A role she needs to live in Campbell to prepare for." I didn't like the way he said "currently" as if that could change. "I don't like her as much as I like you."

Weird, she actually likes you. "You don't know her." My voice betrayed my defensiveness.

"That's true. I had to choose based on limited information."

Which left me no choice.

Holding the reins in one hand, he ran the other hand through his hair. "Lanie seems tiresome at times, and I think she would get on my nerves always blathering on."

Excuse me. "She's smart and energetic, easy to please and beautiful—"

"Don't be offended."

"Don't be offensive." I turned back to face forward.

He sighed, and his breath ruffled the fine hairs on the back of my neck, sending a shiver down my back. He was much too close. "What kind of an answer did you expect? What did you want me to say?"

I was stupid to have asked.

Hours passed in miserable silence. Pain spread over my legs and up my back. Pressure built in my bladder. When I could withhold the jarring no more, I said, "Please. I need to use the lady's room."

He turned to the man riding at our right. "We're riding ahead for a piss stop. Give us a tick."

Angus tucked his free hand under my coat and gripped my ribs. I jolted at the touch of warm fingers through thin cotton, my breast heavy over his thumb. He kicked the horse, sending us on a mad charge down the slope. I swallowed the howl clawing up my throat as my stomach lodged in my spine. With a steel arm, he held me against his chest, the only thing separating me from sudden death. We tore down the road in a frightening rhythm. I nearly peed my pants.

We rounded a bend, and he reined in. Coal pranced to a stop while I sucked in a staggering breath, nerves aflame.

"Why did you do that?" My anxiety came out as anger.

He chuckled, flaming my rage. "You were safe."

Safe. Ha.

He swung off and held up his hands to me. Near tears, I gratefully tipped into his arms. My feet hit the ground, and my legs gave out. With a grunt, he caught me before I hit the dirt. I clutched his solid waist, trying to will strength into my legs. Balancing precariously, I let go as quickly as possible.

Holding the reins loosely through his arm, Angus walked to the side of the road and watered a tree. I stared in dismay.

"If you wait too long, you'll have an audience."

Muttering obscenities, I crunched through tall grass, dirt marring my new boots. I wanted to go home. I found a thick tree and crouched behind it. My thigh muscles screamed. I could do this. It took a long time, but I finally emerged, disgusted and triumphant.

The other riders caught up, dismounting gracefully, except Koda. I took perverse satisfaction in his wobbly gait. A man handed me cold potato slices that had been cooked in oil and nuts. It tasted better than it should have. Washing it all down with spiced juice helped.

Like an inconvenient piece of luggage, Angus lifted me onto a horse with a strange woman, and too soon we rode north again. Sitting with Angus was bad. Sitting with this sour-faced woman was worse. I found I did have the strength to lean forward and not relax against her chest.

I passed the day without coming up with any solid plans for freeing the Campbells and me from the Glenns. It would be near impossible to connect with Watt's Laboratory now. Trista had been my only contact with the other rebels. I had no way to reach people who could help me. I lost my hair ribbon and my braid fell out of its bun, hanging down my back like a limp tail. I was too tired to cry when we finally stopped for the night at a meadow.

Men and women threw out blankets, built a fire, and brushed out the horses. One tent stood ominously near the edge of camp. Helplessly I watched the commotion while leaning on a tree. My legs hurt, and I felt as unsteady as I was exhausted.

During the two days I had to mentally prepare for this new life, I couldn't've imagined it would be this bad. Ignorance had kept me from factoring in the bugs and blisters, or the hollowness in my heart. I'd taken so much for granted, and now all the comforts, luxuries, and kindnesses of home were gone.

Hunger chewed at my stomach as a simmering pot sent tempting tendrils of sweet onion over the clearing. An eun flew down and dropped a flopping fish into the hands of the cook. The man sliced chunks off, flicking them into the pot. The Glenns gathered around the fire and passed around bowls. Angus saw me, but he didn't move from his relaxed seat in the grass. His piercing gaze challenged me to join him, but I hovered in my tree shadow, not wanting to be near any of them.

Koda ate quickly. He refilled his bowl and walked over to me. "Here." He set the clay in my hands. My blisters from gripping the saddle stung against the hot ceramic. "It's gross, but you need to eat."

Angus's eyes followed Koda as he left my side and traipsed over to the bedrolls.

I ate, trying not to focus on the lumps of soft meat. Koda's kindness warmed me more than the soup. Empty dish in hand, I jolted over to the Glenns. Every harsh face watched me.

"Thank you," I said to the man who'd made the soup. I set my dish in the growing pile. Smoke puffed into my face, burning my eyes and choking my throat. How could they stand it?

"Come upwind," Angus said.

I coughed, eyes watering as smoke clouded my vision. I didn't want to *come* anywhere near him. I wanted away. "Is that tent for me?"

A man nodded, a glint in his eye.

"Good night then." I weaved through the small camp and crawled into the tent. I cringed at the musty smell, but smiled at the size. Definitely not room for two. I imagined the canvas walls were made of impenetrable steel, keeping out predators of any kind.

I wanted a shower. I wanted a bed. I wanted to go home and eat dinner with my family. Leaving my coat on, limp-limbed, I dropped to the hard ground.

I slept. Panic jerked me awake at rustling near my feet. Darkness blanketed the camp. Insects crackled and popped. Angus crawled up my legs. The shadow monster loomed above me. My pulse ratcheted up. *He can't possibly want that now. Here.* Only a thin barrier separated us from all those people, and Koda. Angus's hand went under my coat and his thumb brushed my breast.

"Please no," I whispered.

"Why?" His face stopped inches from mine. The smell of campfire and sweat washed over me. "I'll be quiet."

I never wanted to *that* again. "Because I feel like I've been kicked between the legs." I couldn't imagine how I was going to sit on a horse ever again, or do anything else down there.

He dropped on top of me, his body so heavy all the air whooshed out of my lungs. He nuzzled his face into my neck. The new growth on his chin scratched my skin, and the smell of woodsmoke itched my nose. He groaned in frustration. Chills ran down my spine and fear pricked my heart.

Was he going to anyway? Of course he was. He was Angus Gray. He took what he wanted, everyone else be damned. I blinked at the canvas ceiling in surprise when he rolled off to my side. His back remained a wall between us the rest of the night.

In the morning, I forced myself to sit up when Angus rose. Crouched in the musty tent, I put on my boots and sucked in sharply when my raw fingers clasped the leather laces. He took my fingers, examining the blisters. Wordlessly he left.

I hate you too.

Eyes watering, I tied my boots and crawled out of the tent. The other riders had packed up and prepared the horses. Angus strode up to me.

"Give me your hands."

I held out my angry red fingers and palms. He scooped orange cream out of a jar and worked it into the blister on my index finger. I gasped and jerked away as stinging pain tore through my hand. With a look of determination, he gripped my wrist, ignoring my attempts to pull free, then he smeared the paste into my raw skin. When my hands were fully on fire, he released me.

I seethed and hissed.

"Don't clutch the saddle." He tromped to his horse.

I slumped after him. Mounting the dread horse hurt worse than I'd feared. Muscles I didn't know existed complained. Minutes passed like hours as yesterday's nightmare day repeated.

In my head, I drew landscapes and the faces of men and horses. Hunger slashed at my stomach. I squinted at the eun scouting high overhead. It soared in circles, its wingtips fluttering. It dove, shooting down like an arrow. I flinched when it narrowly missed smashing into the dirt.

The bird flapped up, a rabbit in its talons. It snapped the rabbit's neck midair and landed a few feet later. The sharp beak ripped the limp animal to shreds. My hunger receded with a wave of nausea. I could only hope for a better fate than that poor bunny.

Angus stopped the horses before a dense forest where a narrow, rocky trail disappeared into the shadows. The group dismounted. A man passed around brown rolls that tasted like sand and crumbled like dirt on my tongue. I wandered near the trees, stretching my legs, and peered in wonder at the thick trunks, vibrant undergrowth, and dense leaves.

Koda strutted from a thicket, buttoning his pants. He startled when he lifted his head and saw me.

"Excuse me, Lady Vera."

I chuckled. What would have been appalling at home was becoming commonplace. I reached up and plucked a twig from his messy ponytail.

"The forest is beautiful, don't you think?" I asked. Koda looked back at the trees. "Makes me want to paint."

"I'd like to see it when you do." He looked at me now.

Angus trotted over. "How's the ride, Koda?"

"Fine, Highness."

Angus coughed. "You can call me Angus or chief, like the rest."

Koda nodded.

"You're sitting well."

Koda's chest rose. "Thank you."

Angus turned to me. "You're going to have to ride with Hayln through this part."

I pursed my lips in annoyance. Nestling against his broad chest was a thousand times more comfortable than the cold, bony Hayln.

Angus chuckled at the face I must've pulled. "It's steep and uneven. Coal's got his work cut out carrying me."

I sighed.

"You could ride Pearl."

"Can I walk?"

"If you want to sleep in the forest tonight."

I glanced up at Angus. Maybe I did.

"You don't."

Humph.

Koda offered, "She can ride with me."

Angus's neck nearly snapped as he turned to Koda.

"I'm not much bigger than Hayln," he said.

There was an awkward pause as Angus studied Koda. "You think you can handle a passenger?"

"Yes, chief. I won't let anything happen to her." Was the eagerness in Koda's voice as clear to Angus as it was to me?

The coldness in Angus's eyes told me that he saw it all. No way he was going to let me ride with Koda. He looked at me. "It appears you have another option now."

"I'd choose Koda over Hayln any day."

"Then mount up." Angus turned and marched away, but not before I caught the hardening of his jaw. I should have felt thrilled, but instead I felt guilt.

Koda chewed his lip as we walked together to the dappled mare they'd given him for the trip. Several of the riders had mounted using a broken tree. Koda led the horse to the side of the trunk.

"Do you need help up?"

Yes. "No." I couldn't let Koda pick me up the way Angus did. Could he even lift me that high?

We were the last to mount, and my face burned under the scrutiny of a dozen waiting Glenns. My gaze flicked to Angus, who sat leisurely on Coal, the reins slack. The image reminded me of when I'd seen him ride into Cromarty years ago—arrogant and entitled, and so damn good at everything.

Straightening my shoulders, I put my foot in the stirrup, gripped the saddle, and jumped. I groaned as hard leather rammed into my stomach. My top half folded over the horse's back.

Koda's hand wrapped around my calf, pushing me up.

"I can do it." My voice was a hiss of sound.

He let go.

With a grunt and a heave, I wiggled up and threw my leg clumsily over the horse. What little pride I felt in my accomplishment died with the chuckles of the Glenns. What did they look like their third time getting on a horse? I schooled my face into waxy pleasantness.

Koda stepped onto the log, and the horse jolted forward, out of his reach.

"Whoa." I yanked back on the reins as the horse tossed her head in annoyance.

The chuckles turned to outright laughter.

Grabbing the reins from me, Koda dragged the horse back. Hooves pranced as he swung onto the saddle, slamming into my back with surprising force. I folded over the horse's neck.

"I'm so sorry," he said as I straightened. "Are you okay?"

That hurt. "I'm fine."

"Ready now?" Amusement laced Angus's question.

"Yes." I forced my chin up.

"Terry," Angus said. "You're behind them."

"I don't need a babysitter," Koda said in my ear.

Angus led out, and Koda held his horse back until we were second to last into the forest. The trail was narrow, so there wasn't much for the horse to do but follow.

I inhaled cool air, fragrant with loam and pine. Propriety kept my back straight along with the worry Koda would tire if he had to hold me up. Face tilted over my shoulder, I whispered to him, "Worst part so far?"

His breath warmed the back of my neck. "Seeing you with him."

Heat spread down my spine. "Worse than sleeping outside?"

He chuckled. "Worst part for you?"

All of it. The barbarians, the exile, the discomfort, the food, *the husband*. "Feeling trapped. Like I'll never be free." I bit my lip to stop more unwelcome truths from spilling out.

He loosened his hold on the reins, and his arms tightened around my coat. His nose brushed my ear as he whispered, "I promise I'll get you out. No man who uses his power to steal a woman deserves to keep it or her."

My body threatened to turn in the saddle, wrap Koda in my arms, touch his lips, and disappear into caramel eyes.

Shame punched me in the stomach at the forbidden desires. I pushed the guilt away. I wasn't alone. We would topple the Grays and we'd leave together soon enough. I didn't focus too closely on what success would actually require. For now, I was heading into the heart of the enemy. It seemed like a good start.

"Let me take a turn." I tugged at the leather straps in Koda's palms.

"No way. I'm responsible for keeping you safe."

Annoyance flared, and I barely stopped myself from telling him he'd entirely failed in his responsibility so far. Instead, I reached up and plucked a handful of leaves from a low branch. Beautiful veins and pale green diamonds patterned the softness.

"Best part?" I asked.

"This ride."

"Really?" My voice betrayed the pleasure I took in the compliment.

"Yes. The forest is a delight." Out of the corner of my eye, I caught a glimpse of his teasing expression.

The horse slipped on a loose rock. We jolted in the saddle, straining to stay mounted as the horse shuttered forward. As we steadied, cackles bubbled up my throat. I laughed at our near fall, at our painful predicament. I laughed because it felt good.

Up front, Angus rounded a hairpin turn on the steep trail and appeared through a thin row of trees above us. Grimly, he looked down at us and our mirth. My merriment died as quickly as a bug under his boot. Like a coward, I looked away first.

The delightful forest ended too quickly. We emerged at sunset on a flat field of tall grass. Angus dismounted. I thought for a moment he'd come help me down, but he didn't look my direction as he called out instructions to make camp.

His indifference bothered me. I was his *wife*.

Then it bothered me that I'd let anything he did or said bother me.

Koda swung off the horse and shook out his legs. He held his hands up to me. I shook my head. I hadn't let Hayln lift me off the horse. I had no honorable reason to fall into his arms.

He held the horse's head, and slowly I lowered myself off the side. He walked the horse away, and I traipsed into the trees. Walking was sweet pain. I took my time watering a clump of mushrooms. By the time I'd returned, the group lounged around a raging fire. Koda and Angus sat opposite one another.

I settled on the log next to Angus, but not close enough to touch his thigh. I had something I needed to say. I held up my remarkably improved hands for him to see. "Thank you."

"It was my pleasure." His face was solemn, but I caught the jest in his eyes.

"At least someone enjoyed it."

He chuckled, and the hardness in his brow melted.

Embers popped. Horses munched. Stars flickered. A scene straight out of a storybook. It would've been beautiful if I didn't feel shackled.

A young Glenn named Gent handed us each a steaming bowl. I cradled the warmth and poked at the thick stew with my spoon. I took a tentative bite of a smooshy blob. The flavor wasn't terrible, but the texture was. I rolled the strange chunk around my mouth, unsure whether to chew or swallow or spit.

"They're wild mushrooms," Angus said, watching me. "Gunther found some near the trees."

I spat the bite out at my feet.

He quirked a brow.

I leaned close to his shoulder, my heart leaping. I forced the words out in a low voice. "I peed on some mushrooms over there."

He blinked at me, the firelight dancing over his wide eyes.

My lips pulled down in a grimace, and Angus burst into laughter. He clutched at his abs, sucking down air to fuel his glee. Every single face had turned to him. To us.

"What's the story, chief?" Gunther asked.

"Something wrong with Gunther's soup?" Gent asked.

Angus looked at my appalled expression, and more laughter burbled up. After long moments, and with what appeared to be extreme effort, he reined in his howls. "Nothing." He waved a dismissive hand. "The soup is well tidy scran."

"It's not that good," Gunther said.

Angus picked up his spoon and took a large bite.

"What are you doing?" My voice was a quiet hiss.

"I'm eating dinner. Thank you for providing the entertainment."

"But—"

"I wouldn't worry about it. The chances are extremely low he picked *your* mushrooms. I can't taste anything weird. Weirder than Gunther's soup usually is. Besides, if he did use your mushrooms, heat kills germs, right? That's what they taught me at Cromarty. That stew is good and boiled." He gave me a wink and took another bite.

I recoiled.

"Don't think about it," he said.

I brought a spoonful near my lips, and despite my empty stomach, I set it back down. "I can't."

"Not a lot of options tonight, dear wife."

I held the bowl as far from my body as I could.

"Well, don't waste it." He took it, callous fingers brushing mine.

Stomach grumbling, I trudged to the lone tent. I didn't know when Angus came in. Tonight, he didn't rouse me with his attentions.

I woke the next morning with my face and chest pressed tightly to the warmth radiating from his back. I rolled over, embarrassed to be caught holding him. Missing his heat and the comfortable place to rest my head, I didn't allow myself to move until he woke a short while later. After a too-small bowl of porridge, we packed up camp. I stood watching how he bridled Coal, apparently without fear of the horse's teeth.

"Coal is rested and this morning is easy going." He looked at me in question.

I wished I could sense how he felt behind that tight brow. Was he asking me if I'd like to ride with him? Was this a test? I considered telling him I could ride with Koda again and spare Coal, and me, but something stopped my tongue. Maybe it was the flash of vulnerability in Angus's eyes. Maybe it was the realization that if I wanted to take down the Grays, I would have to play the game. The long game.

"Great." I stepped next to Coal's high flank. "I would like a boost."

A twitch of his lips was the only reaction I got, but I sensed I'd passed the test. Hands tight on my waist, he lifted me onto his horse.

After miles of rolling fields, the landscape changed. Flat roads turned steep and rocky. A city of tents frosted the valley to the west of our high trail. I lamented my final destination would be a tent, which might possibly be the worst part of this marriage. I wanted a bedroom with sturdy walls.

"Did you enjoy your time at Cromarty?" I asked Angus. "Or did you feel trapped by the roofs and doors?"

"I don't have a problem with buildings."

"You know what I mean."

"If you mean did I miss Alta Glenn, riding my horse, having space and privacy, then yes. It was hard for me to focus on equations when the sun was shining." He tugged Coal to the right, avoiding a divot. "The south garden was my favorite place to study."

"That's a good spot." The perfect outdoors experience—contained and smelling of roses.

"I got a scolding for stripping an entire raspberry bush once."

"You got a scolding?"

"Tasha hit me in the shoulder with her cane. I think she was aiming for my head, but couldn't reach that high." He chuckled, but I was too surprised to laugh.

"What did you do?"

"I apologized and stopped eating her raspberries. What do you think I'd do?"

Kill her for treason. I didn't answer.

"Here." He dropped the reins on my hands. "You take a turn."

I snatched the leather.

"Gentle." Strong fingers pried my tight grip open. He adjusted the straps. "Like this." His hands encased mine as he led me through the motions. His chest pressed against my shoulders as he leaned in. "Slight tug to the right."

Coal changed course.

His hands fell away, and I was on my own.

Little nudge left, and the horse obeyed. "Yay, Coal," I gushed in delight. I led him safely around a boulder. Not that I thought he'd have been dumb enough to walk into it. Still, I yipped at my success.

Angus's chin rested on my shoulder.

My body stilled.

"I'm going to take a little nap." He closed his eyes and nestled his face into my neck. Arms tightened around my waist, holding me close.

I attributed my rising heartbeat to the excitement of controlling an enormous beast. Absolutely not from the tickle of Angus's unshaven jaw or the warm puffs of breath sneaking down my coat.

The grass turned thin and brown. Pieces of grimy hair jetted from the braid I'd worn for three days. I didn't dare touch it. I gawked at the first real mountain. She loomed above me, majestic and fierce and breathing down a cold wind.

Angus lifted his weight off my tired back, and I straightened gratefully.

"Stop here."

I pulled back, but nothing happened. I pulled harder.

"Coal," he said with disapproval.

The horse stopped.

Even the beasts obeyed him.

I had a long way to go.

At the mountain's foot, we ate a lunch of strapples and nuts. I declined the dried meat. The Glenns eyed the gray sky and fast-moving clouds with frequency. Gent approached Angus. Angus and Gent acted like brothers, Gent being the younger of the two. Watching their easy conversation and comfortable interactions over the last few days had made me wistful and sad. What I wouldn't give for a trusted friend right now. I missed Lanie. I could barely think of Trista or Emilia without wanting to strangle the Glenns.

I could hear Angus and Gent's conversation from my seat outside the group's circle.

"Should we tent down here, chief?" I took pleasure in hearing Gent's low voice. He spoke as well as any virtuoso from Cromarty. His polished accent was soothing relief after listening to the Glenns' thick garbling all day. "Join up with the Oscars for the night?" Gent gestured to a spread of tent dwellings peppering the hills.

"No," Angus said.

Gent sent a meaningful glance at me, as if I weren't ready to face the mountain. I wasn't, but I didn't like him thinking it.

"We ride," Angus said. "Let's hope we reach Cabin before the snow."

The word cabin and snow hit me at the same time. Hope and horror colliding.

Gent shook his blond head, but didn't argue.

Angus stood and called to his crew. "Pack up." He strode over and crouched next to me. "Can you ride your own horse if I hold the lead rope and guide you?"

No way. I nodded my head.

He gripped my thigh. "Good girl."

My stomach tied in knots as I approached Pearl. "Hi there, big lady."

The mare's nose steamed. I turned to stone and pinched my eyes shut as she sniffed my hair. Footsteps crunched gravel behind me, and the horse shifted interests.

Angus helped me mount. "She'll go wherever I go."

She and I both, though she seemed eager to follow, and I wanted to flee. I nodded, my tongue heavy with unspoken invectives.

We started up the mountain. My pleasure at not being smashed in the saddle with a Glenn soon overcame my anxiety and I relaxed. With her gait even and soothing, Pearl dutifully followed Coal. My seat no longer barked in pain. I soaked up the beauty of the massive purple-streaked boulders. A tree sprouted from a sheer piece of granite. The sapling curved around a ledge, and proudly faced the sun.

I would be like that little tree. I would find a way to thrive among these people with hearts of stone. I clasped the pebble at my throat. I could do this.

No sooner than I had the thought, the snow began to fall.

Soft white flakes danced to the ground. Within minutes the poetic display turned to gruesome torture. I pulled my face into my furry hood and tried to disappear. My world shrank to blind cold swaying. We plodded on.

My teeth chattered so hard I thought they would break off. I couldn't feel my legs, which at least was a change from constant soreness. Horseflesh shifted beneath me. The darkness of my hood was my view. I wouldn't have known if I walked off a cliff, and I didn't care. My numb hands grasped the saddle and my spine shivered violently. Wind clawed at my hunched back and battered my head. The storm froze time. I wanted to go inside—anywhere inside.

The horse stopped. Frozen solid, I feared. Winter screamed through my tightly drawn coat. I tipped sideways. My fingers lost their gripping on the leather. Bloody hell. I was falling, and my muscles refused to fire.

"You in there?" Angus's voice penetrated the fog. I jostled in his arms like a cube of ice in a glass.

"Aye. Over here, chief," a voice said. "No dry wood."

He set me on the ground with a thud. I rolled, stiff as stone. I wiggled my face out of my coat and peered through the frozen furry hood. I lay in a cave.

Why must we still be outside? I was done with nature.

Angus disappeared into the white sheet of snow.

Left to die.

He returned a moment later with a canteen and blankets. He gripped my coat and pulled me to sitting. He poured the partially congealed drink between my trembling lips. It tasted like fat. I gagged.

"Don't cowk." His brow pinched tight and his tone was hard, as if I could control it.

I swallowed back bile with difficulty and obeyed.

He forced another gulp down my throat. I tried to focus on the hint of rosemary and not the oil slick. He set the drink aside and swept away pebbles and straw with his boot, revealing rocky ground.

"You're not cold?" I managed to get out through chattering teeth.

"This is merely a little late snow. Nothing to a winter storm." He chuckled at my horrified expression. "Your blood will thicken."

That sounded unpleasant.

He laid a blanket on the ground, took off his coat and spread it on top of that. His shirt came off next. I took some satisfaction in at least seeing chills run up his chest. Nimble fingers unbuttoned my coat.

"What are you doing?" I came as close to yelling as my scratchy voice would allow. "Who takes a coat off a freezing woman?"

"I'm warming you up, dear wife."

"Don't call me that."

"What would you like me to call you?"

"You may call me Lady Vera."

"No."

He ignored my feeble protests as he quickly and efficiently stripped me of all my clothes. Shivers racked my frame. A naked Angus lay next to me and wrapped us in coats and blankets. He drew me against his body. I pressed icy hands to his warm ribs. He hissed. I snuggled closer to his radiating flesh fire. Nothing had ever felt so good in my life.

"You stink," I said.

"So do you."

Slowly, my convulsions stopped, and my muscles relaxed. I burrowed closer, too tired and comfortable to care it was Angus Gray who held me. I melted against his warm skin. Oh, he felt so good.

Calloused hands explored my back, and I felt his body shift gears.

"Stop getting ideas," I said.

"Too late."

I had the sickening feeling this had been his plan from the beginning. "I'm still too sore," I lied.

Large hands widened their range. "Best thing for soreness is to work it out." He made certain we moved, but not in concert. He'd taken his pleasure within the span of my held breath. He was right about reducing the ache. When he pulled out of me, I felt my body and heart callus over.

CHAPTER 8

Truth

Tucked against Angus's hot skin, I felt like I'd slept mere minutes when a Glenn butted into the cave.

"Sky is clear," he said with a thick burr.

Angus lifted his head. "How many hours of daylight?"

"Three."

"I want to make it to Cabin before then."

"The cuddies are saddled. Wer ready when ye are."

I meant to glower at the man's suggestive tone, but instead a giggle escaped. Angus raised a surprised brow, and a pleased look passed over his face. I replaced my smile with a scowl.

After the man left, Angus got up. I almost called him back as frozen tendrils penetrated my cocoon. He lifted his coat, and my hair went with it.

"Ow." My head jerked to the side. I sat up, clutching the blankets to slow the fleeing warmth.

"It's caught." He showed me the button tangled in a messy blond braid. He tugged.

"Don't rip it like you did my dress."

He dropped the coat on my lap. "Your hair is impractically long. Let me cut it."

"No." Angry, I worked my frayed braid free and flung his coat at him. I made a mad dash to get into my clothes before the shakes overtook me again.

Back home, my hair had been a beautiful thing. I despaired that now it was an ugly impractical mass. Towing the blanket, I marched into lightly falling snow.

Perched on Pearl, engulfed in the blue plaid quilt, I finished the day's ride. I swooned when low stone buildings came into view. Smoke waved happily from the chimneys. Three people ran out of the biggest building as we approached. They looked like everyone else from Alta Glenn, strong as beasts and dressed practically with canvas pants and sturdy boots.

"Welcome," the woman said.

"We expected you hours ago," the man said.

"Snow held us up." Angus pulled me down from my horse onto wonderfully solid ground.

The man stopped in surprise. "It was that bad? It's dreich here, but we didn't get a storm."

They'd stopped for me. The soft one from Campbell. I stood a little taller, waiting for Angus to admit his *dear wife* was a thin-blooded weakling.

"No, it wasn't bad. We stopped to enjoy it." The side of his mouth turned up.

The man gave Angus an odd look. "I'll see to the cuddies."

"Thank you. Marna, please see to the lady." He motioned to me. "I believe she'd like a bath."

I skipped to Marna's side. I'd never felt so vulgar, and never imagined I could smell this foul.

"Welcome to Cabin." She had a round face, dimpled cheeks, and short white hair. "How was your ride?"

Such a simple question compared to the full catalogue of possible responses that rose to my tongue. "It was my first time on a horse."

She halted, her brows rising. She put a thick hand on my forearm. I leaned toward her touch. "Oh, you sweet thing. That's a long ride." She nodded her head toward my group. "Even for those tough-assed brutes."

She looked as resilient as the rest of the Glenns, but my lips curved up for the first time in days. "Thank you."

Her dark eyes crinkled in delight. She seemed to draw my emotions out of the hole I'd locked them in. As she held the door and ushered me into a warm, homey-smelling building, I felt the urge to bury my face in her soft shoulder and cry.

She hesitated in the hall. "Will you be rooming alone tonight?"

I wished. "With Angus. We're newly married."

Her eyes widened, and I braced myself for her condescension.

"He's a lucky man."

The knots in my belly unspooled, and I lurched forward, throwing my arms around her stout shoulders.

She patted my back. "There, there. Men aren't always easy partners. I've nearly nailed my precious Douglas to a tree more than once, but you've got to swallow the vinegar with the honey. After a bath and some dinner, you'll feel right as rain again."

I leaned back and nodded, rapidly blinking watery eyes.

Marna opened a door. "In here's the chief's room. Your room."

I sighed at the sight of the large bed and fluffy blankets, thinking only of peaceful sleep and not how I'd have to share it with a brute.

I followed her to the lavvy. She turned the spigot above the large tub. "Dinner is down in the largest building in the middle. I'll make sure your bag is brought into your room right away."

"Thank you."

She gave my hand a reassuring squeeze before stepping out.

Sinking into the hot bath was pure bliss. So, all Glenns weren't demon spawn. I hoped there'd be people like Marna in Pinehearth, and that Angus's mother would welcome me as kindly.

Freshly clothed, scrubbed pink, and hair combed, I joined the group for dinner. Angus wasn't there. Gladly, I found Koda at the end of the table and sat at his side.

"How are you?" he asked.

"Hungry." I accepted the stew and hardly tasted it before the bottom of the bowl appeared.

"I'm worried about you."

I gazed into his warm honey eyes, unsure if it were a compliment or an insult.

"This is tough," he said. "Even for me."

"You having second thoughts?"

He smiled. "I'm up to about a thousand of those by now." His gaze traveled over my face, and his voice lowered. "But I won't leave you."

I turned to my bowl, thinking the warmth in my core wasn't from the soup. "Home seems far away, doesn't it?" I jolted when his hand found my leg under the table. Just as quickly, it was gone again. Little more than a phantom comfort.

"I'll get you back there. I'll figure out a plan."

I clung to his promise, grateful to have an ally in this sea of enemies. I ignored the niggling voice in my head, reminding me of Marna's kindness.

Angus entered the dining hall. I wasn't the only one improved by a bath. Wet brown hair curled around his ears. He scanned the room, his gaze landing on me. Before he could sit next to me, I stood. "Good night, Koda."

"Lady Vera."

I walked away without a word to Angus.

I threaded my way through the chilly night to the comfortable room, and sprawled over the bed. Being clean and warm helped with my misery. I'd survived the first few days, barely. I hoped to make that trip one more time—on the way home to Campbell. Koda and I would figure out how to destroy the Grays and free my country.

Angus didn't knock when he interrupted my musings.

"Marna brought these out after you left." He held out a tray of figs rolled in crushed pistachios.

I stood and drew near. "Glenn treats." I picked one up and took a bite. It wasn't bad, but it wasn't dessert. I took the whole tray. "I'm sneaking these in my pockets tomorrow."

"I won't tell." His gaze landed on my mouth. "You've got something." His thumb brushed a crumb from my lower lip. His fingers lingered, and he bent down.

I slapped his hand off and ducked away.

His eyes darkened. "Stop acting the victim. You made your choice. You chose me. Stop making it miserable."

I rocked back. "Chose you. Ha. I had no choice. You were going to kill my father."

His jaw dropped. His brows pulled up, revealing shining silver eyes. "What?" After a tense pause, his face turned to hewn steel. "We were never going to kill anyone."

I humphed at his asinine lie. "If I didn't marry you, you were going to kill my parents. Like you did Trista."

"Sit down, Vera."

"No."

His expression changed, and I read frustration on his handsome face. He put his hand on my shoulder and pushed me down. I thumped onto the bed. He crouched, and his stormy eyes bore into me. "We came to Campbell to removed Hugo's title, not his head."

I blinked.

"His actions have bordered on treason for some time. He begged for a second chance—third or fourth really. He offered you as a show of his loyalty—assuming you *agreed*."

Betrayal washed over me like burning acid. Father had given me away. Offered me to them like a trussed pig.

"Hugo argued he would never move against his own daughter." The room spun at Angus's words. "My father has been a burr in my side about getting married so I thought this was a good way to silence him for a while. He couldn't say I wasn't trying. It wouldn't have been my fault when my choice denied me."

Each word was a punch in the stomach. My voice came out like a rasp. "You never wanted to marry me?"

"The only thing I knew for sure about you is that you hated me."

Stunned, I whispered, "So, you don't want to be married to me either?"

His jaw tightened at the word *either*. "I expected you to spit on my offer."

"Answer my question," I insisted.

"You're doing a good job of making this unpleasant."

Self-pity welled up like black tar clogging my chest, and I held my tongue.

His lips softened. "I wouldn't have risked it if I haven't seen brawn and courage in you. You're well bonnie to look at, besides."

I flung off the kind words I ached for. "That's not a good enough reason."

"My duty is to the Realm." How could he be so calm? "Campbell is vastly important, and yet your domain has been troublesome and unhappy. I hoped that joining our lands through marriage would strengthen the bonds of loyalty."

In other words, make Campbell easier to rule, but the way he said it made him sound almost noble.

Confusion churned, making my head ache. Father had twisted my thoughts, manipulated me. He'd let me think he was going to be killed. He'd played the victim so well. He'd lied, and I wanted to know why. I heard his answering voice in my head, *I've been chamberlain for twenty-two years. My father for thirty-seven. My grandmother for twenty-nine. Before the Grays, my family ruled*

Campbell for centuries. They won't give my right to someone else, even if it's merely a puppet title.

My father loved being chamberlain more than anything, more than me. I rubbed at the pinch in my chest. "Was it my Father's idea for me to come to the gathering?"

Angus looked surprised. "Of course."

Bloody hell. How deep did Father's deceit go? I was physically sick. Heat licked my sternum and up my neck. "I thought Bear forced me."

Angus frowned.

My fingers, icy and quivering, wrapped around my throat. "If you weren't going to kill my father, what were you going to do?"

"We offered him the Matheson Laboratory and intended to install a more loyal chamberlain."

"You threatened his life." I swallowed back bile, unwilling to accept I could be so ignorant or wrong.

"No." He rested a hand on my knee. I shoved it away. The crease in his brow deepened.

"You're lying." My voice rose.

"Just because you were lied to doesn't mean I'm lying." His voice was infuriatingly calm.

Betrayal clawed into my heart, and I washed it away with fury. I stood, my limbs shaking. "You forced me from my family, and now you wish to turn me against them." My hot voice blasted through the room. "You're a liar and a killer, and I hate you."

Angus stood to his full height and stared down his noble nose at me.

I fumed, too furious to care that I'd goaded a murderer. He could end my life in seconds.

His jaw rippled as he worked his teeth. "I'll *never* lie to you." His voice was low and deadly serious. Eyes ablaze, he strode out, the door slamming behind him.

Anger abandoned me, taking my strength with it. I dropped to the bed like a corpse, and gasped at the pain grating through my chest. His revelations were a nightmare on repeat.

Father had offered me up to keep his trifling title.

I buried my face in my hands and bawled. Ugly sobs tore from my chest in violent waves. I tried processing my family's betrayal as Angus's lies, but I knew better.

Father had never used the word kill. I had assumed that, and he'd couched his words so I would think it the truth. Bear and Angus had seemed truly shocked when I accepted the marriage proposal. Angus's story fit too well for a fable. His words settled over me with the weight of truth.

Shouts from outside pulled me from my wallowing. Wrung out, I jerked on my coat. I pulled the hood down over my stinging eyes and followed the noise. The chilly night air kissed my hot cheeks. A spotlight illuminated the crowd gathering outside the main lodge. I darted to the side of the building and into the shadows. I halted at the sight before me.

Angus and Boratio, wearing only pants, wrestled in the muddy snow. Boratio was thicker than Angus and had his arms wrapped around Angus's dirty back. They slammed into the ground, and Angus rolled free. The men crouched, circling the cold ground with bare feet.

"Come on, chief," Gent yelled.

Angus charged, ramming Boratio. The bigger man slipped onto his back. They rolled in the mud, all muscle and male. Angus ended up on top. His knee pinned Boratio's chest. The spectators clapped and hollered.

Angus panted like Pearl on an incline, more beast than human. "Again?"

That was the monster my father handed me to for a title to a conquered country.

Repulsed, I ran to my room and wedged a chair under the door handle. I didn't feel much like freeing Campbell only to hand my home over to a lying bag-of-garbage father.

That night, while I waited for a husband who never came, I decided to lock it all away. Forget past pain and move on. I needed to get smart. Get strong. Learn.

With his slippery persuasive words, Father sold me for a government position. I hoped he would make the most of the bargain. I certainly would.

After I brought down the Grays, I'd settle things with my father.

I was going to be his chieftess, after all.

CHAPTER 9

Choice

Tense with determination, I woke before the sun, dressed, and strode to the main building. Rounding a corner, I halted before our saddled, half-mounted riding party. Dressed for travel, Angus adjusted Coal's bridle.

Anger flamed up inside me, making me want to punch his pretty nose. He stood only three steps away, but I yelled, my shrill voice ringing in the crisp morning air. "Were you going to abandon me?"

Every face turned to me. Mouths hung open in shock.

Angus draped an arm over Coal's black neck and turned a grim face my way. "Gent will take you back to Campbell. You'll be safe. I'd trust him with my life."

I squashed the hope blooming at the thought of going home, wondering if I'd be welcome there. My parents had rejected me. Angus wasn't going to as well. I folded my arms. "How rude."

His brows shot up.

I made a show of looking around. "Where's my horse?" How I wished for the skill to leap on Pearl's back and gallop off in an impressive display of temper. *Someday.*

Instead I waited in humiliation while a man coaxed my obedient animal forward. The Glenn handed me the lead rope. I steeled my spine, willed Pearl not to make a fool of me, and snatched it. "Thank you."

Angus smirked. "Now what, dear wife?"

"Now you will kindly tie this terrifying creature to yours."

"Which terrifying creature?"

My cheeks pinked, and my voice came out soft. "Both of us." I forced an apologetic smile.

Even the wind seemed to hold its breath while Angus stared me down. For long dreadful moments, I feared he would send me away in shame. Finally, he exhaled and stepped up. He took the rope from my hand. I jumped out of the way as he pulled Pearl forward.

"Gent," Angus called. "Get yourself and my dear wife some scran. You're coming with us." He turned to me. "I intend to make it to Pinehearth by sundown."

"I can do it." I had no idea what I'd promised. Clearly, I needed to get out of the habit of making blind commitments.

He looked skeptical.

"I will." My tone was fierce.

"Then go get your bag."

I darted back to my room, worried they might still leave without me. I wrapped the figs in a cloth and stuffed them in my coat pocket. I threw my nightshirt in my bag. The bottle of pills from Lanie clacked against my fingernails. I halted, pulling out the small jar labeled *For Constipation.*

A lie.

Father was a liar.

Hurt, betrayal, and anger churned through my gut. I would not be like him.

I am not a liar.

Before I thought about the consequences or lost courage, I tossed the Preprep into the rubbish bin. My duffle went over my shoulder. I shot out the door and rammed into Koda.

His arms flew around me, and his attempt to steady me felt more like an embrace. "Please reconsider."

"Reconsider what?" I inched around him, but he blocked my path.

"This is your chance to escape. Go home."

"No." I'd go home when the Grays no longer owned it.

"I'll handle the Glenns."

I huffed in disbelief. "Not without me."

"You'll be safer and happier at home."

How presumptuous of him to presume what would make me happy. It certainly wasn't going home to my backstabbing, traitorous, daughter-selling family. "I am going to Pinehearth. Father sent you to look after me, so help."

"Hugo sent me because you're not strong enough on your own."

Screw you, Father. And you too, Koda. "Get. Out. Of. My. Way." I shoved past him and ran outside.

Angus had waited for me. A flush of warmth washed through my body when I saw him standing next to the horse he'd given me.

I came to his side and looked up at clear gray eyes. "Thank you," I whispered. For the first time, I meant it.

He nodded, face solemn. He held out the stirrup. I put my foot in and reached for the saddle. He palmed my rear and heaved me up, sending a jolt through my core. It seemed last night's honesty had broken down my shields and awoken my body to a world of sensation. He didn't walk away when I'd settled in the saddle. He stepped close and wrapped a hand over my thigh. Tingles danced under his touch.

"We were both lied to." His quiet voice rumbled. "Manipulated." His serious eyes locked on mine. "We're making our own choice right now." His hand moved down to grip my calf, as if pleading, but I wasn't sure for what. His heat penetrated my pants and blossomed through my body. "I meant what I said. I won't lie to you. I accept this marriage. I'm yours, and I'll welcome you to my home."

Why? Perhaps he didn't want to lose his bedmate. More likely, he didn't want to lose his leverage with Campbell.

His upturned face shined in the golden dawn.

I had to clear my throat to get the words out. "I'm not a liar. I gave myself to you. Now take me home." *Home.* I didn't have a home.

"I hope this isn't a mistake." His hand fell away, and I missed the heat and the comfort of it.

"Me too."

He handed me warm bread.

Arms folded, Koda watched us from near the building, his frown fixed and evident.

We waved good-bye to Cabin and headed north. The first time we galloped, I was too scared to even cry. I clung to the saddle horn and counted my breaths. My legs shook like leaves when we stopped for lunch at a friendly town. This community was a combination of tents and wood cabins. I didn't dare hope I might find more than canvas walls at my final stop.

"Why don't you blast a train through here?" I asked Angus as we ate sausage pies outside a small tavern. We didn't even go inside to eat.

"We enjoy riding. It's beautiful. A train would destroy the land while giving enemies easy access."

I picked at the grass. Good reasons.

"There's a longer route the supply caravans take that's wider and easier."

I chomped on mysterious gristle in the sausage. I swallowed the lump without further chewing. *Gag.* "Sounds nice." As did a fresh persickle tart.

"Soon this journey will seem easier and shorter."

That seemed hard to believe. Even harder to believe was that Angus believed it. My lips tipped up and my belly warmed at his confidence. I dug in my pocket and pulled out a fig. I set it in his palm as I got up.

We rode past more sprawling developments with various degrees of permanence. Apparently many Glenns actually *preferred* tents so they could migrate periodically. The housing stopped abruptly with the start of a steep slope.

Midafternoon, we crested the mountain and looked down the other side. The world lay before me in majestic splendor. I was as high as the sun, and I felt why she would wish to shine brightly on such beauty.

Angus turned Coal toward the downward path on the northern side.

"Wait," I called.

He looked over his shoulder, his brow raised.

"One more minute."

Coal stopped and so did Pearl. He watched me while I soaked up the scene. Rugged mountain peaks filled the skyline. Tucked down in a wide valley, below the snowline, lay a city like a nest of jewels. Large brown timber homes, *real homes*, pushed up against glittering white cliffs. Lower in the mountain's bowl, buildings were clustered together, surrounded by fields and farms.

"Pinehearth," he said.

Sweet paradise. Delight spiraled through my body, fighting back the despondency that had taken residence in my breast. "I'm ready."

The horses seemed ready too. They tore down the mountain in a suicidal rush, as if they could smell their oats waiting. Sweat-slicked horses and humans emerged onto a wide flat road winding between pastures of sheep, cows, goats, and horses.

Farm workers waved and shouted greetings. The horses walked on a path through the fields, and then we started up the opposite slope. A grand house with steep roofs and wide wood panels rose before us. Not exactly the tents I'd imagined and dreaded.

Campbell profits had made the Glenns rich.

The others in our traveling party veered right toward a stabling barn. Angus continued toward the stern woman waiting on the front steps of the large home.

Bloody skies. The chieftess.

She was not pleased.

Angus tilted his chin over his shoulder. "I can never beat the birds."

I couldn't speak over the marble in my mouth. Naira Gray was trying to kill me with her glare. An eun stood at her side. It was small, coming only to her knees, but it stood like a soldier at attention.

Angus drew Coal to a stop and dismounted. Ignoring his mother, he fitted his hands around my waist and gently lifted me down. Like a coward, I hovered near Pearl's side, thinking it a safer place than following him up the short stairs.

"Hello, Mother." He stopped a step lower, his face now level with hers.

Naira had large brown eyes and graying hair. Deep wrinkles did little to diminish her natural beauty. Keen intelligence radiated off her, and a straight back bore evidence of strength and cunning. A blue plaid shawl was layered over her tunic. She placed her hands on Angus's shoulders and kissed his brow. "For your safe arrival home." In a flash, she swung a hand back and slapped his cheek. Angus didn't move, but I flinched. "For marrying a soft Campbell lassie without my permission or presence." Her sharp tone failed to hide her hurt.

"Forgive me, maw."

"I don't."

"The decision was a bit rash, but I don't think I made a mistake."

Why defend me?

"Look at her." Naira's disdain cut straight through me.

I straightened as two grim faces turned my way. I imagined I resembled a mouse cowering in the corner looking for an escape route.

"You'll see." His expression wasn't encouraging even though his words buoyed me.

"I see quite well."

I dipped into a low curtsy. Without billowing skirts, it felt wrong. "Please to meet you, highness."

She grunted.

"Fleming," the bird said, its round navy eyes never leaving my face.

Words failed me. Was that his name? Should I have bowed to him too?

Naira turned her back on us. "I'll see you at dinner." She and the bird went inside, and she closed the front door firmly behind her.

Angus hopped down to my side. "That could have been worse."

"You have a red hand mark on your face." Then I remembered the thin scar on his back.

"I'll walk the horses down."

"I'll come with you." Anything to avoid going inside with her, and that bird.

As we walked, I fought the urge to apologize for being a substandard wife. I didn't belong here. I'd come to kill him and his parents and free Campbell from the Glenns' murderous rule. I wasn't going to apologize for something I'd never admit.

Angus scanned the road and the houses lining it, as if looking for something—or someone. He passed off our horses to a man near the barn.

Rest well, Pearl. I shouldered my pack with all my meager belongings, feeling like a peddler.

A young woman approached. "Welcome home, chief." She took his pack.

"Thank you, Lily. Please escort my dear wife to the house."

I still didn't know if he meant to mock me when he used those words.

Her dark cold eyes flicked to me. She did not appear to like what she saw.

"Be ready for dinner in two hours." He strode away without a backward glance.

Lily and I stood awkwardly for a long moment before she motioned me forward. A female voice calling for Angus stopped my progress. I looked back. The setting sun lit up a young woman's joyous face as she flew up the street. Black hair framed strong cheekbones and almond eyes. The beautiful girl sailed at Angus, throwing her arms around his shoulders.

My stomach curdled.

Angus tensed. Tenderly, he took her arms off his neck. He held her hands in the space between their strong bodies. Her face showed the terrible journey of her emotions. Joy crumbled to confusion, then sadness and pain. They were too far away to hear, but I knew what dreadful news he shared. I couldn't see his face, only her beautiful stricken one.

"Who is that?" I breathed to Lily.

"Ana Sky."

"She loves him."

It wasn't a question, and Lily said, "Aye."

In a cruel strike, I saw with clarity all that I was not. Angus had mistakenly fallen for my father's tricks and married me, missing out on strength, grace, beauty, and a woman deeply in love with him.

My chest caved in, and I curled away, feeling weak, alone, and unwanted. I shuffled behind Lily, who thankfully did not lead me to the chieftess's home. Angus, it seemed, preferred to live alone.

It was a brutal climb for my already spent legs, but it was worth it. His home was perched on a large ledge on the side of the mountain. The house appeared nailed into the white granite rock face. Broad windows lined the front, providing a sweeping view of valley and forest.

My boots clapped against the wooden porch. Lily opened an unlocked door and flicked on the lights. I exhaled a relieved breath when no dead animals haunted me from the walls, although the couch was leather, the rug appeared to be a headless bearskin, and there was a fur blanket covering the bed, which I spied through an open door.

Only Angus and me all the way up here.

There were no single-bedroom freestanding homes in the city of McAndrew. My family shared the East Tower of the Cromarty Institute with a hundred virtuosos.

Lily handed me a letter and left me in my new home. I dropped my duffle near a dresser in the bedroom and unfolded familiar peach parchment.

Little Sister,

I've never sent a letter to Pinehearth before. How's your new home? What are the walls made of? Do you have a shower? Send me some sketches.

We left the gathering early. It was too depressing. Although Fitz did his best to cheer me up.

My eyes wavered on the words. Exactly how did he cheer her up? I shouldn't care.

I was married.

Misty stopped talking to me. Not my fault you're so much prettier, smarter, and braver than she is. She never had a chance with Angus. She's also steamed that I accidently dropped the Preprep in the toilet. I'd say you owe me, but I can imagine your eyes flaming if I did.

Our room is too quiet without your joyful presence.

Love you. Lanie.

Also. How was it?

Paper crinkled as I fisted the letter. *It?* How was it? We were not huddled in bed giggling and gossiping anymore. This was my life. Messy. Painful. Miserable. Real.

The second letter was from Mother.

Dear Vera,

We're so proud of you. We miss you so much. We think about you all the time. I saw a Trille yesterday and thought of your green-rimmed blue eyes. Even the flower couldn't compare. You're so brave. Remember the necklace. You're strong as granite. If you want to tell me all about your first few days, I'd love to hear it. Don't forget how capable you are.

We love you, Margaret and Hugo Wilson.

Oh, stop it. I knew the terrible truth. And *really* with the full name signature.

I threw the letters away and stripped. The shower jetted out ice chunks. I shivered and hissed as I scrubbed furiously at the rank smell of horse clinging to me.

Finally clean, and nearly hypothermic, I rummaged through my clothes. I felt like the one dress I'd packed from Campbell: out of place, cumbersome, and wrinkled. I put on one of the outfits Angus had given me of practical pants and a warm flannel shirt. Fighting against the tangles in my hair warmed my arms. My hair reached my hips, and was a pain. Angus didn't have any hair oil, and I finished combing out my mane with a sore scalp and frizzy hair.

I tied the wad up in a bun.

In a comfortable seat by the window with nature safely outside, I wrote Lanie a letter. Only Lanie.

My ears steamed, and my heart hurt at the thought of replying to my parents after that farce they performed at the gathering.

Twenty-two years their daughter, and nothing more than a commodity to be traded for a title worth little or nothing.

CHAPTER 10

Unwelcome

Angus found me in a large armchair hunched over my sketchbook, pencil flying. I flipped over the page, hiding the depiction of Ana Sky's stunning and heartbroken face.

He motioned to the sitting room and kitchen. "What do you think?"

I thought he used Campbell's money well. "It exceeds expectation."

He turned away and hung his riding coat near the door. Face blank, he strode over to me. "May I see?"

I flipped some pages and held up an old drawing of Lanie playing polisque with two friends.

"It exceeds expectation." He swept into the bedroom.

Well played.

Ten seconds later, he appeared with a towel around his waist and surprise on his face. "You took a frozen shower?"

I nodded.

"Lily doesn't usually forget to start the water furnace when I return."

She hated me.

Fifteen minutes later, next to a fresh, clean-shaven prince, I walked down the steep path to dinner with Naira. The chieftess. Who also hated me.

It was only the three of us. I didn't include Fleming, the bird, in the count. No long dining hall feeding hundreds every meal. I might've enjoyed the peace and privacy if Angus and his mother weren't there.

Ten bowls spread between us on the table, each filled with something different. When Naira picked up the first bowl, I lifted the one directly in front of me. She scooped some carrots from her bowl onto her plate. I spooned red beans onto my plate. Angus handed me a flat, warm circle of bread. I took my first bite of beans and nearly swooned. I no longer heard Angus or Naira, I only heard my hunger leap up and grab my attention. I glanced up in surprise when I heard my name.

Naira and Angus focused on me, and I figured one of them had asked me something.

She spoke. "I'll take it as a compliment that you like my reds."

Blood flooded to my face. I'd wiped the bowl clean with my flat bread before passing it. "Please excuse me. Dinner is quite good, thank you."

Amused, she passed me the other bowls. Reluctantly, I took a small portion of each, including the goat. Fleming got up from his nap on a feather-strewn pillow. He waddled over to Naira's elbow and looked at her with round dark eyes.

"Yer so spoilt." She dropped him a piece of meat.

"Not spoiled," Fleming said with a gravelly voice. He swallowed the chunk. "Overcooked."

"Your meat's over there." She pointed to a bowl of raw meat. "Go eat it."

"Not hungry."

"Because you're lazy."

"Smart," Fleming said. "No wasted energy."

She narrowed her eyes, but I sensed she loved that bird. "He's the smarted eun I've ever trained. I wish he didn't know it." She looked at me. "What are you good at?"

I tried not to cower before the straight nose she stared down. Angus had inherited that noble nose. "I'm good at drawing, reading, writing, cataloging…" I faltered at the cold look from the chieftess. I wracked my brain for more. "I did well in biology, although not as well as my sister."

"What do you intend to do here?"

End her tyrannical reign over Campbell. "I am at your disposal."

She let out a high incredulous laugh. "I have no use for you." She might as well have slapped me as she had Angus.

He said, "We'll find a good place for you to contribute." He didn't look quite as skeptical as Naira.

"I'll like to learn to ride Pearl properly."

His brows rose, revealing bright pale eyes.

Naira said, "Join the training at the stables at eight." She turned and asked Angus about the gathering, dismissing me.

Hogg had a serious outbreak of red velvet. Campbell had the vaccine, but not nearly enough of it and not yet the cure. The Glenns hadn't gotten vaccinated on their trip because of the treason at Cromarty. Hogg was given more freedom and hopefully they wouldn't use it poorly and decide to rebel again. Chamberlain Wilson was still considered a rebellious threat. I nearly snorted in disbelief at that one.

They spoke as if I weren't there, except when Naira asked Angus about some missing rifles. His gaze flickered to me, and he didn't answer.

He didn't trust me. The feeling was mutual.

"Father plans to be home in four weeks," Angus said. "We'll have my wedding celebration the day after his arrival."

Naira pursed her lips. I held my breath. He waited, his jaw set. She exhaled. "This is not what I wanted, son. Is this truly what you—"

"This is what is."

She nodded stiffly. He stood and held out a calloused hand to me. I latched on.

"Thank you for dinner, maw."

"Yes, thank you." I now sounded like the mouse I'm sure I resembled.

We left the grand house through a side door. The moment we got outside, he dropped my hand. I folded it into my armpit to replace the loss of warmth.

The sun had set and trees loomed like giant ghosts. He strode purposefully up the path. I jogged at his side, my focus entirely on not tripping in the darkness. Wordlessly, he led me inside his home. Our home.

He flipped on a lamp in the bedroom and starting take off his boots. Maybe it was this handsome home, maybe it was the look of desire on Ana's face, maybe it was the walls we'd broken down this morning, but I was not afraid of the night with him.

Horrified revulsion didn't beat at me as I prepared for bed. On principle, I still slipped into my nightshirt when he went to the sitting room. Exhausted, I crawled under the heavy blanket and into the wide comfortable bed.

I jerked awake a few minutes later, groping the cold sheets filled with worry. I sat up and scanned the darkness. "Angus?"

"What is it, dear wife?" His voice came from outside the bedroom door.

I tiptoed to the door. He sprawled over the couch in the main room. Bare shoulders peeked out of a blanket. A pile of clothes heaped on the floor. Pale feet stuck off the end of the sofa.

"Oh." Surprise and several emotions I wasn't ready to acknowledge hit me. "Okay. Good night." I bolted back to the bed. This was good. But I didn't feel like it was good. Guilt and hurt coiled in my belly. This was his home, and his bed where I curled contentedly.

This had to be about Ana. After seeing her, he didn't want me. The thought dug its claws into my chest and wouldn't let go. I flinched with each howling animal sounding off in the distance, each creaking tree swaying near the house, and each haunting whisper of wind.

***

Angus traipsed into the bedroom with the sun, dragging me out of sleep.

"Lily brought breakfast," he said. "She'll come clean and launder this morning. Put your clothes in the basket."

"Thank you," I said, feeling appreciation I didn't communicate. I didn't know how to cook or clean.

"Pearl is stabled at the east barn. Do you remember where that is?"

I nodded.

"Good. Then I won't take you. I should get started on the one hundred and seventy-two reports that came in during my absence."

Apparently, ruling was a lot of work. I'd like to relieve him of Campbell's portion of the job.

"You can find me at the large bit with the flag if you need me."

I didn't intend to find it. He didn't want me, and I certainly didn't need him.

CHAPTER 11

Rider

At the door of the stables, a thick-legged woman with tight leather pants addressed a group of eight children. I might have been insulted Naira had invited me to join six-year-olds if I hadn't been so relieved. I knew about being a student in class, even if this one was out in nature and possibly dangerous.

"Aye," she said to me when I'd inched close enough to be intrusive.

"Good morning. My name is Vera."

"Minerva."

"I'd like to join your riding lesson."

The woman's jaw dropped. All eight young faces stared at me with shameless curiosity. The little girl with red pigtails giggled.

Minerva regained her composure quickly. "Aye, Vera from Campbell."

So, everyone in Pinehearth had heard of me. Not Vera the future chieftess. Not Angus's wife. I had a journey if I wanted to change the tide of negative opinions. I doubted it would be worth it.

"You don't know how to ride a horse?"

"I'd like to learn."

"Off you go then." Resigned, she motioned me toward the line of children.

After a lecture on treating the animals with respect, Minerva let us into the barn. Stable hands helped us saddle our mounts. I rubbed a tentative hand along Pearl's bony white nose. Glossy black eyes sent a smile spreading over my face. "You missed me, huh. Well, I suppose it's nice to see you too."

My only friend here, I thought with a pang.

Minerva approached as I nervously led Pearl to where the class waited for me next to horses that looked more likely to eat the small girls and boys rather than submit to them. Minerva thumped Pearl's neck.

"She's a good cuddy. One of the best mares we've had in years."

Angus gave this treasure to me. He'd brought her to the gathering in case I said yes. A bridal gift for *me*. Guilt seeded in my stomach. I intended to repay his generosity with mutiny.

"Take good care of her."

I didn't know how.

Minerva turned and yelled, "Mount up. Walk your horse round the pasture along the right. Hug the fence. Let's see how close you can get. I'm watching posture."

Nerves firing, I sat on a horse without someone else controlling it. Turned out, I need not have worried about Pearl galloping off with me. She wouldn't budge. I coaxed and pleaded and gave the reins an unpleasant jerk. I told Pearl how embarrassing it was that the little boy who couldn't reach the stirrups had his horse hugging the fence like a champion. Minerva's flat hand on Pearl's rump got us moving.

After a rough two hours, I gratefully gave up the reins and trudged away. Angus hadn't mentioned lunch, and I didn't dare approach Naira or Lily for anything. The cracking of guns led me to the training fields.

Koda and nine others were shooting muskets at wooden targets. I had the sudden urge to try it too. He saw me as they packed up, and he split from the group.

"What are you doing for lunch?" I asked.

"Headed there now. Want to join?"

"Yes, please." The words poured out in a grateful rush.

He sent me a meaningful glance.

"I'm fine." *Enough.*

He squeezed my shoulder and led me into a low cabin, dense with the smell of grease and garlic. Strangers eyed me with curiosity before getting busy with the task of eating. I sat timidly at one of the long tables. This felt more like eating at home, yet I felt totally out of place.

Koda handed me a bowl with flatbread and delightful-looking beans mounded next to chunks of chicken and dark greens.

"Thank you," I said, eager to stuff my face as the others were.

"Haud," a deep voice bellowed.

I froze.

A man strode forward. He was older than most of the others in the room and smaller, but by the sharpness in his eyes and the straightness of his spine, I didn't think it would be a good idea to underestimate him. "Who do we have here?"

"This is Lady Vera," Koda said. "Vera, this is Bale, the weapons master."

I bowed my head and swallowed a nervous lump. "Pleased to meet you."

"We earn our scran here."

The music of scraping forks and conversation silenced.

Bale's eyes glinted with challenge, but I sensed an invitation instead of hostility. Or maybe I dreamed it, but I accepted it anyway.

"What must I do?"

His look of approval warmed me. "It's wrestling after lunch. You'll join us."

Koda tensed.

I nodded. Whatever I would find in the training room couldn't be worse than walking out of here a hungry coward.

"Eat up," Bale said. "You'll need yer brawn."

CHAPTER 12

Fighter

Dread and excitement mixed like oil and water.

"You don't have to do this," Koda said as we followed the trail of people out of the dining hall and over to the training yard.

"Yes, I do. How else can I earn their respect? I must get stronger."

He pursed his lips.

"I won't walk away in shame."

"What if you get hurt? There's no shame in your upbringing, which didn't include fighting."

"I'm not in Campbell anymore."

Soft spring grass carpeted the field, and a cool breeze blew the scent of trees and dirt up my nose.

"Pair up for the basic warm-up," Bale said. "You two Campbells partner. Ye can learn together."

Koda balked, but I smiled. I'd already looked over the other competition, while carefully avoiding Ana's burning gaze, and found Koda the easiest target. We lined up for deep breathing and then a series of flowing body movement that left me sprawled on the ground more than once. No one laughed—that I could hear anyway. No one looked except Koda and Ana.

"Grab yer partner and ten paces of open space," Bale said when I was warm and breathing hard. He stood by Koda and me and put a wiry hand on our shoulders. "Watch first."

Gent and another guard, Scotsbane, circled each other, legs bent and hands up. They scuttled in and out, trying to get a hand on their opponent.

"See the legs," Bale said. "Muscles engaged for a stronger base. Harder to tip someone squatting then standing stiff."

Scotsbane was a mountain of a man while Gent was a tree. I thought Gent would splinter under obvious superior strength. I was wrong. Gent lunged with inhumane speed. He grabbed Scotsbane's shoulders. Scotsbane twisted, but Gent was stronger than he looked and would not be dislodged. Scotsbane wrapped an arm around Gent's ribs, catching Gent's shirt, which lifted to reveal hard, lean muscles.

I did not look like that underneath. My weak abdomen tightened.

The men slammed to the ground. To my shock, the bigger Scotsbane ended up on his back with a painful grunt. Gent grinned down at his prey.

I didn't want to do this anymore.

"Now try," Bale said to us.

Koda and I faced each other. I gave him a nervous grin that he didn't return. Feeling awkward and stupid, I bent my legs and tried to tackle him. I slammed my shoulder into a wall of flesh. My breath hitched when his hands found my waist and pushed me away. I stumbled back. I tried again, and this time he clamped me against his chest and held me there. I wiggled and strained, but couldn't escape. I succeeded only in feeling my attraction rise as I explored his chest and abs with my hands. He chuckled.

"Stop laughing at me." My tone held the force my body lacked.

"Koda," Bale barked. "Yer with Gent."

Ha. That was going to hurt.

Koda dropped me. I wobbled, unsure whether my heart raced from exertion or the moment I'd spent in the protection of his wing.

"Ana. Come teach Vera something."

I went as still and cold as prey. Her angry brown eyes locked on mine. She sauntered forward.

"Hello," I said, a little too cheery and loud.

"Bend your knees."

I didn't see her move until I was staring at azure sky. My head spun, and my spine barked. The beautiful wild woman loomed over me. She held out a hand and easily pulled me to my feet, only to slam me into the ground again.

"I said *teach* her something," Bale yelled from across the yard.

Green stained the elbows of my white shirt.

"Fight back," Ana said.

"I'm trying."

The next time she pinned me to the dirt, she did it in slow motion while commenting on what she was doing. I got up in even slower motion.

I wouldn't cry.

"Vera," Bale said. "Come here."

Like a student heading to the head office expecting expulsion, I approached Bale. He put a hand on my weak shoulder and led me to a series of bags. He picked up the smallest one. I staggered under the unexpected weight when he dropped it in my arms.

"Squat."

My leg muscles trembled. He adjusted my feet wider. Sweat broke out on my brow.

"Stand."

I forced my legs straight again and dropped the bag.

"Do that twenty times, then ye can bolt. It'll be archery tomorrow."

"Yes, sir." He'd invited me back. I wasn't expelled. Sheer willpower got me through the squats. That and maybe a little bit of Ana watching, as well as Koda.

I was glad no one saw me trudge up the path to Angus's—my house—like a drunken mouse. Lily had washed my clothes and stacked them on the dresser. A hairy brown spider the size of my palm blinked at me from the collar of my shirt.

Lily still hated me.

I did the only rational thing I could think of. While sitting a safe distance away, I drew the spider. I retreated to the kitchen and wondered briefly if Lily poisoned the food before I shoved nuts and cheese in my mouth. I sat on the couch to finish my snack, intending to shower immediately. The next thing I knew, Angus was nudging me awake.

"What happened to you? Yer loused." He perched on the ottoman, fresh-faced and in a clean shirt.

I peeled my grimy head off the leather. "I met Minerva. Then I met Bale."

He laughed, a deep rumbling sound that revealed large straight teeth. For the first time today, I didn't feel like the laughter aimed at me was mocking. I relaxed. His laughter made me smile, but pain quickly killed it. I clutched my barking abs.

He sobered. "Cold tub for you tonight."

"What? No hot water again?"

"Not if you want to walk tomorrow."

I held up my spider sketch. "Is this going to kill me?"

A lock of wavy brown hair fell over his tan forehead. "Looks like a taran. So no. Where did you see it?"

Prying my aching body off the couch, I motioned him toward the bedroom and pointed where the monster still nested in my shirt. He strode over, picked up the shirt and spider, and went outside with it.

"Brave," I said when he returned and handed me my de-spidered shirt. "Thank you."

"You're welcome, dear wife."

If only our words didn't feel so stilted and shallow. It was easier this way, I told myself as I hobbled to the bathing room. He followed. He turned on the bath—only cold.

"I really don't think that's necessary. I'll be fine after a good rest."

"Get in."

"No, thank you."

His brows pinched together. "I'll help you if you want."

I hugged my shirt. I didn't doubt him. "I'll do it."

He looked disappointed. "Soak for twenty minutes. I'll fetch dinner."

When the front door closed, I stripped. I stepped into the freezing tub and yelped. It was torture lying down. Horrible invented-by-the-Grays torture. By the time I got out, I thought I would never feel warm again. I debated whether to put on my thin nightdress or a fresh set of clothes. I was tired and hopefully going to bed soon, but I chose the clothes. I still had to sit at dinner…with Angus.

Dressed in pants and a tunic, I shuffled to the kitchen. He came through the front door, and I had the sudden urge to press against his hot skin. I sat at the oak table and gratefully accepted the dinner plate.

"How was your day?" I speared a soft potato.

"Long and tedious. I hate being chained to that desk."

"I'll trade you."

"Be careful what you say. One of these days I might take you up on it."

I grinned. Yes, I intended to take his office.

His gaze lingered on my lips before he returned his attention to his steak. "I'm glad you've joined the training group. You'll learn a lot from Bale."

"If he doesn't kick me out for being weak."

"I have a feeling you won't let that happen."

My ribs expanded with pleasure at his encouragement.

"Ana is in that group. She's good at leveraging her smaller mass against the lads."

And just like that, my chest collapsed.

After dinner, while Angus washed the dishes, I drew Gent and Scotsbane wrestling. Blond-haired Gent, long and lithe, wrapped around the redheaded Scotsbane, thick and strong.

I slipped into the bedroom and changed into my nightdress. Surely he would join me tonight. A part of me wanted him to seek me out. There would be no pleasure in it for me, but I found perverse interest in his desire for me and in the act. I ached for more power over him, and I wouldn't get it with muscle, no matter how long I spent at the training yard.

I peeked my head out the door. He was reading a book on the couch. The muscles of his thighs splayed over the ottoman and were outlined by tight pants. I recoiled against the memory of his weight crushing me.

No, I did not want him pinning me. "Good night," I said.

He looked up, his face blank, though his gaze dropped down my figure. "Good night, dear wife. Oh wait."

I went taut as canvas stretched over a frame.

"Letters arrived for you this afternoon. I meant to give them to you first thing, but you looked so peaceful asleep, and then I forgot." He pointed a small table near the door.

Nightdress billowing, I darted out and retrieved the letters. Back in the bedroom, I closed the door and read a peppy note from Mother and Father. I tossed that garbage aside and picked up Lanie's letter.

Dear Little Sister,

How's the new home? Write me all the details. With pictures. Are you making friends?

My eyes prickled with tears. I wouldn't be responding to that question.

I'm seeing a new place too. Father and I are in Porto.

Rage dried my sadness. That was supposed to be my trip.

I hate you're not here. The Marshes were thrilled to see us. I'm sure it's because of the two full train cars of medicine and supplies we brought. Although Misty got a little extra something from me. She's found a handsome boy in NewGate so now that she's got her Preprep, she's back to being as friendly as ever. She's been busy with him. Father's been meeting in private with Chamberlain Marsh. I'd be annoyed at being left out, but Fitz has been so good to me.

The shops here are incredible. Beautiful fabrics. The variety is amazing. I'm still in shock from what some of the women are wearing, though. No sleeves. Skirts as short as their knees. Trousers are popular (I blame Alta Glenn). I'm having a hard time being too appalled by their immodesty.

It's really hot here. I'm sweating through my corset every day. Fitz talked me into buying a dress that doesn't have a petticoat. It's pink and the sleeves are as soft as baby skin. It's so much cooler. I wore it last night. He took me to dinner overlooking the sea. It's so beautiful, Vera. You need to see it. I even ate seaweed, though I don't recommend it.

There have been a few cases of red velvet near the Hogg border. Father's going with Chamberlain Marsh to see if there's anything we can do to help. What they really need is to come to Cromarty for the vaccine. I'm staying in NewGate with Fitz and Misty. They're going to take me on a fishing boat. I'm so nervous I can't sleep. Hence the long letter.

I'll let you know how I do. I'll be so embarrassed if I get motion sick in front of Fitz.

Love you, Lanie.

I flopped onto the bed and stared at the wood-beamed ceiling. Giant pinchers clamped at my chest, and I decided I'd rather not examine the reasons. They felt ugly, like envy. Instead I thought about Father and why he'd visit a red velvet outbreak, and why Lanie wasn't going to the meetings. As the next chamberlain of Campbell, she should be learning instead of flirting with Fitz. I rolled over and counted out slow breaths.

I was a world away. Home and the comforting scene of Father, Mother, Lanie, and me in Campbell seemed to be dissolving into a distant memory.

Angus slept on the couch again that night. Thank the stars. At least that's what I told myself, even when I woke in the middle of the night shivering from the chill. In the morning, I felt as if every square of me had taken a beating. His cold tub was a lie.

***

The last five days had been torture. I didn't even know parts of my body existed until they'd started screaming at me. The pain distracted me from my loneliness, my homesickness, and my subjection. Bringing down the Grays with no help but Koda was going to be harder than I thought.

I tied up my hair in a bun, refusing to admit it really was a nuisance. I padded into an empty front room and found nutty crackers and bean spread in the fridge.

By the time I reached the stables, my gait was mostly normal again.

I needed to learn to ride well for when I made my escape.

CHAPTER 13

Fallen

I sat perched atop Pearl. When I asked her to walk, she walked. When I nudged her left, she obeyed. When I kicked her into a trot, she trotted, during which my entire body seized into a knot and I clung to the saddle.

"Walk," Minerva hollered from her station on the far side of the field.

I gladly pulled on the reins, and Pearl jostled to a smooth walk.

"We did it, girl." I patted her thick silvery mane in triumph. We had trotted. Without help.

"First time—"

The girl's voice over my shoulder caught me off guard, and Pearl jumped in surprise. I shifted with a jolt and fell.

My spine cracked against hard dirt, and my head snapped back. Hooves pounded the dirt inches from my face.

"Are you okay?" The child peered down from atop long, monstrous legs.

No. I was not okay. Pearl bucked me off. I curled up and held my hands over my head. I didn't want to watch the horses trample me to death.

Wet lips nipped at my elbow.

"What were you thinking?" Minerva's angry voice made me lift my head in surprise.

But she wasn't looking at the six-year-old. Minerva's flashing eyes bore into me. I got to my knees, dumbfounded.

"Pay attention, girl. You are responsible for Pearl and keeping yourself in the saddle." She grabbed Pearl's dangling reins and thrust them at me.

I took them with trembling hands.

"Mount up and stop daydreaming."

I wasn't dreaming. "She bucked me off." My voice came out in a croak.

"She did not buck." Minerva shook her head. "Horses move. You can't fall off anytime something spooks them. It's dangerous. You could get hurt."

I did get hurt.

"What if you'd been out on a trail where Pearl needed a responsible rider?"

"I'm sorry."

"All right then. Don't let me catch you napping again. Let's go." She motioned to the mounting block.

Apparently, I had to get back on. Nerves taut and muscles tight, I turned from Minerva's wide stance and heated face. Pearl bobbed her head over my shoulder as I dragged my feet across the field. I imagined her large marble eyes were looking at me with sympathy.

I humphed and rubbed her neck. "It's hard to stay mad at you, but I'd appreciate it if you'd go easy on me."

Pearl waited patiently by the mounting block. I took three deep breaths. *I could do this. I could do this.* Left foot in stirrup, I flung my right leg over.

For the rest of the hour, I paid attention with the intensity of a lab technician using potassium chlorate. By the time we dismounted my jaw ached from clenching. I rubbed the bruise forming on my side as I trudged to the stables.

Pearl nose-bumped my shoulder. I forced a smile for her benefit, wondering if it did benefit her. "You're the one who knocked me off." I glanced sidelong at the long white nose and unrepentant dark eyes.

Up ahead, Gent stepped out of the stable and held the door open for me. His blue eyes reflected the sky as he smiled. "Nice dusting, Lady."

I glanced at the smattering of dirt on my side and frowned.

"I've been there plenty myself."

"I don't believe it." I'd seen him ride. "Thanks anyway." I tugged Pearl into the shade of the stable.

He followed. "Don't let Minerva get you down. Believe it or not, she's trying to help."

I couldn't hide my half smile. "I have too many helpers around here. I could hardly walk after Bale's first day of *helping*." I took off Pearl's bridle.

He took the reins out of my hands and hung them on their peg.

"Ana's help is—"

"Let's be honest," he said, "she's not really out to help you."

I grimaced. He chuckled. Kind eyes and a playful expression cracked my gloom.

"You headed to lunch?" he asked.

I nodded. Together we ambled to the trainers' dining hall.

"Thanks," I said.

He stopped staring at the clouds and turned to me. "For what?"

"Being nice to me."

"I like you."

"You do?"

A goofy grin split his face. "Don't be so surprised. I like Campbell too."

I stopped walking. Lots of youth from Alta Glenn went to the Cromarty Institute. Angus did for a few years, but Gent had never mentioned it before.

"I considered staying on at Cromarty and applying to become a medical virtuoso. I worked in the red velvet lab for a few months when they were starting research on the vaccine, but in the end, the call of the mountains was too strong."

"My sister Lanie works in that lab."

"I met her a few times. Tried to meet her a few more times." He winked. "She wasn't going for the younger assistant."

I laughed in delight. Someone else knew Lanie. Someone else liked Campbell.

"Gent," Bale called.

We looked to where the weapons master motioned him over. He stood up the road visiting with an older woman.

"I'll see you later." He trotted off.

I watched him go, wondering if maybe I'd made a friend. I frowned. I hadn't come here for chums. Befriending Glenns would only make my job harder.

In the dining hall, with my plate of chicken salad, I settled at the end of the empty table. Trainees trickled in through the double doors. Koda's attention snapped to my spot in the back where we'd sat yesterday. A smile lit his face when he saw me already waiting. I smothered my returning grin with a bite of cucumbers. He hustled through the line and joined me.

"How was your morning?" I asked, eyeing his mountain of food with interest. How was I even considering wanting more chicken?

"Blah. Scar's lecture on the unification of The United Realm went long. Double die."

"What did he say?"

"He talked about the history of the wars, and then of course he couldn't close without spouting on about how the domains are stronger together. We're all pieces of a great whole." He tore off a bite of bread as if the roll were Scar's head.

"The Glenns are certainly better off," he whispered.

I could almost hear Ian's voice in my head. *What does Campbell get in return? What does Hogg need from Alta Glenn?* "What did he say the benefits are to the conquered domains? Did he get into specifics?"

Koda scowled, as if he didn't want to talk about it. "They seem to think that the domains aren't strong enough to fight off foreign attacks, but that's only because they don't allow us to grow our armies. They destroyed Hogg's army so Hogg would have to depend on Alta Glenn."

Three years ago, Father had taken me to visit Hogg. Ian had shown me sheds full of guns and ammunition. Factories, smiths, and forges, all melting blades and shields. "Hogg can help protect Campbell," Ian had said to me. "Together we can conquer Alta Glenn and take back our lands and our profits." The next year, the Grays had emptied Hogg's weapon stores, punishment for the Wallaces' treason.

"Would they have disbanded Hogg's army if Hogg hadn't rebelled?" I asked.

Koda's voice was an angry bee in my ear. "Gads."

I didn't point out his use of the Glenn's slang word.

"They sell us expensive timber, granite, and marble," he said, "but rob us of our inventions and medicines, and call it *taxes*. We don't have to be under their rule to be trade partners."

"I know." I tried to calm him with my voice, and tipped my head, reminding him we had company, all Glenns.

He looked at me and nodded. "I'll get you out of this—" Two Glenns sat down across the table from us. Koda shoveled chicken into his mouth. "How was your morning?"

I pursed my lips. "Possibly worse than yours. I fell off Pearl."

His fork clanged against his plate. "What?" His gaze snapped to me at the same time his hand found my thigh under the table. I jolted at the demanding touch. My knee banged the table leg.

"She jumped when one of the girls brought her horse in close, and I lost my balance. I got a tongue-lashing from Minerva. Apparently, it was my fault."

"How could it be your fault? You've never ridden a horse before. What kind of a teacher is she?"

I should move his hand. It wasn't that I didn't enjoy his concern, and his fingers on my leg. It's that I did. I relished it, and it made me uncomfortable.

"I'm fine. Minerva's not bad. She was right anyway."

"She should be more careful with you. You aren't made for this life."

I shoved his hand off, annoyed at his coddling. "I'm getting stronger."

"You shouldn't have to go through this."

I feigned interest in the last bits of sunflower seeds at the bottom of the bowl. Maybe I shouldn't, but life served up shit sometimes, and Koda's overprotectiveness bordered on insulting.

CHAPTER 14

Cold

I walked with Koda and a dozen others to the training yard. Bows hung on a rack next to a table with arrows. Targets dotted the field.

"Don't pass that white line." He pointed to the rope spread over the grass.

Obviously.

My feet grew roots as each person, Koda included, selected a weapon and stalked to the shooting line with confidence. He set the arrow between his fingers, pulled it back, and let it fly. It hit the second ring of the nearest target with a *thunk*. He winked at me before cocking another arrow and sending it toward the next target back.

Ana didn't bother with the close range. She hit the far bull's-eye. Every time.

"Ye can't learn to shoot by watching," Bale hollered.

I turned. "Why bother with arrows when you have bullets?" It made sense to use the more effective weapon.

"It's our history as archers. It's tradition."

"Not my tradition."

He ignored me and held out a complicated black device. He laid it in my hands. "Compound bow." Wiry fingers pointed to parts as he spoke. "Idler wheel, sight piece, grip, bowstring, string suppression, cable slide."

Hopefully he didn't expect me to remember all this.

He motioned me to the rope line. Taking the bow and fitting an arrow, he spoke as he demonstrated. Then he handed the contraption to me. I dropped the arrow. Twice. The string didn't draw back as easily as the others made it appear.

Looking through the eyepiece, I let the arrow go. The fletching cut my thumb as it passed and dove into the grass a few feet away. I sucked in through tight teeth and shook out my stinging hand. Thin lines of blood beaded on my thumb.

"Ye nocked too low." No apology. No concern. He pointed to the bow. "Keep the arrow up here. Again."

Sweat dribbled between my breasts. I could do this. Straining, I pulled the bowstring as far back as my trembling arm would allow, which was not that far. The arrow didn't cut my hand. It arched high before diving to the ground, not much farther than the first.

"Yer nocking is too high, and yer pull is toaty. You won't have proper aim that way. Again."

After a dozen arrows peppered the ground halfway to the closest target, Bale took the bow. I sagged like an old balloon.

"Ten push-ups over there, then yer done for the day."

I turned my back on the group and whatever judgments they decided I deserved. Down in the grass, dirt oozing between my aching fingers, I lowered my body closer to the ground. My arms gave out, and my face dropped to the muck with a grunt.

"Do them on yer knees." Bale's voice rang across the field.

Blood seeped into my dirty cheeks as dozens of faces glanced my way. I glared. Anger fueled my knee push-ups.

Finished, I marched to what was now my house.

Pinehearth was the worst place on earth. I wanted to go home. Sit in my art room. Walk the groomed garden. Eat honey-drizzled figs. An image materialized of my father giving me away at my wedding with hardly a backward glance.

Thorns dug into my chest at the realization that I didn't have a home. Father had taken it from me.

Back at the house, I took a hot shower and buried my sorrow in drawing the evening away.

Angus came home late. "Fit like?"

I stared blankly.

He sent me a pitying look and dropped his accent, now a common habit when we were alone. "How was your day?"

"Mingin," I said, in appreciation of his efforts.

He smiled at my use of a Glenn word.

I lifted my tired body off the couch. "I don't want to talk about today."

Silently, he handed me a letter on peach parchment.

Sister,

Pinehearth looks incredibly wild, but the nature is lovely in your drawings. Those trees are enormous. It must be lonely you and Angus in a home by yourselves, but I'm glad it's a house.

Father moved me out of the red velvet lab. Actually, he moved my entire team. I'm steaming. We had almost figured out how to preserve the vaccine for an extended journey. Short trips have been no problem, since we learned how to keep it stable and cold for up to three hours outside the lab. We were so close to a longer time/distance solution. Now the new crew—I don't know a single one of them (where did they come from?)—will get credit for the discovery.

Now I'm working on cataloging the growth of magi fungus in various life forms, and how fast it mutates into poison. It's sooo boring.

I lowered the letter for a moment, not able to read any further. Why would Father remove Lanie and her team? He'd never told me they could transport the vaccine short distances and long distances was the next step. Deep simmering rage at my lying father boiled and frothed inside me. Something was going on.

That night, the crushing feeling of helpless isolation plastered me to the mattress. I lay awake long into the night, but no answers came.

The next morning, I hurt even when holding still. The lessons that day weren't worth recapping. I was utterly useless.

That night I took a cold shower and felt like a new woman. Begrudgingly, I admitted that Angus had been right about the restorative properties of freezing water. I didn't tell him. Thursday was knife training. Bale didn't let me participate. I stood at the side and did infernal exercises the whole afternoon.

After eating too-tart yogurt from the fridge, I took a cold bath, which was now an integral part of my day. What would Lanie think? After toweling my neglected hair, I tied it into a braided bun. I hung up the towel and padded into the bedroom, eyes fixed on the drawer where my clean clothes waited for me. I looked up at the soft gasp.

In the doorway, Angus froze, mid-step, his eyes riveted to my bare body. The need in his gaze stopped my impulse to fling on the nearest shirt or dart back into the lavvy. I saw the inviting looks females, young and old, sent Angus. Ana's unwelcome face popped into my head.

True, Angus was my enemy, but I didn't want to share him. The twisted realization nearly stopped my heart. I dropped my arms. The hope on his face bolstered my wounded pride.

"Go ahead." If it would keep him from seeking her, I'd endure his "visits."

In the six strides it took him to cross the room, he'd stripped. I gaped at his body, strong and hard with wanting me. My blood warmed as he drew me against his front. His arms wound around my waist and hips, and he scooped me up then laid me across the bed.

I tilted my chin, waiting for those wide lips to find mine, wanting to feel something besides hollow and cast aside. He closed his eyes and tilted his face away and lowered his head by my ear. I blinked back tears. He must be imagining someone else, and I could guess who. Soft dark hair brushed my face as he efficiently satisfied his base needs. Ultimately, I was nothing more than a vessel for his release.

Spent, he climbed off the bed, leaving me without a word. He picked up his clothes and left the bedroom. The thump of the door closing behind him was a punch to my frayed heart. I pulled the fur blanket over my cold body and curled into myself like a dying rose. Naked and utterly unsatisfied, my silent tears dripped onto the pillow.

Angus's powerful body, the smell of his salty skin, and the feel of warmth spreading up my body from the memory of his touch should've brought me comfort. In that moment when he'd held me close and lifted me in his arms, I hadn't felt alone. Then he'd used me and left. Now I felt more alone than ever.

I hate you, Angus Gray.

CHAPTER 15

Jealous

Dancing practice. I'd been dreading this since Angus had told me about it last week. At least my limbs responded normally and were no longer sore. I trudged beside him into the valley and around the side of a popular tavern.

Outside again. Why must everything be done in nature? A bonfire illuminated a circular arena of packed dirt.

"Haw, Maeve." Angus strode up to the thin woman and kissed her on the cheek. It was more affection than he gave me. "Meet Vera."

The fire lit up a wrinkled face and sharp eyes. "Not as hopeless as I feared. Gossip has not been kind. Ye have graceful lines and hold yer spine properly. You have potential. We'll get ye moving like water."

Oh. Okay. Hello to you too.

"Dancing is an important part of our culture. We celebrate the strength and beauty of our bodies. Dancing celebrates community, health, and prosperity. I understand ye do not dance in Campbell."

We danced, but I sensed it best not to argue.

"Dancing is a critical part of the marriage rite," Maeve said. "Dancing becomes meaningful when we share," she motioned to the space around her body, "with a loved one."

Loved one. Ha.

Maeve motioned to a group of twelve musicians, each with a different size or shape of drum, set up on the patio by the wall of the building. I jolted in surprise when they started to play. At home, we danced to violins, bells, and tinkling pianos. My heart seemed to match beat with the low pulse of the drums.

"Watch me." Maeve's command was unnecessary. She clapped with the slowest of the beats and held her hands above her head. Moving her hips, she turned into a snake of flowing yellow silk. Her feet touched the ground when the fastest stick hit the drum. She tapped and turned with dizzying speed. Then stopped as abruptly. "All right. Now ye."

I told my body to obey, but the only response I got was the sarcastic cackle echoing inside my head.

She turned to the musicians. "Half speed."

Thank you for that.

"I smell port sauce and kidneys," Angus said. "You good? I'll be back." He jogged over and disappeared into the restaurant.

Thank you for that too. I loosened up without him watching. I clapped and tapped and suffered through Maeve's endless corrections.

"It's not random movements," she said. "Count in yer head. Follow the pattern of my feet. Be precise, the rest will follow and the rhythm will become habit."

I counted. I copied. I cried—not really—but I wanted to.

Angus emerged. Ana, Koda, Gent, and three more followed him.

It gutted me to see Angus with Ana, who smiled at him with ease and love. Did she know he was a murderer? Surely she'd never watched her precious chief kill *her* friend in cold blood.

"They want to join," Angus said.

Now that was plain mean.

"The drums always bring them out," Maeve said with a thin smile. "Partner up."

I jolted in surprise when Angus's palm wrapped my hip. He slipped a finger though my belt loop and tugged me against his side. "Will you be my partner?"

Did I have a choice?

Koda's eyes darkened as he watched us. Ana approached him and held out a tan hand.

"Dance with me, Koda?"

He nodded, but didn't smile.

The drums started again. They pulsed in my brain and through my blood. Angus's strong hands gripped my ribs, my waist, my hips, turning me, pushing me, pulling me. I tried to ignore my body waking and focus on the pattern his pounding boots left in the dirt. I was always a beat—or seventeen—behind.

All thoughts fled when his hot hand slid up my sternum and wrapped around my neck. I was stiff as a board when he curled me into his chest. His eyes shone with pleasure. I blinked in surprise. This brooding barbarian loved to dance—if one could call this stomping, sweaty activity dancing. His face was a breath away from mine. Golden light played over his lips. I had the inexplicable urge to arch forward and kiss him—to claim what was mine.

This dancing was dangerous.

"Haud," Maeve demanded.

I hopped out of his arms and wiped the moisture from my brow.

"Maybe it would help for ye to use your yaks and watch," Maeve said. "Ana, show her how it's done properly."

If I heard those words again, I was going to explode. It was bad enough that Bale said those words every day, but I nearly vomited at the look of pleasure on Ana's face when she glided up to my husband. The drums' pounding filled the world around us. They *danced*. I couldn't look away.

Maeve stood at my side. "See how they move in perfect synchronization? See their feet? See how she follows him?"

My mouth was too dry to speak. Yes. I saw it all.

Her body molded against his. He lifted her off the ground. She rolled over his back and landed without missing a beat. Firelight painted their beautiful faces in warmth. Their bright eyes and strong bodies emanated heat and power. Ana's wide smile radiated her joy. She didn't have to look at her feet as they flew over the dirt. She looked at Angus.

Well, I could see who'd practiced for their wedding dance. Sarcasm didn't stop my heart from breaking. Why did I even care? I wanted Angus to suffer for the many terrible things he had done, but a sharp pain speared through my chest, and I didn't know why.

The song ended with Angus holding Ana in his arms, faces close, their breath intermingling.

"Well tidy," Maeve said, breaking the spell.

Angus set her down and turned to find me.

I was no Ana Sky. No wild creature who could call down the stars when she danced and wrestle grown men to the ground.

He held out a hand to me. For a split second, I saw past my hatred. I saw an achingly handsome man reaching for *me*. The fire turned his eyes a bright gold and gilded his straight nose and high cheekbone.

Oh no. Oh no. No. No.

With my stomach in my throat, I whirled around and ran. I sprinted down the main street of town, fear fueling my feet. *I hate him. I must hate him. I can't stop hating him.*

My hatred was all I had left. I would not let it abandon me. Not when I hadn't freed my country or avenged my friends. I ran past the lights at the edge of town and into darkness. I stopped. Trees loomed like monsters. Shadows reached for me. Leaves rustled. Moonlight silhouetted an eun patrolling the sky.

Adrenaline coursed through my body. Out in the dark. Alone. What a coward I was. For the second time within minutes, I gave in to my fears and ran.

I didn't stop until I was securely in my bedroom in Angus's house.

CHAPTER 16

Dresses

Relief loosened my shoulders when I heard Angus come in a few minutes later and hit the couch. He hadn't left me for Ana yet.

When I exited the bedroom the next morning, he was sitting at the table, eating a spinach and sausage scramble.

"Did you make that?" My sister liked to spend time in the kitchens, but I hadn't joined her.

He nodded. "Would you like some?"

"No."

"I thought you might say that. There's fresh bread and berries."

"Thank you."

We eyed each other as we ate, but neither of us spoke. He cleaned his plate at the sink and leaned against the counter.

"Would you like a new dress for the wedding party?"

I set down my spoon. I'd worn the three outfits he'd given me every day. Yesterday, I went through the clothes I'd brought from Campbell, and each item seemed overly heavy, impractical, and wearing them was a horrible way to stand out around here.

"Are you planning on wearing one of your dresses? I was thinking that you might be more comfortable in a new one." He didn't say Glenn made, but I knew what he meant. "Isla can make one in time. She's already offered, but I told her that you might not be interested."

"I would be willing to wear a traditional Glenn bride's dress if you would like." I stood and carried my plate to the sink.

"It's up to you, dear wife. Whatever you like."

Drat. I turned to face him with a half smile. I'd hoped he'd consider my acceptance as doing him a favor, but he wasn't going to fall for that. "I would like a new dress."

He smiled, and I couldn't look at it, not when last night's sudden attraction still smoldered at my core. "Do you know where her shop is?"

"Yes." I'd seen it on the main street with swatches of fabric draping the front windows, and a beaded purse I'd swooned over.

He tilted forward, and for a flash I thought he might lean in and kiss me. Desire flashed through my body, hot and unwelcome.

"Get whatever you want."

"Thank you." Since it was Campbell's money anyway.

He drifted over to the bedroom while unbuttoning his shirt. "May I use my lavvy now?"

Heat bloomed over my face. He grinned and ducked into his bedroom.

I submerged my plate in the soapy water, feeling like I was the one drowning.

After riding lessons and grooming Pearl, I strolled over to Isla's shop. A fifteen-year-old boy, who introduced himself as Pax, Isla's son, greeted me at the front door and led me inside. Tables of leather bags, wide hats, and beaded belts tempted me. Plaid shirts and skirts hung on the racks. Riding pants were stacked high up the wall. Furs and coats lined the back.

"Maw," Pax called. "Vera's here."

Isla swept into the storefront, followed by a young woman. Isla was the shortest adult Glenn I'd seen. She came to my shoulder, although her hips were wider than most.

"Welcome, Vera. These are my twins, Pax and Peony. How can we help ye?"

"Ye owe me," Pax said to Peony. "She did come."

"Wheesht," Isla hushed her children.

"Please. I'm looking for a dress for the wedding party. I know there isn't much time."

"Aye, I can make one in time. I'd be honored and delighted."

Finally. Someone who didn't seem to automatically want me far away.

"Do you have any ideas of what ye fancy?"

Worry caused my lips to dip into a frown. "Not really. I was hoping you would."

Peony clapped.

Isla brought her hands to her chest and spoke in a gush, "Of course, we do."

I smiled. Pax led me to a private room in the back with a plush loveseat and three full-length mirrors. Peony brought me spiced orange tea. Isla pulled out several things for me to try on. I had my own gallery of ohs and ahs as first I modeled a green gown, then a silver one that was too thin by half. They assessed me as if I were deaf.

"Hate it," Pax said. "Red is not her color."

I twirled the heavy skirt. I'd picked this one out. "Red is for funerals."

"Oh gads," Isla said. "Take it off." She held up a bolt of pale blue fabric and draped a piece over my shoulder. "Bonnie." She sighed. "Look at yer yaks now." The silk matched the light center of my irises inside the green rim.

"I love it," Peony said.

"Great," I said. "Thank you."

Isla read my measurements off to Pax, who took notes. "I think I'll make ye something long and flowing. Ye'll want to move and dance."

"I never want to dance again." I'd only meant to think the words.

Isla reeled back. A pencil dropped from its perch between her lips.

"I can't do it." My hands came up as if to ward off an attack. "I tried to learn last night, and I'm a total failure. I'll embarrass myself and Angus." I burst into tears, surprising us all.

Isla clucked like the hens outside the training yard. She tugged me to the couch and held me in her arms. I allowed myself the brief comfort of resting against her soft shoulder. She smelled of oranges and laundry.

I thought of the kind Marna back in Cabin, and how she and Isla showed compassion even though they didn't know me. The last time my mother had hugged me, I hadn't felt anything near this infusion of peace and warmth. Mother had acted like I'd saved her and Father's life, when, in fact, I'd saved a stupid title. She had no warmth to give.

"I'm so sorry." I sat up, wiping at my face.

Peony handed me a pale pink handkerchief and knelt on the floor next to my feet. Her round eyes traced mine, concern written in her pinched expression.

"Thank you."

"Can we help?" Peony asked.

"Not unless you can succeed where Maeve failed."

Isla pursed her lips and tilted her head. "Maeve is a wee severe."

I snorted out a laugh.

"We'll teach ye," Peony said, her face radiant with excitement. She scrambled to her feet. "I'll fetch music."

I braced myself for more failure.

She pulled a record player out of the closet and brought it to the floor. Deftly, she engaged the needle, and music filtered through the small room. This time, violins and bagpipes joined the ever-pounding drums.

"Aye, here." Pax held out his fingers, and I let him pull me to my feet.

Their smiles and nods relaxed my nerves. It felt almost as if I were home at Cromarty with younger classmates playing a game or celebrating a holiday.

"Follow me exactly," Peony said. She stood at my side and motioned for Pax to join her. They slowed their steps dramatically, and she counted off each beat. After a few minutes, they stopped and turned to me.

I pulled a face. "You make it look easy."

"Take my hand," Pax said. He wasn't much taller than his mother.

I giggled as his narrow hand rested on my waist.

"Eh, what?" Pax deepened his voice. "Just because I'm not big and broad like Chief Angus Gray."

Peony burst out laughing.

"You're quite handsome, Pax," I told him solemnly.

His dark cheeks pinked. "Watch yer feet."

I focused intently.

"Weight on yer toes," Isla added.

Pax patiently directed me through several turns and across the room.

"Yer doing it," Peony said. "Yer doing it."

Her exuberance filled me with encouragement. When the song ended, I flung onto the couch with a tired thump, smiling real and wide.

Pax dropped next to me. "Now I'm hungry."

I lurched forward. "What time is it?"

Isla glanced at the clock on the wall. "One fifteen."

"Oh no. I'm late." I hopped up. I'd missed lunch. "Thank you so much."

"Come back tomorrow?" Peony asked.

"Yes." I waved as I ran out the door.

I would definitely come back to this little haven of fabric and giggles.

I'd had more fun in that shop than I'd had since my class got to paint the walls under the Clover Bridge.

CHAPTER 17

Beaten

I sprinted past a group of warriors training in the yard and swung into the low building behind it. Koda looked up. He was punching the heavy bag closest to the door. He stopped and turned to me. "You okay? You weren't at lunch."

"Sorry," I managed between heavy breaths.

"Yer late," Bale said with a voice sharp as one of the knives on his belt. He folded wiry arms.

"I'm so sorry."

"Aye, I believe ye will be. Get yer gloves on." He looked over my flushed face and heaving chest. "Ye seem plenty warmed up. Yer first. Into the ring."

I swallowed a sense of impending doom and wished I had more than air and acid in my stomach. My first time in the ring.

"Koda, ye can join her."

Koda tightened his lips and followed me onto the fighting pads.

"No clypes to the face," Bale warned. "Ye can batter yer enemies. We're friends here. Work yer reactions. I want fast jabs. Quick feet. Fast hands."

I rocked to the balls of my feet and held up my hands, stubby and padded from the thick gloves.

"I can't do it." Koda looked at the floor.

"Wut?" Bale said.

"Come on, Koda." I jabbed, hitting his arm.

He didn't react. "I can't hit her," he said to Bale.

"Why is that, Koda?" Bale's sharp gaze bore into him. "Ye have naw trouble working with Ana, Revka, or June, or even Ivy, who's smaller than Vera."

I swallowed.

Koda's jaw tightened.

"Bampot." Bale's lip curled in disgust. "It's sprints after practice if ye don't."

"Hit me." Anger sharpened my voice.

He ignored my pleas. "Fine," he said to Bale and walked off the mat.

I had to force myself to keep from running after him and kicking him in the kidney. By now, he had to know he wasn't doing me any favors by treating me like a hothouse flower.

"Scotsbane." Bale's voice carried through the room.

Koda flinched as Bale's retaliation hit its mark. Scotsbane was the biggest man in our group. Scotsbane grinned, revealing gaped teeth too small for his mouth. He tromped forward like a boulder: a mass without much muscle definition. Koda would rather this ox pummel me? He glared at me over his folded arms. He didn't want me to fight Scotsbane. Koda wanted me to quit. He expected me to back down.

No way.

"Ready, Lady?" Scotsbane's deep voice rumbled. They'd all taken to calling me Lady since the first day they overheard Koda call me Lady Vera.

"Not in the least." I attacked with all my strength. Scotsbane held up his forearms, and I punched them as hard as I could.

"Hit me," Scotsbane said in his gravelly voice.

I increased speed, but he blocked all my jabs with his gloves.

"Have ye started?" he asked with a goofy grin.

Angry and embarrassed, I kicked him in the shin.

"Ow." He feigned pain.

"No kicking," Bale said. "Fists only today. Come on, Vera."

I sucked down air, my arms complaining when I positioned. Fists up, I went after Scotsbane again. He blocked my punches and threw my arms up. I didn't see his hit coming, but I felt it land on my side. I jumped out of the way, narrowly missing the next jab. Quick dancing feet would sure help me right now.

My arms trembled, and I don't think Scotsbane even felt my gloves peppering his arms. He waited patiently. It didn't take long for me to sag. I forced my gloves up as he watched me, waiting for an opening. He took a turn jabbing at my gloves. I was going to hurt tomorrow. His punches gained strength, and I bobbed side to side. He landed a solid hit on my ribs. I shuffled backward. His glove hit my shoulder. I slipped.

His eyes widened as I fell. He pulled back his punch, but not before knocking my nose.

I hit the mat. Pain seared through my face and into my brain.

"Sorry. It was a blunder."

"It's fine." Blood dripped over my mouth. I pinched my lips shut.

Koda rushed to me, his eyes wide and his expression pained. He gathered my shoulders onto his lap.

Warm liquid slid over my closed mouth. I held up my hands. *Get these stupid gloves off.*

Bale bent over my face and ran his fingers over my nose, feeling at the bone. *Ow.* I swatted away his unwelcome prodding. He unwrapped my hands and pulled off the gloves. My sweaty fingers flew to my wet face and came away dripping red.

"It's okay," Koda said. "You'll be fine."

I knew that.

I didn't see Angus until his face appeared above me. He usually trained in the later afternoons with a few of his friends. I noticed Gent often joined them. "First bloody nose, dear wife?"

Koda jerked at the voice near his ear. I nearly rolled off his thigh in his rush to loosen his hold. Angus pinned Koda with a serious glare.

"I didn't hit her," Koda said.

"Of course not." Angus's voice grated like dry sand. He had to have seen how Koda looked at me, and how he didn't hide his growing desire. My husband was a lot of things, but a fool wasn't one of them.

Scotsbane handed me a towel, and I shoved it against my nose. I reached for Angus. He gripped my blood-splattered hand and deftly pulled me to my feet. Bale's fingers clamped my nose again. I grunted in pain.

"It's not broken," Bale said. "Pressure will help stop the bleeding."

I knocked Bale's hand away and used my own, more gentle fingers.

"Come with me," Angus said. "I want to show you something."

I nodded, sending dizzy waves through my aching head.

"Back to work," Bale yelled to the group standing around watching the spectacle.

Holding the bloody rag to my sore face, I walked away with Angus.

CHAPTER 18

Helpless

We traveled down the main road, lined with shops and spring flowers.

"I'd like your opinion on a report I received this morning."

My nose will be fine, thank you ever so much for your concern.

Angus stopped in front of a large brown wooden building with twin pines standing tall out front. The Gray flag hung from the roof. "This concerns the safety of Alta Glenn. Mother thinks it's a mistake to include you. Is it?"

I wiped my lips with the towel as my thoughts churned. The bleeding had subsided, and I no longer dripped blood into my mouth. I didn't know the answer to his question. "I can't imagine how I could help."

"I'll show you."

An eun flew past and landed on the arm of a woman wearing leather gloves. She took the package the eun carried, fed the bird, and released it.

Angus opened the door for me, and I stepped onto a rug with swirling blue designs. A heavy chandelier hung from the high circular ceiling. I followed him as I looked at the paintings covering every wall: landscapes, battles, hunts, and portraits. We went upstairs and down the hall before we entered an office space with large windows showing off the forest.

"Sit down." He motioned to a leather chair.

I glanced at my red-splattered shirt and hands and stayed standing. He picked up some papers on his desk and walked over to a large map of the United Realm.

"Red velvet has hit Alta Glenn," he said.

A series of thoughts flew through my head. This could be good news if it weakened the Glenns, but I didn't actually want people to die. I feared I was more my father's daughter than I'd thought.

I wanted the Grays to leave Campbell and Hogg alone. For things to go back to the way the history books said they were before we were conquered. Yet I didn't want anyone to die a gruesome, painful death. I thought of the sweet children in my riding class, and Pax and Peony, who were lovely and kind. "I'm sorry to hear that," I said truthfully.

Angus pointed to the region of Alta Glenn touching Perth. Perth, where the dreaded disease started when some really stupid people ate some really rotten snake. "There's been four cases in the border town of Stuartsyard. The disease moved up through this corridor of Perth and into Hogg's capital."

"We don't have a cure."

"But you have the prevention."

"I don't." I wiped at my bloody nose. I had nothing.

"Would your father listen to a petition from you?"

"No." *He threw me away.* "We haven't been in contact." I wanted my knuckles to be bloody from having made contact with my father's face.

"He lied to us," Angus informed me of something I already knew. "He said they didn't have any vaccines ready, but he snuck ten thousand vaccines into Porto last month." This was a new and more egregious lie.

"What?" It didn't make sense to hide that they could transport the vaccine long distances, if that was truly the case. The people of Alta Green didn't deserve to die because of what the Grays did. The thought startled me. Weeks ago I would have celebrated the entire country's destruction. Or maybe I told myself that as another cover for my soft center.

Angus was studying me. "I'm glad to see this is a surprise to you. You didn't inherit your father's ability to lie."

"My father's not rebellious. He's spineless." The floor seemed to be moving out from under me. Father was sneaking vaccines to the other domains. If this was not a mistake, my father was committing high treason.

Angus snorted. "Slippery as a snake, but not spineless."

I chewed on my lip. "Are you sure your report is accurate? It could've been something else."

"Aye. It's been verified twice. This isn't the first time Hugo has fooled us." Angus laughed, cold and harsh. "I'm still not sure how we went to the gathering intending to replace him, and he wound up keeping his title *and* he planted his daughter among us."

I bristled against the stinging words.

Angus sat down in a high back chair. "What is he planning? Does he think he can pick who to protect? Is he hoping red velvet will sweep through and kill us all, leaving the Realm to him?"

It would be a heinously effective plan, but no one was that cruel. "I don't know." I was still trying to wrap my mind around this reversal and wondered what Father could possibly be planning. Was he sending Porto vaccines because they were closer and he could keep the vaccines cold that long? Was he doing what he could to save lives, not take them?

At least I was inoculated against the horrible disease, and could help if it came to that. "As far as I know, they can't transport the vaccine for longer than three hours. Alta Glenn is too far."

"How do we know that's true?"

I shrugged, ashamed that I didn't have any answers.

"It's the weak and the young who will die," Angus said. "We won't be wiped out by this disease. We will do what we must to stop it spreading, but the vaccine would save countless innocents."

"I'll write a letter," I said, devastated by the thought of dead children, and torn apart by strained loyalties.

"Thank you." He laid out papers and a pen.

I held up dirty hands.

"Lavvy down the hall."

I took my time washing my hands and face. I didn't have a clue what to write. *Hi. It's the daughter you gave away. Are you planning a rebellion? Will you stop red velvet killing innocent babies? Do you remember me? By the way, I got punched in the face today while training to fight.*

I trudged back to Angus's office. He was reading and didn't look up. I leaned over the paper and scrawled a short note.

Dear Father, I am healthy. The Glenns may not be if red velvet continues to spread. The Grays are planning their return to Campbell for vaccinations. The sooner we travel, the sooner I'll get to see you all. I know you can't support innocent children dying. For how long can you transport vaccines? If you're working on making it longer, do that fast. Can't wait to see you, Vera.

I dropped the note in front of Angus.

"Eager to leave Pinehearth?"

"What do you want me to say? Hi, Father, they know you're a liar. I know you sold me for a title you'll lose anyway if you don't get the Grays the vaccine before winter. Watch your back. Thanks for writing. Oh wait. You haven't."

Mother's meaningless notes with his name at the bottom didn't count.

Angus laughed, low and round. The pleasing sound penetrated my aching bones. I would enjoy hearing that more often.

"Nothing like the truth. You could add that the threat isn't from the North. It's from the South. I'm curious how Hugo intends to defend himself from the Churrys after he's killed us off with red velvet."

I leaned away from the desk and thumped against the back of the chair. "What threat? Why would Churry attack? We've had peaceful relations and trade for years."

"Why would they build sixty battleships and outfit them with weapons if they don't intend to sail the sea? They've shot down the last two euns returning from our ambassador."

My mind reeled. War with Churry? It hardly seemed real. "Porto is well defended."

"Is it?"

Well, I'd never actually been there. Lanie got to go instead. "Why are you telling me this? Are you lying to try to get me help you?"

His face hardened. "I said I would never lie to you. I'm not your father." That hurt. "I didn't know I'd have to manipulate my dear wife into helping her country."

I'd do anything for Campbell, including saving it from his knife. I grit my teeth, lest I said anything regrettable. Then I did anyway. "Why did you kill the entire Wallace family?"

His head snapped back as if I'd punched him.

"You could have spared the two youngest. They didn't deserve to die."

Slowly, he leaned back in his chair, his eyes dark. "You must truly hate me. Think me a real dobber."

Adrenaline tingled through my veins as I berated myself for my wayward mouth.

"I didn't kill the Wallaces."

"Not your hand—"

He held up one of the large hands in question. "Nor my father's. Nor any Glenn acting under our command."

I shifted in my seat, confused and agitated. If the Glenns didn't kill the Wallaces, who did?

"We had evidence of plots against us." His voice was calm and steady. He looked me in the eye as if to prove his honesty. "Hogg had been stockpiling ammunition, meeting in secret, and gathering support. There were large holes in their plans. Things that didn't make sense to us. Missing pieces.

"When the Wallaces came to the gathering, we intended to speak with them. Use the euns to get the truth. On the day of their questioning, we found them dead in their beds." He shuddered. "Except for the cold skin and silent hearts, they appeared to be peacefully sleeping. No evidence of violence or strain. Dead. All nine." His cheeks paled, and he looked away.

My fingers wrapped around my throat, and my tongue lay heavy in my mouth. I'd imagined their death too many times to count, but as Angus retold it, grief and horror flooded through me anew.

His voice was soft. "There was a note saying they'd rather die than tell us anything. Down with the Grays. Freedom for the domains."

I wheezed in shock. "They killed themselves?"

He shrugged. "I wish I knew what really happened."

Me too. My father never mentioned a suicide note. Confusion warred with what I knew. Emilia wouldn't do that to herself or allow her family to do it to themselves. No. This was all wrong.

Angus cleared his throat, then told me, "I'd guess they didn't knowingly take the poison. Well, not all of them, anyway."

"Poison." I'd known it was poison, but the word clanged around my head. Something rang false about Ian using poison. Or Angus. Or any of the Wallaces. Hogg was a place of steel and fire. Strength and grit. Ian would've died for his cause. He cared that much, but he wouldn't've used poison. He never would've killed his sisters. He wouldn't've willing done anything like that.

I frowned. Frustrated at my ignorance and craving the truth, I tried to remember what Father had told me about their deaths. He'd said the Grays had killed them as traitors. End of story. Now knowing my father's duplicity, I wondered what really happened and if he'd had a hand in it. He'd been as upset as the rest of us, crying while holding a series of memorials for our dear friends.

"We didn't kill the Wallace family," Angus repeated.

I stared at his calm gaze and steady chin. "I believe you." I did.

With a subtle shift in his mouth and eyes, his whole countenance brightened. My words pleased him.

All of Campbell and Hogg believed the Grays had poisoned innocent children. Knowing they were wrongfully accused made me sick with regret and exasperation. Now I was desperate to know who'd killed my friends. This truth would have changed many things these last two years, not to mention the way I treated Angus.

Knowing that the Grays didn't kill the Wallaces, I never would've encouraged Trista to destroy the vaccines. I pressed a hand against my stomach where pain flared red hot. If Trista hadn't destroyed the vaccines, she'd still be alive. The scaffolding around my rebellious heart began to crack. What did I have left to support my hatred?

Eerie emptiness rattled through my hollowed-out rib cage.

"You hungry?" he asked, and for a moment I thought what a strange question to ask when my whole world had shifted.

Practicality took over my emotional turmoil. "Starving," I answered. "Bread and berries don't hold up for long around here."

Angus held out a hand, and I latched on to it like a lifeline. His thick palm tethered me to this world, an anchor against the despair that threatened to carry me away.

We met Naira and her bird at the bottom of the stairs. She eyed my red face and bloody shirt with curiosity.

"Bloody nose," Fleming said.

"My first time on the mats," I explained.

"Good for you." It might have meant more if her tone hadn't been so condescending.

Unfortunately, Naira accepted Angus's invitation to join us for a meal.

Fleming said, "Hate Frank's. Go home."

He flew off without waiting for a response.

CHAPTER 19

Worries

Every night, Frank's offered dinner to the hearty appetites of Pinehearth. Besides eating alone at Angus's house, I preferred Frank's to the other taverns. Frank led us to a small table in the corner. Naira and Angus sat across from each other. I hesitated for a heartbeat before squeezing onto the bench next to Angus. There would've been more room with Naira. As it was, my arm and thigh pressed against Angus's. It seemed a long time ago that I'd sat with him at Cromarty the night before Trista's death, keeping the fabric of my puffy skirt from brushing him.

"We've got lake trout tonight and pheasant pie." Frank's chapped hands rested on his wide belly.

"Trout please," Naira said.

"Pheasant," Angus said.

Frank nodded as if he'd expected as much. He looked at me, and I sent him a tight smile. "Red beans again?"

"Yes, please."

He ambled off, picking up empty plates from a nearby table on his way to the kitchen.

"What have you heard from yer da?" Naira asked me.

"Nothing."

Her mouth turned down.

I squirmed like a bug under glass. "I learned from my sister that the vaccine is transportable as long as it's kept cold. Three hours or so. Lanie isn't in the red velvet laboratory anymore. My father moved her team out."

"Why?"

"I wish I knew."

"Find out what more you can from Lanie," Naira ordered.

I intended to. I swallowed the lump in my throat and nodded, hoping to prove my worth and trustworthiness to this woman while discovering my father's perfidy.

She turned to Angus. "Ye won't be returning to Campbell without your father. I heard word from him this afternoon." Angus leaned forward at the tightness in her tone. "He's delayed in Porto, checking on defenses."

Were the Churrys really coming? The bloodthirsty tribes lived across the Katrine Ocean to the south of Porto and Hogg.

"He felt confident in Hogg's progress," Angus said. "They've built watchtowers from the cliffs. Although the Churrys would be unwise to attack at Hogg. They'll hit the weaker harbors at Porto."

I puffed in pride for Ian and Emilia's country. Hoggs were strong and hardworking, despite the Grays' harshness. I stopped myself. The Grays didn't kill Emilia. I'd believed Angus when he told me that, but I was having a hard time accepting the truth. I'd been certain Angus was Emilia's murderer for so long. Without that sure knowledge, I had nothing to hold on to to keep my anger alive.

I'd been blind long enough. I could no longer deny that the Grays were not the tyrannical savages Ian had described them to be. My heart sagged, limp and gutted. What now?

A young woman brought three steaming plates, and my stomach nearly sang in delight. I burned my tongue in my rush to assuage my hunger.

Angus speared a piece of meat. "Da's going to want to station a unit in NewGate."

Naira nodded, her expression tight at hearing they were sending soldiers to Porto.

My thoughts were a jumble. I didn't want Glenn soldiers trampling through the conquered domains, living off our means, but the thought of Churry attacking Hogg or Porto cooled my indignations. The Grays were defending us. Going to war for us. That was if the Churry reports were real.

"We'll postpone the wedding until Bear's return," Naira said as pleasure flickered over her face.

Tough luck, lady. Unfortunately, we were already married. Her party mattered not a whit.

Frank appeared alongside us and set a small sizzling crock on the table. "A little something you might like with your beans. Freshly made this morning." Small slices of speckled meat glistened a dark crimson.

"Thank you," I said.

Frank didn't leave. Reluctantly, I lifted the smallest piece to my mouth. Juicy flavors exploded over my tongue. Pepper. Anise. Garlic. Apple. Salt. I grinned. "Now this is good meat."

Frank flushed with the pride of a validated artist.

Angus snorted.

"What is it?" I asked Frank.

"Yev never had black sausage, lassie?"

"No," I said, trying to ignore Naira's smirk.

Angus had his knuckles to his lips, chewing back laughter.

"It's delicious," I said. "What animal is this?"

Frank's brows furrowed in thought. "Let's me think what bits I had this mornin' from the slaughter...." He paused.

"Why is it called black sausage if it's red?" I asked.

"Black for blo—"

"Thank you, Frank." Angus held up a forestalling hand. "I'm hoping you have more of that for us. I don't think Vera's going to share."

Frank nodded happily and retreated to his kitchen.

I rounded on Angus. "What is so funny? Why didn't you let him finish explaining?"

"I have only your best interest at heart when I suggest don't get curious about what goes into Frank's food."

Naira chuckled.

I soothed my irritation one piece of black sausage at a time.

It was at home later that the sausage turned against me. I spent the night sweating and sick on the floor of the lavvy, cursing Pinehearth, Naira, Angus, and most of all, the demon spawn Frank.

CHAPTER 20

Cook

I woke up the next morning to the disgusting smell of bacon. My wrung-out stomach tightened threateningly. I dressed, cinched my hair bun, washed my face and mouth, and padded into the kitchen. I stopped at the counter and watched Angus's blade destroy a small potato with a few rapid slashes. He dropped the chunks into sizzling grease and looked over his shoulder at me.

"Would you like some?"

His tone seemed a touch too innocent. I couldn't tell if he knew I'd been sick all night or if I was being too sensitive. I lifted my chin. "Would you teach me how to cook?"

Angus's face blanked.

"Nothing fancy," I said in a rush, thinking I'd overstepped somehow. "How to do some basic dishes to start."

He shook off his wariness, his mood lifting. "Aye. Come over here."

I edged around the counter and stood awkwardly at his side.

Angus turned off the burner. "First you need to know how to light the stove." He handed me a box of matches. "Turn the gas on, and stick the match up close."

I turned the knob and fumbled to light the match. I stuck the match up, and a puff of flame plumed. Heat licked my face, and I jumped.

Angus chuckled. "Aye. You want to get to that match quickly or the gas builds."

Nerves jangled, I set the matches on the counter.

"All right. The potatoes take longer to cook than the onions, so I've got them started. They're cooking in a little bacon fat. Helps with the flavor and they don't stick to the pan. Pinch a little salt over them." He held out a bowl of salt.

I stuck my fingers in. He grabbed my wrist, and I dropped my salt.

"Not a handful."

"Oh sorry." This was a dumb idea. I felt dense as a rock.

"It's all right. Brush the bits off your fingers into the pan."

He held up a peeled onion. "Chop this."

Anxiety sped my heart as Angus pressed the handle of a knife into my palm. My fingers clenched shut.

"Not so tight." His brow furrowed. "Here. Like this."

He stood behind me, his arms encircling mine. He peered over my shoulder. His breath warmed my ear, and his thighs bumped me. His strong hand covered mine, and he pried my tight fingers off the handle and adjusted my grip.

"One hand holds the onion, other hand the knife. Watch your fingers. Slice." His hand pressed mine down, and the blade pierced onion flesh. Intent on the chopping, but fully aware of his body encompassing mine, I made the next slice. He jerked my left hand away. "Careful of your fingers. Try curling the tips under, like this."

As we chopped, my eyes stung. A little at first and then they turned into a raging fire. I wormed my hands out from under his and rubbed my knuckles into my eyes. Turning into Angus, a breath from my face, I lifted watery eyes filled with dismay.

His eyes widened. He caught my wrists as I brought my hands up again, intending to scratch my eyes out. "That makes it worse. It's the onion's acid."

"Am I going blind?" Tears streaked down my face.

He laughed, and it sounded so free that I might have joined in if I hadn't been so angry and scared.

"Why isn't it doing that to you?"

"I'm used to it, and I didn't have my face hovering right above it."

"I didn't know not to."

My anger ebbed at the softness that suffused his expression. "I know. It's my fault." He brushed his thumbs over my cheeks, wiping away the wetness. "I'm sorry."

Oh. Well. That was nice.

"Wash your hands with soap and then splash cool water over your eyes. It'll help."

I darted to the lavvy, and when I returned, my eyes were red, but no longer stinging. I sat at the table, and Angus set a plate of potatoes, onions, and scrambled eggs in front of me.

"What is your favorite breakfast?" he asked.

"Oat porridge."

"That's Coal's favorite too."

I chuckled.

He grinned, showing straight teeth. "I'll teach you how to make that tomorrow."

I lifted watery eyes. "No onions?"

"I promise."

I smiled, surprising myself. I was actually looking forward to it.

CHAPTER 21

Hunt

As spring melted into summer, my softness melted into sinew. I had been in Pinehearth eleven weeks and three days without a single word from Father. I pretended I didn't care, but a cherry pit wedged in my sternum I couldn't dislodge. Angus slept on the couch, only visiting me on nights when it seemed a biological need drove him to ask if he could join me. He remained in my bed as long as it took for him to hurt my heart a little more each time and leave my body wishing he would stay so I could find some pleasure in the act he seemed to enjoy so much.

He hadn't kissed me for eleven weeks and three days.

I'd failed to plan a revolution for Campbell. My heart was no longer in it. My heart, it seemed, was dying.

On a warm summer morning, I led Pearl, saddled and bright-eyed, to the training yard. A considerable group gathered, humming with excitement. No Angus. I chided myself for being disappointed. Koda found me immediately.

"I thought we decided yesterday you weren't going to come," he said.

"Then why were you keeping such a close watch for me this morning?" I ran a hand down Pearl's neck.

He scowled. "You can't hit a target, how are you going to hit a wild animal?"

I didn't intend to kill anything, but I didn't appreciate him reminding me that I couldn't. "I'm coming, Koda."

"Stay close by me," he said.

By now, I was a better rider than he was.

"Vera." Bale's welcome call interrupted an unpleasant conversation.

I left Koda to grump alone. Pearl followed me to where Bale stood by a cache of weapons. No guns, per Bale's rules. He handed me the compound bow I'd barely learned how to use properly. At least I'd hit the near target by now. A few times, at least.

"Be careful with this." He sent me a sly grin. "Don't hurt Pearl."

"No one trusts me around here." My voice came out harsh and exasperated.

His weathered face turned serious. "I wouldn't give it to ye if I didn't trust ye. Everyone must remember to be careful when holding a weapon."

I calmed. "I'm sorry. I didn't mean to lash out at you."

Bale's eyes flickered to where Koda mounted a borrowed horse. "I know. For what it's worth, you're getting stronger. You've got guts and courage. I'm proud of ye."

Tears pooled behind my eyes as his words washed through me like hot tava tea on a cold day. I looked at the ground, muttered my thanks, and fled.

His booming voice followed me. "Mount up. To the hills."

We'd divided into small hunting parties. I was with Gent, Scotsbane, Koda, and Ana. As our leader, Ana had picked the groups. I could only guess at the perverse pleasure she took in watching me struggle with tasks that came easily to her.

We'd studied the maps yesterday. Our group had a swath of forest to the northeast of town. I'd told Angus where we'd be in case he finished work and wanted to join us. I felt dumb inviting him, but he'd smiled at me, igniting an unexpected ember in my belly.

He didn't come.

Mounted and holding the bow across my thighs, I led Pearl after Scotsbane's enormous horse. Koda rode too close. It was only because he cared so much about me, I told myself. Be grateful someone does.

Ana led us into sun-dappled woods. The shade welcome in the summer heat. Intent on spotting prey, I searched the trees. After a fruitless hour, my focus wavered. If only we'd been allowed to take an eun, we'd have found game immediately, but that wasn't part of Bale's game.

Ana stopped and held up a hand. We reined in next to her. She pointed to fresh deer droppings and then along a narrow trail leading through the undergrowth. With a finger to her lips, she motioned us forward.

Not anxious to find the poor deer, I pulled my canteen from my saddlebag. After a long drink, I smeared a slick of cool water on my neck and unbuttoned my collar. Sweat drenched my shirt beneath the quiver of arrows heating my back.

"Come on." Koda turned in his saddle, motioning me to move.

I urged Pearl forward and we trotted to catch up to Gent and Ana. The path ran along a creek. Up ahead, a large lake glistened. Leaves waved, and birds chirped greetings. A cool breeze kissed my cheeks. It felt lovely.

Then I saw it.

A young buck who still had spots on his back, and the cutest furry antlers sprouting from above his brow. His head popped up in surprise from where he nibbled on soft wet greens at the water's edge. Ana pulled an arrow from her quiver and silently drew it across her bow.

No.

I kicked Pearl, and she jerked forward, startling the deer and knocking Ana's mount. Her arrow went high as the deer plunged into the grass.

"Vera." Ana's shout was sharp with accusation, but I didn't care.

I kicked Pearl again, and we bolted into the grassy trail, following the deer before anyone else. Koda called out to me with a plea for me to stop and wait. I urged Pearl to a canter. I was going to chase this sweet little fellow until he was out of Ana's range. The trail narrowed, tight with vegetation on either side. Branches struck my face and arms. Ana's panting horse beat the air behind me. I slowed Pearl, and Ana nearly crashed into us as she dropped out of a canter.

"What are ye doing?" She failed to find space to pass us.

Pearl's head jerked side to side under the pressure from the horse pressing from behind.

"He's gone," I said.

"He's not gone. Move, dunderhead."

I stopped and halfheartedly tucked to one side of the trail, leaving not nearly enough room for her to pass. She slapped Pearl's rump.

"Whoa," I yelled as Pearl jolted forward. We burst out of the trees. The lake spread before us, majestic and serene. For a moment, all thoughts fled as the beauty hit me, and then Ana hit me. Her horse bumped Pearl, shifting us fully out of her way. My bow fell to the grass. With a shout, she took off down a narrow trail in a hurry to kill that innocent young buck.

I did what I could, little one. Run.

"You all right?" Gent asked as he rode up.

"Great."

He sent me a friendly smile and galloped after Ana. With a sigh, I slid off Pearl's back, picked up the bow, and wedged it into the saddle. I unslung the useless quiver and hung it on the bow.

I stood atop a rise. My heartbeat tripled as I stepped around Pearl and realized we'd come mere feet from falling off a sheer cliff and dropping into the water where we'd drown. I stood on the edge and looked down a white rockface to the mysterious blue thirty feet below. Pearl chomped on soft grass. I wiped my wet brow and inhaled clean air. My new favorite place. I wish I'd brought lunch.

My head twisted at a shout from the forest. Scotsbane burst through the trees. Koda, his face red and his eyes frantic, followed, too close and too fast.

"Stop," Scotsbane yelled, but it was too late.

Koda's horse rammed into Scotsbane's and his gelding bucked. Pearl jerked out of the way. Her rump slammed my chest. I pitched back, arms wheeling. Time slowed and I saw Scotsbane's wide frightened eyes, and Koda's sheer horror as he leapt from his horse. His hand stretched out to me.

Golden sunlight danced over the glittering cliff, and I heard whistling wind. I drew in a sketchy inhale before a sharp crack sounded as my back hit a cold sheet. Frigid lake engulfed me.

My body cut through the water, barreling down. My boots hit dirt, and my legs crumbled. Terrified, I rammed against the lake floor. I shot through bubbles and broke the surface, gasping and sputtering. Koda screamed my name from above. I slipped back into the quiet cold.

Hitting the bottom again, I shot up, gaining another life-saving breath before sinking back down. My back stung and my arms felt paralyzed. I closed my eyes and focused on one thing: staying alive. I'd barely cleared the surface and sucked down a hurried breath when I felt the splash next to me.

I blinked through green murk.

Koda thrashed in the water, sinking as he paddled toward me. He grabbed my arm and hauled me up. I panted as he kicked the water, holding our heads above the surface. His face was taut with determination. His neck strained.

We slipped under. Boots and clothing had to be weighing him down, as they did me. He jerked us up to the surface. Gasping, I searched for the shore that looked so far away. A moment before the water claimed me again, I saw him. Ripping his shirt off as he ran barefoot down the muddy banks.

Angus.

My heart leapt. He came.

Save me, Angus.

Koda seemed to be doing the opposite. He pulled me up, but not with enough power to reach the surface. I fought against his hold. If I sank to the bottom, I could kick up. He let go and pumped up. I dropped like sodden sand.

When I hit the bottom of the lake, I thrust up with waning strength. I blinked at sun-streaked ripples. I wasn't going to make it. I started sinking again, without the gulp of air my body screamed for; my lungs threatened to explode. Koda dove, but Angus reached me first.

I stretched out my numb fingers, and his strong hand latched on to my wrist. Angus pulled, and I shot up, erupting from my watery grave. I coughed and choked, gasping for air. My trembling fingers clung to his chest.

"It's all right," he said. "I've got you."

I kissed his cold neck and flung my arms around his shoulders.

He chuckled and peeled me off. Water churned around our bodies as his legs worked to hold us up. "Roll over." Numbly, I obeyed. His arm wrapped around my ribs, holding me against his chest.

"Can you make it to shore?" he called to Koda, who floundered nearby.

Koda turned angry eyes to Angus.

Whoa, Koda. We were drowning

"I'll come back for you," Angus said.

"I can swim," Koda spat. He pumped forward, as if to prove it, but his sodden boots tugged him down. He didn't go far.

Angus leaned back. With rapid kicks, we glided through the water, leaving Koda struggling to follow. I nestled my face against Angus's neck and relaxed. I closed my eyes, exhausted, but safe. Chilly waves rippled over my breasts.

"I'm glad you came," I said.

Angus chuckled, but with his labored breathing, it sounded like a cough. "Me too."

His words permeated my numb chest. He didn't want me dead. He didn't want me gone. "Thank you for saving me."

His grip tightened on my ribs. Despite the cold, heat flickered in my core.

His legs stopped churning and he stood. He turned me around and with an arm under my thighs, he gathered me against his chest like an infant. I pressed my ear against his bare muscles and listened to his pounding heart. Dripping, he plowed up the shore and set me on shaking feet. He ran a hand through his dark curls. Rivulets of water traced the contours of his nipples, his abs and down. I wanted to follow their dance with my fingers.

"I'll be right back." He marched back toward the cold expanse.

My shoulders curled in, and my body trembled.

Koda shouted from halfway to shore. "I don't need help."

Angus shrugged and turned back to me. His gray eyes were filled with concern. My lips shook, and my teeth clacked. He picked up his shirt and with an arm around my cold shoulders, he led me behind a thick clump of trees.

"Put this on." He held up a dry shirt.

I wanted it on me already. "You need it." My voice was raw and quivering. Chills carpeted his skin.

His fingers found the hem of my shirt and tugged up. My numb limbs felt like glass as I shifted to help him peel off my wet shirt. A clump of sodden hair seeped down my back. A breeze buzzed over my breasts. I leaned forward to give in to the urge to press my skin to Angus and hold him tight when warm cotton fell around my head and chest. I hugged the soft shirt against my ribs instead.

"Thank you," I whispered.

His hand found my lower back, and his eyes were dark despite the sunlight. "My pleasure."

Warmth flooded my body, pushing away the residue of fright.

He drew me closer. His lips were flushed and dark.

Kiss me.

Coughing and cursing snapped me from my growing desire. I stepped away from Angus and whatever was happening there. I rounded the clump of trees and a soggy, sputtering Koda came into view. He steamed with anger and uncontrolled jealousy.

I rushed to his side, thinking maybe I could assuage his emotions before Angus took too much notice. "Are you okay?"

"Of course, I'm fine," he snapped.

Okay. Different approach then. "Thank you for coming after me."

"Aye, I'm the real hero here." His voice was taut.

"It means a lot that you jumped off that cliff for me."

Angus appeared. We turned together and watched the prince approach. Koda glared, surely noting, and hating, the naked torso and corded arms, and the way Angus's wet pants clung to his heavy muscles. Angus's thick hair and wide lips… Koda might not've been noticing those as much as I was.

Angus opened his mouth and then closed it. Wise choice.

Koda marched past. I glanced at Angus, who, to my surprise, rolled his eyes in mockery. I laughed and then immediately regretted it when Koda stiffened. I hurried after him. Angus picked up his boots and followed.

Scotsbane met us on the trail, bringing Pearl and Koda's horse. He dismounted and rushed to my side. "Lady. Are you all right?"

I flushed at his nervous tone. He'd been worried about *me*. "Yes, I'm fine."

"I was glad when I saw Angus. I wasn't excited about making that jump."

Koda's nostrils flared.

That's when I noticed Scotsbane's boots were untied, his shirt untucked, and his knife belt hung over his saddle. I smiled. He was going to jump for me. To save a weak girl from Campbell.

He handed me Pearl's reins. She nuzzled against my neck as if she'd been worried about me too. I sighed in delight. I looked for a tree or rock to mount, but Angus stepped behind me and gripped my hips. A thrill raced up my spine as he lifted me into the saddle.

"Where's Coal?" I asked.

He shrugged. "That monster probably went home. Left me for a bowl of oats without a backward glance."

"Do you need a ride?"

He grinned. I couldn't stop my lips from returning the gesture.

I turned my chin at Koda's annoyed voice. "I'm headed back." With a sharp tug, he moved his horse and charged down the path.

"I'll go find Gent and Ana," Scotsbane said. "See if she got her kill." He trotted off.

"I hope not," I said.

Angus looked up at me.

"It was a baby buck. He has a life to live. Forests to run. Babies to make."

He raised a brow.

I flushed. "I tried to help it escape. She's really steamed at me."

He belted out a hardy bark. His abs rippled as his laughter rolled. "Is that how you ended up in the lake?"

"Not exactly, although she'll be disappointed she missed seeing me fall." I smiled in spite of myself. "Koda was trying to catch up with me, and he knocked me in."

Angus howled. He laughed so hard he cried.

Leaves rustled, and Coal pranced out of the branches.

"Thought you were missing a party, did you." He stepped forward and took the dangling reins. "Well, nice of you to come back for me."

My chin drooped in disappointment. I'd wanted an excuse to ride nestled in Angus's arms again.

Coal puffed out a wet breath. Angus mounted and turned Coal's nose south. "Nothing like a cool swim to work up an appetite. Let's find lunch."

"As long as we don't have to kill it."

As I followed my husband back to Pinehearth, my home, Koda's stricken face appeared in my mind.

As my heart was softening, his was hardening.

Koda was a greater threat now than ever before.

CHAPTER 22

Oppressed

The supply caravan arrived the next morning, and I joined the throng watching horses guide crates up the valley. They stopped when they reached the town center. People unhitched the tired horses and led them away. Others stepped up to the large black trunks and opened the lids. An assembly line formed. I stepped nearer for a better look. The first crate was from Perth. Bags of sugar moved quickly from hand to hand. Salt and spices followed.

Stomach uneasy, I moved down the line. From the glint of metal and the clink of tools, the next enormous crate was from Hogg. I should've looked away, but then my gaze fell on boxes engraved with the Campbell insignia—a red *C* with crossing pens underneath. My limbs trembled as I marched closer. Entitled men and women passed the goods up the lines. Our wealth slipped easily between their fingers. A hand landed on my shoulder. I whirled, fists up.

"Are you all right?" Angus asked. "You've gone white."

My nostrils quivered. "No, I'm not all right. Look at this stuff. You're stealing from the domains." He tilted back as if I'd slapped him. I considered using my tight fists on his face. "Did you pay for any of this?"

His mouth parted, but he didn't speak.

"What does Campbell get in return? Those medicines are expensive. Those books represent hard work." My voice had gotten louder, and I glared at the curious faces turning my way.

"I know," he said quietly.

I lowered my voice, but my tone was sharp. "What do you know? That you're being unfair? You're a tyrant?" I inhaled a ragged breath. "You don't give Campbell your wood or leathers, or stones for free. You can't take whatever you want. It isn't right."

"This is how we tax Campbell. We protect them and work hard to keep peace and issue fair laws to that end."

"That's not good enough. You don't know Campbell. Why should you get to make all the rules?"

Angus didn't respond, but he didn't cower either.

My feelings had been changing in favor of the Grays, but I'd been fooled, duped. I'd been taken in. Even if they didn't kill the Wallaces, they killed Trista. They ruled without restraint. My hatred of the Grays' power over Campbell flared back to life in a burst. How had I ever thought I could like this man? I turned my back on a stony Angus and my gaze landed on Koda. He gave me such a piercing look of understanding that I nearly ran to him. He nodded almost imperceptibly, and I held his gaze as he did.

This robbery would not continue.

Campbell would not be treated with such abuse.

CHAPTER 23

Plans

I said hello to Minerva as I saddled Pearl the next day.

"I'm headed east," I said.

"Watch for the river." She patted Pearl's flank. "It's a lot faster than it looks this time of year."

"Thanks." I had no intention of taking another swim. I waved to the young children perched on their mounts as I set off. I'd been venturing on my own lately. I hadn't been brave enough to go far into the forest alone, but I felt comfortable trotting over the rolling fields and open valley floor. I felt less alone out there in the fields than I did in town with all the Glenns who weren't my people, and they let me know it. They plundered my people and had the temerity to act as if I didn't belong. Talk about not seeing the nose on your own face.

I rode far enough that Pinehearth was barely invisible. Pearl grazed. I spread my blanket out on the grass. I wasn't ready to lie on the earth without any protection quite yet. The sound of an approaching horse, its hooves thundering on the soft earth, interrupted my cloud study. I sprang up as Koda came into view. He dismounted a brown mare and tromped over. He kicked up an insect, which shot at me and stung me in the neck.

Yelping, I swatted at the tiny beast. So much for improved reflexes.

Koda jumped to my side. He peeled my fingers off the spot.

"Hold still."

"It hurts."

"The stinger is still in there."

"Get it out." I tilted my head, allowing him better access to my neck. Stupid outdoors.

As he laid his hands on my skin, I felt uncomfortable having him touch me. His fingers prodded at the fiery spot.

"It's too small for my fingers," he said in frustration.

I jolted when his mouth met my neck. Chills skittered up and down my spine. Gently teeth and tongue worked over the hot spot. His breath tickled, and his warm tongue made my knees feel weak. He straightened with clenched teeth, then spit a tiny stinger into his palm. "Got it." He grinned.

I stepped back, out of the space that made me forget I had a husband. I rubbed my neck. "What are you doing out here?"

"I saw you leave. I need to talk to you. I have a plan to get us home."

My chin jerked up. "What is it?"

"I'm not going to tell you yet. You're not a good liar. All I can say is be ready in two weeks. There's no moon, and we'll have the best chance of escape. Everyone will be distracted."

Why wasn't I elated? Hadn't this been what I wanted all along? Uninvited dread coated my body. I moved my hand over the worry and fear clutching my chest.

"I'll get you home safe." It'd been his mantra this summer. "You won't have to be near Angus anymore. You won't have to pretend anymore."

The problem: I wasn't pretending. I never pretended. I wasn't any good at it. Koda took a step forward, and I held up a hand, indicating he should come no closer.

He pressed his chest against my palm. His rapid pulse beat underneath my fingers. "No one's here. No one can see us. Let me hold you."

"No, Koda."

"Fine." He exhaled his disappointment. "I can wait another two weeks. Then I'll hold you the whole way home." His fingers wrapped my wrist. "My love."

I jolted. Frost iced my veins.

"I love you, Vera."

His words were like one of Scotsbane's punches.

"I know you won't say it back. Not yet. But I can't keep it in anymore." He retreated to the horse he'd borrowed. "Two weeks."

Frozen to the spot, my hand remained straight out in the air where moments ago it covered Koda's heart. I turned my fingers into a weak wave, and waited until he disappeared over a ridge before I fell onto my blanket.

What was he planning? What distraction or destruction would possibly be large enough to prevent the euns from chasing us down before we left the valley? Anxiety caused my heart to skip beats, warning me to fear the worst. I couldn't let Koda know how much I'd changed. I had to find out what he was planning so I could stop it.

I flinched when Pearl's ivory nose appeared over my shoulder. She lipped my hair. I straightened from the fetal position I'd curled myself into. As if that could protect me from the riot of worry pounding at my brain.

"I'm scared," I told my equine friend as I stroked her face. "I can't let him kill these people." I swallowed and got to my feet. "I can't let Bear kill Koda." Tears rolled down my cheeks. Please. Not another friend dead. I buried my face in Pearl's neck. She leaned into me.

"I'm sorry, Emilia." I'd failed to avenge her death and, worse, I'd stopped thinking about her every day. Her face had gone faint in my memory. I didn't even bring a drawing to remind me of my best friend. I wondered if the many sketches I'd made of her over the years were still in my study at Cromarty, or if my family had gone through my desk and seen the hidden drawer with details of weaponry from Watt's Lab.

I hugged Pearl for a long time. "Come on," I said with a sigh. "Let's go get lunch."

She agreed with me.

CHAPTER 24

Tight

I sliced bread and scrambled eggs, but they still didn't taste as good as Angus's. I'd taken to making breakfast while he showered. Dressed in his typical blue plaid button-down and brown pants, he emerged from the bedroom. As he sat at the table, he rubbed at his neck with one hand. I set a plate in front of him.

"Looks good, dear wife."

The toast was burnt on one side, and the eggs were too runny. "Better than last time, at least." Burnt eggs were disgusting.

He picked up his fork with a smile that sent a memory charging into my mind.

I was fifteen, sitting in the dining hall at Cromarty, my head bent over my notes, cramming for my astronomy test. I picked up a quiss from the fruit bowl on the table and took a bite. I chewed the crisp sweetness, thinking only of constellations.

"Ew."

My head had jerked up at the harsh voice above me. Four students stood across the table, leering down at me.

Eldridge, the boy in the middle, said, "Vera ate a gurg."

I'd glanced at the fruit in my hand. In the middle of pink fruit flesh, a plump brown gurg oozed out of the tunnel it had been burrowing before I chopped it in half with my teeth. My stomach turned, but it was the laughter that made my belly boil.

"Bug-breath Vera," Eldridge called.

I'd swallowed half-chewed fruit along with my shame.

Victoria—not my friend anymore—covered her mouth in disgust. "Why would you eat that rot?"

Cheeks hot, I'd opened my mouth to defend my mistake when I heard Angus's voice say, "The only thing rotten in here is you."

Laughter had died as the group turned to him. Even at seventeen, he had an angular face and powerful gaze. White fingers gripped the book in his hand tightly. Eldridge flinched.

"You can either stop," Angus had warned, "or earn the right to mock by eating the other half."

The hecklers had appeared paralyzed.

Angus had shrugged, sat down at my side, took the quiss from my hand, and ate the other half—gurg first. He opened his book and began to read, a dribble of juice on his chin.

The mockers fled.

My jaw had become unhinged. "You didn't have to do that."

He'd glanced up, pale eyes dancing. "It's the most meat I've had in weeks."

I'd thought him frightening and wild then, but now I relished the memory of his kindness as I watched him shovel my pitiful breakfast enthusiastically into his mouth. He turned his head toward my chuckles, or tried to. His hand flew to his neck, and he grimaced.

"What's wrong?"

"Nothing. A wee cramp. Must've slept on it wrong."

Because he slept on an uncomfortable couch. Guilt punched at my conscience. He wasn't sleeping in his bed because I was no more a wife than he a loving husband. Then there was Koda, who planned to take me away from Pinehearth, a place I'd come to call home. My teeth sank into buttered bread, but I tasted nothing but bitterness.

I wasn't leaving Angus.

He looked at me, his expression serious. "I've been thinking about what you said about being unfair to the domains."

My eyes widened in surprise.

"I always thought if we didn't take too much, it was our right to expect goods and services from the conquered domains." His eyes were hooded and his brow grim. "I think you make some valid points." My mouth dropped open. "If we listened more to the chamberlains, maybe we wouldn't be fighting with Hugo for a simple vaccine."

"The chamberlains have no real authority," I said. "Wolfton shouldn't have power to overrule my father."

He studied me. "I trust Wolfton."

"But the regent shouldn't have more authority than the chamberlain."

"I'm going to think more about this. I'd like you to come up with ideas on how to improve our Realm." *Our* Realm. "Then we'll compare notes."

He valued my opinion. I was so stunned I couldn't say anything.

He stood and picked up his empty plate. He held his body stiffly as he cleaned it at the sink. As he strode toward the door, he called out, "I'll see you tonight."

Guilt wormed its unwelcome way through my thoughts. It was my fault he walked like a frozen tree. I knew how to help. He picked up his hat and reached for the door.

"Wait."

He turned in surprise. Then scowled, his hand finding his neck again.

"Come sit." I pointed to the chair he'd vacated.

His brows arched in question, but he left his hat and obeyed.

"Where does it hurt?" I put my hands on his neck. He tensed. "Found it." A round knot of muscle at the base of his neck bulged beneath my fingers. I jabbed my thumbs into it, and he gasped in pain.

Bracing my boots on the floor, I dug into the tight cramp. Pressing deeper, I rooted around the muscle. He arched his back and grit his teeth. I stepped to his side, leaned against his shoulder, and kneaded the sore spot. He wormed and wheezed.

I didn't want to appear mean, but I couldn't help smiling at his noises.

"Do I need to be worried at how much pleasure you're taking in this?" he asked through a tight jaw.

"Probably." My smile grew.

Ramming my thumbs into the cramp, I pressed harder and kept working at it until the knot unwound. The muscle sighed and so did Angus. With softer strokes I smoothed out the muscles in his neck. I shifted to his front, standing between his knees, checking for any other spasms.

"Good now?"

He turned his head with ease and looked up at me through thick lashes. "I don't think you quite got it all."

His heated gaze caught me like a trap. I slipped my hands under his shirt collar, felt his neck was still warm from my ministrations. I leaned forward and kneaded the heavy muscles on his shoulders. My fingers worked up his neck and into his clean soft hair. His eyes rolled back, and he tipped his head forward, burying his face between my breasts.

He groaned, and I stiffened as his breath filtered through my shirt, tickling my skin. Desire rolled down my core. I wanted him to wrap his arms around me. Hold me like he was glad it was me. I took a tiny step back, and he lifted his head. His heavy-lidded eyes tilted up, and his lips were red and thick.

Kiss me.

His gaze dropped to my mouth.

Yes. Time seemed to stand still.

He didn't move. His focus slid away.

Rejection's cold fingers worked inside my chest and squeezed my heart.

He shuddered and stood.

"I should probably get to the stables," I murmured, my voice gravelly.

"I'll walk down with you."

I nodded to the floor.

"Thank you," he said.

Somehow he'd ceased being my enemy, and would someday be my ally.

Though I'd take a husband who loved me body and soul over anything else.

CHAPTER 25

Ready

My wedding party was tonight. A second wedding. The first one was miserable enough for two lifetimes. I hoped this one would be better.

Bear had returned home last night, gave me a long look, and said, "Well don't that beat all." Then he walked away, looking tired and travel-worn.

My brain hurt from failing to figure out how to save Pinehearth *and* Koda. I went to Isla's, as I did most days. Pax and Peony had been patient and entertaining while they taught me to dance. Sweet and unaffected by our differences, they reminded me how to laugh.

Isla had outfitted me with well-made Glenn clothes. I never wanted to wear my stuffy heavy Campbell garments again. Peony squealed when I entered the shop. Isla locked the front door after me.

"No customers today," she said. "I'm busy."

I smiled at her exuberance. She hadn't let me see the dress yet. Peony dragged me into the shop and pushed me into the dressing room. She ordered me to take off my clothes, and came back with a long swath of cloth. She thought it was great fun to blindfold me while they made adjustments. If it had been anyone else—no way.

I had washed and brushed out my hair this morning. This was the first time it had been free of its tight braid bun since I arrived here three months ago. It hung way past my hips. Peony's eyes widened, and she scooped up the locks in her hands.

"Pretty. So blonde and so soft."

"Thank you," I said, basking in the compliment. "Is this new?" I picked up a full black skirt that looked like it might have been belonged in Campbell, but without the heavy layers. "Can I try it on quickly?"

"Of course, dear," Isla said.

I pulled the skirt over my pants. Peony zipped up the back of the skirt, catching a chunk of my hair in the zipper.

"I'm so sorry." Her slender hands hovered over the mess like hummingbirds.

"It's okay," I said.

She looked stricken.

"No, really." I tugged at the tangled ends of my mane. "It's much too long." I sighed. "Do any of you know how to cut hair?"

"Maw is the best," Pax said. He ran a hand through his brown hair as if to demonstrate. His hair was as long as his jaw and tucked easily behind his ears. Too short to get stuck in zippers, and not so long as to be an impracticability to any husband.

"Yes," I said. They jolted at my statement. "Will you cut my hair like Pax's?"

Isla eyed her son. "That short? Ye sure?"

"Yes." My voice sounded sure even if my heart rebelled against saying good-bye to the long luxurious locks I'd tended for years.

Peony got the scissors, and Pax led me to another room with a chair facing a mirror.

"You're all set up," I said.

"Maw really is the best." Pax patted my arm. His version of reassurance. "She doesn't have time to do much hair anymore. The shop's so busy."

"I'm honored," I said.

"It's not every day I get to be the one to set a new fashion," Isla said as she stepped up behind my chair and ran her fingers through my hair.

It was a nice thing to say even if it was a bold lie.

"Ye set all the new fashions, Maw," Peony said.

Isla didn't respond. She had her tongue between her lips and her hands on the scissors. The first three cuts had my hair falling to the floor in heavy golden sheets. A great weight lifted off my head, and my neck straightened. Methodically, she moved around me, snipping and measuring, turning my head this way and that. Occasionally, she clucked her tongue or humphed. Then she resumed moving around me, yanking on the ends of each side and pulling them under my chin.

As the tangled pieces curled on the floor beneath my feet, I felt like a conqueror. Severing the chains of the past, I could step forward without lugging the heaviness of former mistakes and misunderstandings.

When she was finished, we crowded together in front of the mirror. Without the weight, I was surprised to see loose curls ringing my head. Isla had cut the ends so my hair appeared to dance happily around my face, which now appeared older and sharper. I ran my hands through silk and tossed my light head. The ends of my hair brushed against my chin and the back of my neck. It felt like freedom. Maybe I could use tonight as a fresh start to my marriage and to my life here in Alta Glenn.

"I love it," I said.

Peony giggled. "Yer well bonnie."

Time in the sun had lightened my hair, tanned my skin, and brightened my pale countenance. I supposed Pinehearth agreed with me, and possibly improved me.

I couldn't let Koda hurt this place and these people.

CHAPTER 26

Coward

"Now, for the dress," Isla said.

"Finally." I rubbed my hands in anticipation.

After having endured the last-minute fixes from behind a blindfold, now the pale blue gown hung in the changing room, ready for me to wear. I fingered the long drop of shining silk.

"Put it on, then gawk," Peony said. "Pax, get roamin'."

He pouted, but left me to change in privacy. I wore tight brassieres and corsets in Campbell, but the Glenns didn't bind their breasts or waists in uncomfortable wrappings. One of their barbaric habits I found appealing once I got used to it. The cool silk kissed my bare skin as the dress slid over my head.

"Can I come back in?" Pax called.

"Aye," Isla said.

Pax swung in and whistled. "Marry me instead?"

I grinned, and thought whoever he married would be a lucky woman.

"Look." Peony turned me to face the three mirrors, two angled in at the sides.

I blinked, hardly recognizing the woman before me. The sleeves of the dress ended at my shoulders, leaving bare arms that had tiny muscles straining against my skin. The gown had no ribbons or stitching around the middle. It flowed straight down my body in a column and fluttered around my calves. The neckline scooped in front and back, revealing my collarbone and emerging back muscles. My newly short hair flipped and coiled in delighted freedom.

Lanie would be scandalized. I should've been too, but I was delighted. I was no longer a mouse among wolves. Maybe tonight I would fit in.

"It's incredible, Isla. Thank you."

She smiled with the pride of a sculptor admiring her work.

"Let's go." Peony tugged my hand. "We don't want to miss the food."

I waited in the shop while they changed, and then the four of us headed down to the greenhouse. On this warm July evening, everything had been moved outside. I should've guessed.

Everyone was kind, or at least not unkind. Greetings were shouted at us as we weaved our way toward the dinner tables. Torches and firepits lit the scene of Glenns in their formal wear, which mainly consisted of clean shirts and the occasional dress. Twinkling strings of lights hung between tree branches overhead. Flowers, some of which I'd never seen before, bright and huge, plumed from every table. Airy, soothing music gilded the air. A clean breeze tickled my face and toyed with my dress.

I stopped for a moment, overcome. All of it was fairytale beautiful. The stuffy parties inside the towers of Cromarty didn't feel like this. It amazed me brute tyrants and conquering killers created this. It was in that moment of awe I saw my husband.

Isla and her children left me near the edge of the gathering as he approached. He wore a pressed white shirt and navy pants.

He smiled at me, full lips, white teeth, and silver eyes. I gaped like a fish. He brought a hand up and played with a strand of my hair. He stepped close, his gaze flickering from my eyes to my lips, then to my exposed neck.

Kiss me.

He brushed my hair behind my ear, sending a spark down my spine. He dropped his hand and swallowed, as if remembering himself. Disappointment clenched my heart. What was happening to me?

"You look good, dear wife."

"Thanks," I said, my voice half stuck in my throat.

He inched farther away. "Hungry?"

"Yes." But not so much for food. It no longer felt like a betrayal to desire this man. Ian would've wanted me to join with Koda. Finish what Ian had started and destroy the Grays. *I'm sorry, Ian. I can't do it. Not for you or Koda.* I no longer had a passion for rebellion.

We sat with Gent and some of Angus's friends. Before long, Naira's voice rang over the crowd. Angus and I joined her near a central fire pit.

"I had eagerly anticipated the wedding of my only son," Naira said with a booming voice.

My body tensed, ready to flee, or fight.

"I was sorry to miss it," she said. "But—"

But? In front of everyone this hard, shrewd woman was going to vilify me.

"I welcome Vera Gray tonight."

Vera *Gray.*

"She has surprised me. I admit to underestimating her."

My jaw dropped to my exposed collarbone.

Naira held up a crown of silver bird feathers. "Yer already married, but allow me to welcome ye to our family. Come, daughter."

The words felt too good to be true. Warmth poured from my heart through my limbs and back. Angus's steady hand on my spine urged me forward. I knelt at Naira's feet, eyes watery, as she laid her blessing on my head.

She crowned Angus with matching feathers, then guided us to our feet and clasped our hands together. My heart slammed against my ribs as Angus leaned forward. He pressed his lips against mine. My body woke with a sigh. He pulled away too quickly, but his burning gaze searched my face, a question in his eyes. I have no idea what answer he found, but a small wicked smile turned up his wide lips.

"Dance with me?"

I didn't hesitate to hold his offered hand. The drums started, and a roaring cheer rose from the crowd. He started slow, but I didn't. He gawked as my feet flew in time with the fastest drum.

"I've been practicing," I told him, immensely satisfied to impress Angus for once in our marriage.

"I can see that."

"The Wilson can dance." Bear's voice rolled overhead.

People crowded around us, their feet joining the drums. Angus gripped my waist. My abdomen tightened under his fingers as he lifted me off my feet. My stomach leapt to my throat. I wrapped my arms around his shoulders in fright and clung, all thoughts of keeping the beat forgotten.

Laughter rolled through my embarrassment. "I didn't practice this," I said. "My teachers were all smaller than I."

Angus lowered me in his arms, my front sliding against the solid planes of his chest. He cradled me with a hand warming my hip and another holding my back. My dress turned to smoke under his touch. "I didn't know there were people smaller than you here."

I pulled a face and wiggled free, letting my feet pick up the rhythm again.

"Possibly you'll consider upgrading your teacher," he offered.

"Are you the upgrade?"

"I should hope so." He spun me in close and tipped me back. His breath burned up the skin on my neck. His lower lip grazed my collarbone, and I froze. When he'd placed me back on my feet, I couldn't move anymore. My feelings were a tight knot I could no longer dance around. I wanted him so much it scared me to stone.

"Excuse me." I ran a hand over my brow. "I think I need a drink."

"Are you sick?"

"Yes. All the sudden." I swayed convincingly.

With a warm hand on my waist and a worried look on his face, Angus led me out of the crush and to the shadows. He ignored the whistles and suggestive calls directed at us. We stopped near the wall of the massive greenhouse.

"Like baby sick?"

His voice was so full of hope, tears sprang to my eyes. I shook my head and told the cutting truth. "No."

Disappointment darkened his face.

Don't blame me. He was the one who stayed away from my bed as much as possible. I grit my teeth against the sting of rejection rising through me.

"What is it, Vera?" He never said my name. His mouth turned down and his eyes hooded, matching my rising emotions. "Have you been unfaithful? I see you and Koda."

Anger made my blood boil. Good. Finally, an emotion I could harness. "You're accusing me of adultery? I could say the same thing about you and Ana Sky."

"I would never dishonor myself or you."

I knew that about him. Why he didn't believe that of me was humiliating. "You should think the same of me."

His face softened, and he opened his mouth, but my veins had caught fire.

"I've been honest with you," I said. "Yet you accuse me as if I'm my father. You couldn't've insulted me more."

Again he opened his mouth to talk, but I couldn't stop.

"I don't want a baby. I'm alone and betrayed by my family. I thought tonight could be a fresh start for us, but now I'm happy I'm not having your child."

Pain lanced through his face. It would've been better for me to have kicked him between the legs. I deflated, adding regret to the pain of rejection.

"I'm sorry," I said, trying to erase the forsaken look on his face. "I might not feel ready to be a mother, but I should not have insulted you personally. I didn't mean it."

"Aye, you did." His deep voice quivered.

Now I was truly wretched. "No, I didn't."

His head tilted toward the dirt. I brought my hands to raise his jaw, but he shoved me away. When he tromped back to our wedding party, I didn't follow. I wasn't a puppy to cling to his heels waiting for scraps that wouldn't come.

As I slunk to Angus's house on the mountain, I pulled up memories of what once was home. Of Lanie and art lessons, games, dinners, and sophistication. If I left with Koda, I could have it all back. I'd be a liar and a traitor, but at this point how could it be worse than being shunned by the man who was supposed to care for me best of all? I'd foolishly let my guard down, and he'd stomped all over my needy heart.

Silently I slipped into the empty house. I took off the dress and hung it in the back of the closet. I was tired of trying to figure out my father's motives for keeping the vaccine from the Grays, and I'd had enough of being "other" in Alta Glenn. Campbell wasn't my home, but neither was this.

Two years ago, months after the Wallaces' deaths, my friend told me she'd found a secret room in the basement of the West Tower at Cromarty. She'd seen a cupboard of poison, knives, and scrolls. There was a map of the United Realm, but it had been broken up into four separate countries. I begged her to show me, and together we slipped down there one morning. She opened the door and there sat Father at the desk, writing. He jumped to his feet. My friend's hands curled around my wrist like a vise.

"What are you doing here?" he asked.

"What is this place?" I tried to see into the room, but the cabinets were closed, and there were stacks of paper everywhere.

He swept us out into the hall and closed the door.

"What's in there?" I asked.

Father looked between us for a moment before speaking. "It's Ian's room. I discovered it, and I am most seriously displeased. If the Grays found this, we'd be accused of his crimes."

The girl at my side hitched in a breath.

"How did you find it?" my father asked.

We were silent. I'd never seen such a severe shine in his eyes before, and he scared me.

"Have you been in there before?"

The girl nodded as I shook my head.

Father studied her intently. "Well, no harm done. I'll get this place cleaned out. All is well. Go to class, and don't worry about a thing."

I'd tried to sneak back to the room later that night and search for information, but the room had been scoured, not even the chair or table had been left behind. My friend took sick the next day. She was so ill she had to go home to her parents in Porto. She died three weeks later.

It was only now, with eyes opening to a world of betrayal and lies, that I questioned her death. Did Father kill her to protect Ian's secrets, or his own? What else had he done? Feeling woozy and rotten, I groped for a shirt in the darkness. It fell to my thighs. Angus's. It smelled like him, cedar, salt, and fresh loam. I didn't take it off.

I crawled onto the couch and curled up in Angus's blanket. I woke when he picked me up. Grim-faced, he carried me into the bedroom, dumped me on the bed, and waltzed out, closing the door firmly behind him.

My hand reached out to him only to curl back into my throbbing chest. I'd said I was sorry, but it seemed he wasn't going to forgive me and let us start again. He might never stop hurting me, but at least I was going to save him from whatever Koda had planned.

CHAPTER 27

Shame

I didn't see Angus the next day. Or the next. He left before the sun rose, and came back after I went to sleep. I tried to wait up for him at night, but failed. I knew he'd come home by the rearrangement of blankets on the couch. I ached for him.

Bear found me walking through the trees behind the shooting range. Hunting the undergrowth for bullets felt appropriate to assuage feeling morose and low. The metal balls rolling in my palm somehow calmed my sorrow.

"Bonnie morning, daughter," he said. I didn't deserve to be called that. "Pinehearth seems to agree with ye."

"It is beautiful here."

He smiled, his round face bunching up. "It is, especially since ye expected a campsite." I looked up in surprise. His brown eyes danced. "I'm glad to've proven ye wrong."

In many ways.

He held out his thick hand, and I dropped a dozen balls into the cup of his palm. He picked them over. "The wee barras will be disappointed when they come out to find ye've taken all the bullets."

I could do nothing right. "I didn't—"

His strong hand weighed down my shoulder. He smiled. "Come on. Let's replace them."

My mouth slackened. "Shoot?" My voice was squeakier than a mouse.

"What? You've been here all summer and haven't shot a gun yet?"

"No. I've tried the bow and arrow and haven't mastered it in the slightest."

"Well, that's much harder. Ye don't strike me as an archer."

"I'm not from here. I don't strike anyone as an archer, or an anything."

"I hope ye don't believe that."

A trickle of warmth made its way into my gloom.

Bear tugged a gun from the holster on his belt. "Start with this revolver." He pressed a lever and a round chamber popped open. He took six bullets out of the gun and set it in my hands.

"It's heavy."

"And deadly."

Cold metal weighed against my hands and my heart. I was not a killer.

We traipsed to the far side of the range. Bear adjusted my grip and showed me how to aim. While focused on the target downfield, he had me pull the trigger several times.

"Ready for the real thing?"

The sides of my mouth twitched into a small smile. He made me put the bullets in on my own. I wanted to thank him for trusting me and not treating me like a child. Instead, I lifted the weapon.

"Watch out for the kick."

The instruction was pointless since I didn't have a clue what he meant or how to follow it. I pulled the trigger, and my hands flew up. My ears rang from the crack. "Whoa."

Bear grinned. I did too.

Heart pounding and nerves crackling, I aimed the weapon again. This time I braced against the kick and the blast.

"Ye hit it."

The hole was on the edge of the target, but still, I beamed, my chest expanding in triumph.

"Finish off the round," he said.

I did happily, splattering the target. He clamped me on the back when I handed him back his gun.

"Thank you."

"You should keep practicing," he said. "Forget archery."

"I already have."

We walked together into town, and I was sorry when Bear left me for his "drudgery of duties," as he called them.

I didn't even have a clever retort because I no longer wanted to remove those duties. I was grateful to have such a solid chief, and I hoped he would rule for a long time.

In the dining hall, I sat at lunch with Koda.

"Did *he* make you cut your hair?" His voice was a low hiss in my ear.

I looked at his unhappy expression in surprise. "No. He doesn't make me do anything."

Koda sent a look so full of jealous rage I balked, my mouth gaping open. "That's what I thought. You're lying."

My mouth worked, needing to supply a calming comeback. "My hair was getting in the way." I took a small bite of carrots, no longer hungry.

"It was beautiful."

"What? It's not anymore?" My chest pinched.

He stiffened, and I could see him struggle over the words. He hated it.

"You don't look as dainty or young anymore. You look more like *them*." He spat out the last word.

I stared, not sure if I was insulted or complimented, and not sure when our friendship had soured. I didn't know how Koda and I could see things so differently after we'd both experienced Pinehearth together these last few months.

His face softened. He pressed his shoulder against me as he leaned into my ear. "You're beautiful no matter what, my love. Soon we'll return, and you can live as you used to."

The last thing I wanted to do was stuff myself into a corset and sit with my backstabbing family. I wanted to shoot Bear's gun, ride Pearl, and draw more pictures of Pinehearth. *I want my husband to call me my love.* I sent Koda a soft smile. The girl he'd met on the train was gone forever. The girl who believed everything Ian said without question was gone. I'd seen too much good here, and had learned the depths of my father's perfidy.

We finished lunch and went our separate ways. We'd be doing that forever soon enough.

After training, I went to Isla's. She told me that red velvet had widened its circle of death. Peony helped me make a batch of bean and deer meat-filled rolls, which I left out on the table for Angus that night. After I rose the next morning, I found them gone, the dishes cleaned.

At lunch the next day, Koda whispered in my ear, "Meet me after training." His toxic tone foretold death.

This was it. His plan. I nodded as stones piled in my stomach. When Koda left, I searched for Angus. The threat had sharpened into real looming danger, and I no longer felt I could risk fixing this on my own. Angus would help me stop Koda, and I could only hope for his mercy in sparing my dear friend's life. I wasn't sure what I was going to tell Angus, but I'd figure out how to get the dangerous words out when I saw his honest face.

I looked everywhere and couldn't find him. A woman at the office building told me he went riding with his parents up Lang Mountain. It helped them clear their minds before making important decisions. I swallowed my self-pity. I knew why Angus hadn't invited me to ride with him. He couldn't stand me.

The Grays were meeting with their advisors this evening. Red velvet had killed fourteen thousand Glenns in the border developments, and Porto was in danger of attack from Churry and needed enhanced defenses.

I slipped into Angus's office and wrote a quick note excusing myself from the conference. I should be sitting at his side, making decisions and sticking up for the domains, but I couldn't miss my meeting with Koda.

My heart felt as heavy as the setting sun when I found Koda outside of town. With a maniacal look of hope on his face, he gripped my arm and tugged me down to sit on a rock at his side.

"This place will go up in flames faster than old parchment," he said.

A jolt of fear ran through me. "You're going to burn Pinehearth?" It had been a dry summer, and this town was made of wood buildings throughout.

"We are, love."

No, no, no, no, no. This was so much worse than anything I'd imagined. Ian would've been proud, but I was horrified.

"I didn't think you were going to be able to do it. I thought you'd gotten soft on the Glenns. But then I saw the look on Angus's face when you left him at your wedding party. He walked around like a wounded cat."

Guilt laid heavy on my heart as I remembered the cruel words I'd flung at Angus. I'd been hurt and lashed out. To learn I had any power over Angus's mood surprised me. I'd thought he'd enjoy the party more after my departure.

Koda's face gleamed in delight, drawing me back to the serious threat at hand. Angus's feelings wouldn't matter if he didn't survive the night.

I shuddered to think what would've happened had Koda not chosen to confide in me. He might still go out on his own and start murdering people. I swallowed back bile and rising panic.

Koda ran a finger down my cheek. I sat on my hands so I didn't knock him away, but I shuddered at his touch. The hand he would use to kill my husband now caressed my skin. Until I figured out how to undo his plan, I needed him to trust me.

"It's time, love. Tonight we'll be together and riding home as heroes."

Revulsion swelled like a disease through my entire body. If he'd come to me four months ago, I would've jumped at his offer. Or so I believed.

"What's the plan?"

"The meeting should be starting any time. No one will blink when you walk in the building. Don't let the people in the meeting see you." He leveled his amber eyes at me.

I nodded, keeping my face blank.

"Lock the meeting door from the hallway." He handed me metal wire locks. "We can thank their heavy wood doors, but be quiet about it. Then outside, you'll find the fuel stash under a bush beneath the first window on the west side. Light that fuse first. That will trigger a line carrying the fire to the schoolhouse next door."

My insides curdled, and I did everything in my power to keep my face relaxed. Right now I wished for the ability to lie as well as my father.

"Sprint down to the tavern. Light that one. It will trigger three more. I'll take care of the rest. Then run like the wind to Pearl. She's saddled, and I've got provisions. They won't even see us leave."

Yes, they will. They'll kill us.

He pulled out a small device from his pocket. "This is your igniter."

What a terrible, horrible idea.

He showed me how to flick the metal wires together, causing a spark. "Be careful when you're lighting the packets. Light the end of the lead rope, and hurry or you'll get burned when they explode."

"Where did you learn all this?"

He puffed with pride. "Campbell technology."

Fitting.

He leaned forward, his gaze on my mouth. I tilted back and leveled him with a stern look.

He licked his lower lip. "Light the first fuse in twenty minutes exactly." Koda darted away, leaving me holding the igniter and feeling like death.

Twenty minutes. Icy panic roared through my body. I couldn't let anyone die. Images flashed through my mind: Trista's body going limp. Blood glistening on metal. Hair flopping over her pale face. They would do that to Koda. I needed him to leave. Flee.

I didn't have time.

I sprinted up the hill to the leadership meeting. Tiptoeing up the stairs, I peeked through the open door. Dark smudges underlined Angus's eyes, and strain was imbedded in his furrowed brow. I wanted to kiss it all away.

The seat at his side sat empty. My seat. I would not let Koda hurt these people. I left the door cracked open. The wire lock stayed coiled in my pocket, as did the igniter.

Outside, I cut the fuse ropes, and dragged the fuel packet away from the building. I dropped it in the middle of the dirt road. I ran through the main street, terrified I wouldn't make it to Koda in time to stop Pinehearth from burning. The sun had set, casting the world in shadow. I found him assembling kindling near the stable.

He looked up in surprise as I jogged to his side. "Vera." He scanned the town and seemed to relax when no flames licked the sky. "What's happened?"

"You must go." The panic in my voice was real. I didn't want Koda to die.

"What's happened?"

"They know. I saw some men find the packet at the market." Fear validated my lies. "They'll trigger the alarms any minute, and then there won't be time. They'll kill you. You must go."

The whites in his eyes shown even in the dusky light. "I won't flee. I'll finish this. Did you lock the doors? We can trigger the fires now and still get away."

"Go." I cupped his face. "Please. I can't bear to see you killed. They're coming."

He deflated. "I won't leave you."

"You must. It's your only chance. Our only chance for a future."

Koda hesitated as my words sank in.

"If we both go, we both die." I felt each second tick by like a bomb, inching him closer to death. "Where's your horse?" I ran into the stable and came out with the gelding he'd chosen to *borrow*.

He looked back at me and Pinehearth, his face full of regret. "Come with me. We can light this fire as a distraction and get away. I can't leave you here."

"I'm safer here." I wasn't leaving.

He gripped my chin and planted his lips on mine. My eyes flew open. I froze, holding back anger and shock, as well as the desire to punch his throat. He pulled away. I bit my tongue to kept from spitting in his face or calling him names that would surely reveal my changed loyalties.

"I'll think of something," he said. "It's not over. I'll get my love back."

Please don't try. "Hurry. Go."

Horror paralyzed me as Koda struck his lighter and set the flame to the end of a long rope. He swung into the saddle. With a kick to his horse's belly, he galloped past the stable and along the road out of town.

Knees buckled as I dropped to the dry grass next to the sparking fuse. Oh no. No. No. The fire snaked closer to the packet. I ran into the stable. So many horses. Pearl nickered at me from her stall, saddled and ready to carry me away. I grabbed a blanket and bolted outside.

The fire had caught the grass and spread. I held the blanket wide and jumped onto the flames. Heat slammed into the fabric. Hissing, I pressed and patted at the steaming cloth. When I lifted the charred blanket, the fuse flickered back to life and ate more rope. I needed a knife.

"Help me." I screamed the words and ran frantically into the stables. Grabbing an axe, I darted back outside. I slammed it into the rope and missed. The rope severed on my second hectic swing. I kicked the burning end away from the packet, but the grass had caught fire. A growing line of flame crawled relentlessly closer to the stable. I gripped the packet, but Koda had tied it to the wooden beams. Flames jumped closer.

Shaking with adrenaline, I sprinted into the stable and ripped open the stalls.

"Come on, Pearl."

She pranced nervously and jerked her head toward the young horse in the neighboring stall.

"I'll get her."

I pulled Pearl's reins and with a loud snort, she jolted outside. The other horses had no lead ropes or reins. I opened Ivory's door, but the scared foal retreated to the back. Frantic, I opened the rest of the stalls. Tamping down my fear of the frantic beasts, I slid into a stall and slapped a stallion's high rump and yelled, "Get outside."

Hooves crashed into wood paneling as he jumped. Time slowed as fear sharpened my world. The horses peeled their lips back and cried, their rolling eyes big as moons. I tugged at long manes and hit heavy muscled bodies. I screamed and cried. Smoke curled in the air and clawed at my throat. In a stampede, the skittering horses burst out the back doors at the same time I heard the human shouts.

Oh, thank you.

I coughed and sputtered. The last horse was Ivory, the foal. She clung to the back of her stall. Pearl's baby girl. I threw an arm around her neck and dragged her forward.

The packet exploded.

Ivory dropped. Her heavy body crushed my legs. My head hit the ground with a sharp crack. The front of the barn burned in a wall of yellow heat. I writhed beneath Ivory's weight. Liquid thick and sticky seeped over my knees. The flames gilded the spreading blood in gold. Heaving and straining, I jerked partially out from under Ivory, wondering what, or who, was bleeding. Then I saw it—a spike of timber jutting out of the side of the young horse. Ivory whimpered and thrashed—and then went still.

Nooo. My adrenaline surged as the fire crept closer. Panting and straining, I wiggled free. Ivory's head jostled against the floor. I stroked her nose. "I'm so, so sorry." Nearly strangled by the smoke,

I scrambled toward the back door and fell into the fresh night air. I choked and wheezed. Ashy tears blinded me.

Hands gripped my arms, pulling me away from the blaze. "Lady? Lady."

A blurry Scotsbane scooped me up. I slumped against his thick chest as he carried me toward the safety of the streets. Water spewed from somewhere, a few welcome drops kissing me. People had formed a perimeter between the stable and the town. Water buckets passed along the rows and over the edge of the fire closest to the buildings.

How easily the stable torched. Koda's plan had been truly ingenious...and deadly. I was glad he got away, but I was equally horrified by what he'd wrought. I pressed my face into Scotsbane's chest. Pinehearth was safe now.

"What happened?"

I jerked up at the sharp voice. A terrifying female face bore down on me. "What did you do?"

Scotsbane set me down in front of the woman.

"Nothing." I ran a hand over my gritty face. "I was trying to stop the fire and get the horses out, but the fire spread so quickly."

"How did the fire start?"

I shrugged.

She narrowed her eyes suspiciously. "Ye did this. You started the fire. Why would you have saddled Pearl without intending to leave?"

A man ran up and spoke to the woman I'd never seen before who was accusing me of treason. "Siana. There are explosives planted all around town. We've found fifteen so far. They're all connected by fuses."

She whipped her head back to me. Her hand flew up and struck my ear. My already pounding head screamed. Her ring embedded in my hair, and liquid trickled down my temple. Her fingers dove to my pocket, and she ripped the igniter from where it poked out.

"Bind her," Siana said.

Disappointment and hurt filled Scotsbane's face as he jerked my hands behind my back and held them so tight I feared they would pop off.

Siana searched my other pocket and pulled out the lock. "Bring her." She marched up the hill.

People poured toward the fire. Euns screeched overhead. My shoulders felt torn apart as Scotsbane lugged me behind Siana.

The smoke thinned. They dragged me through the main street bound, a criminal headed to her execution. Hostile faces lined my path. I'd saved their lives. They'd never know, and I didn't blame them for their anger. I was covered in black soot and blood, both horse and human, and I was from Campbell.

Siana led us up the stairs of the main hall. She flung open the doors of the meeting room, and Scotsbane hauled me forward. Every face locked on me. Angus jerked to his feet, his eyes widening. I let myself believe I saw concern for me there. Naira flew from her seat.

"The fire is under control," Siana said.

"What fire?" Naira asked. She stopped in front of me and studied my face.

"The east stables are gone, but we're not in danger of it spreading. We caught her before she could burn down the rest of Pinehearth."

Angus stood next to his mother. I turned my itchy eyes on him. Tears formed at the look of betrayal in his gaze.

"I went to stop it." My voice was a dry as kindling. Tears spilled out. "I went to stop it."

"There are explosives placed all around the buildings," Siana said.

Naira's hand flew up. I was going to die. I curled and tensed. The strike didn't come. I dared a glance up. Angus held his mother's wrist in the air. He'd stopped her from hitting me. I didn't know who looked scarier as they fought a silent battle of wills.

"I will hear her speak." His voice was cold and hard as iron. He released Naira, and she huffed and folded her trembling arms.

Scotsbane let go of my wrists and feeling flooded in. I rubbed my hands and brushed my filthy hair off my face. My fingers came away bloody and black.

"Fleming will do it," Naira said.

"No." Angus nodded to the eun tender by the door. His bleak look sent ice through my veins. The woman brought the silvery-feathered bird forward. The unpleasant creature was thin, tall, and long beaked.

"Bring her here," Bear said.

I couldn't move. My body rebelled against getting close enough to the chief for him to slit my throat. My neck itched with remembrance of Trista's quick demise. I tensed against the urge to flee.

Angus gripped my arm and hauled me to the chair at the table. His fingers didn't bruise like Scotsbane's had, but he held on to me tight as a clamp.

"I'll run this," he said.

Bear nodded and took a seat a few steps away.

"You may request privacy," Angus said to me. He motioned to the curious faces still in the room.

I stared into his familiar gray eyes. "No."

His thick brows rose.

"I'd like them to stay." My fate would be public. If I wasn't killed as a traitor, I wanted the world to know my innocence first hand. "I have nothing to hide." I hoped that was true.

He nodded, but the muscles in his jaw twitched.

I sat with my arms face up on the table. The bird wrapped each wrist with a taloned foot. Round inky blackish blue eyes loomed close to my face.

"I suggest you answer truthfully," Angus said.

"Or blood," Fleming said as he flapped up and perched on a table next to Naira.

My insides wilted. Naira hovered by Angus at the side of the table, leering down at me.

"Did you light the stable on fire?" Angus asked.

"No." I pinned him with a hard stare, willing him to believe me.

His expression was frosted ice.

The bird spoke in its high creepy voice. "Look at me, Vera."

It knew my name. I shuddered but forced my gaze up to the large glossy orbs. "No. I was trying to put out the fire."

"How did you know about the fire?" Angus asked.

I shifted, and the bird's grip tightened. "I didn't plan it."

"Answer," the eun said. A blue tongue quivered inside its dagger-beak.

"I went to stop—" My words jilted into a scream of pain as the bird bobbed forward, and its sharp beak sliced my arm. My jaws jammed together in anger and pain. A drop of my blood fell from its beak when it lifted its head. A red drip tickled down the side of my sooty forearm.

"Answer the question," the bird said, its voice like grating sand.

"I found out about the fires twenty minutes before he intended to torch Pinehearth."

"Who?" Angus asked, his tone strained and tense.

I sniffled, eying the predator. I opened my mouth, and the claws tightened on my wrists in a painful warning. His name came out like a wheeze. "Koda."

Naira jolted forward, but Angus held out a hand, stalling her.

"Why didn't you tell me?"

"I didn't have time."

"That's a terrible excuse," Angus said.

"I did all I could to stop the fires. I ran here and cut the fuses. Moved the explosives away from the building. I should have interrupted your meeting, but I was afraid of what Koda would do if cornered. I thought you would be safer. He has a gun. And—" I focused on a glinting talon embedded in my skin. "I didn't want you to kill him."

Angus's lips thinned. "Koda started the fire at the stable?"

"Yes."

"He planted the explosives?"

"Yes."

My husband's jaw rippled. "Did you help him?"

"No." Despite my discomfort, I was suddenly grateful for the bird, even if it was a trifle bloodthirsty. I desperately needed the Grays to believe me.

"What are these for then?" He held up the lock and the igniter.

"He expected me to lock you in this room and set this building on fire."

Angus's face blanched.

"I was *never* going to do it."

The bird didn't move.

"Where is Koda?"

"He's riding south to Campbell."

"Did you help him escape?"

"Yes. I didn't think he would start the fire when I told him to leave. I thought I could get him out and stop his plans. Prevent everything." Which I saw now was stupid. "I was a fool."

Angus's nostrils flared slightly, the only sign of his anger. "Do you love Koda?"

"No."

He looked at the bird in confirmation, and I barely caught his almost imperceptible relief before his face again turned grim.

"But I don't want him dead, murdered in front of me like my friend, Trista." I glared at Bear. "She's the one you killed in Campbell this spring."

Bear's voice was quiet. "I remember her, Vera. How could I forget? Taking a life is a heavy burden…and responsibility."

I exhaled, some of my rage gone at the sad, heavy expression on the chief's face.

"Because of her actions, we still don't have the vaccine," Bear said. "We can't travel our Realm without fear of disease and death."

I'd helped Trista make those plans. Bile burned up my throat. I'd been so ignorant. So horribly wrong. Regret ate through me.

Naira spoke. "Are ye a traitor to the United Realm or to this family?"

I sighed, feeling tired to the marrow in my bones. I closed my eyes and searched for the truth. I had had every intention of being a traitor, of freeing my country from the imposing Grays, but I had failed. I opened my eyes and locked onto Angus. I held his gaze, wanting him to know the truth. "No. I am not. I am loyal to you and to this Realm."

"That's enough." He gripped the back of a chair and slumped forward like an old man.

The bird hopped off my wrists. I sighed at the flush of blood returning to my fingers. I went limp as the sweet pleasure of relief replaced my terror. The eun rubbed its head against Angus's shoulder, almost as if it wanted to comfort him. I curled my hands in my lap, and rubbed at my aching wrists.

"She aided a traitor's escape," Naira said, looking at Bear.

Bear squished a hand over his face. "She also stopped a traitor from burning down Pinehearth and roasting us alive."

I wanted nothing more than to wipe away the hurt on Bear's face. "I'm so sorry," I said. "I should've told you."

"Aye. You should've." He looked at me with all the disappointment of a father.

Tears swam, blurring my vision. Bear didn't hate me. He cared for me, and he was sorry for me.

"We'll hunt him down," Bear said.

I nodded. They had to after what Koda had done. Why didn't he leave without starting that fire?

"But ye have given him a head start."

I didn't know if that was a kindness at this point.

"Take her home, Angus," Bear said.

I got to my feet, joints cracking, head spinning.

"I'm sorry," I said to Naira. "I thought I could stop him."

Her eyes seemed to glow with fire, and her hands were fisted into hard balls. It seemed only a force of will kept her from swinging for my face. "We're kin. Ye aren't alone. Yer actions affect us. Working together makes us strong."

I swallowed.

"Because ye are my daughter, I will allow you to earn my forgiveness."

"Thank you," I said, meaning it, but afraid what her icy tone foretold.

CHAPTER 28

Fire

Silently Angus and I drifted down the steps and into the night. I made it to the base of the path that climbed to our home before my legs stopped moving. The last of my energy ebbed away. My shoulders caved forward as my body began to quake. Frost carpeted my skin, and the world spun.

A steady arm wrapped around my back, and I curled into Angus's chest with a moan. He scooped me into his arms. I burrowed my face into his neck and breathed in the smell of cedar, salt, and skin as he carried me up the mountain and into the house. He set me down on the counter next to the bath and started the warm water.

"I'll get you a drink."

I glanced at myself in the mirror. Blood caked chunks of my hair. Dried tears streaked down black cheeks. Red painted my eyes.

Angus returned with water and a full glass of wine. I guzzled them both and sagged in relief. He hesitated, before ducking his head and turning to leave me in privacy.

My hand flew out, and I cupped his wrist. "Stay with me." My whisper came out weak and unsure.

For a horrible moment I thought he would reject me, that he was done with me forever. He set the glasses by the door and drew near. He folded his long legs beneath him and knelt at my feet. He took off my boots and sweaty socks. He balked at the blood encrusting my pants.

"It's not mine." I told him about returning to the stable for Pearl's young foal. "I couldn't save her. She died on top of me."

He peeled the stiff pants down my legs. "That could have been you." His eyes said the words his mouth didn't. He wanted to kill Koda.

My desire to protect the fugitive had waned with the death of Pearl's foal and my near destruction. I yelped when Angus lifted my shirt. Gingerly he peeled the material off my sore shoulders, raw wrists, and a bloody forearm. His gaze drifted over my body, lighting a different kind of fuse inside me.

My hand braced against his steady shoulder as I climbed into the tub and sank into the warm water. I washed my face and limbs. Angus knelt next to the tub and washed the blood from my hair. I sighed as his gentle hands explored my scalp, but hissed when he touched the cut.

He leaned closer. "It's not deep." He poked at the laceration. "It's already clotted." He drew my arm out of the water and dried the cut the eun had made. Blood burbled out again, and he winced.

With a hand on my arm, he held me steady while I stood. He was gentle when he used clean water to rinse the bubbles and blood off my pale body. I stepped out onto the rug, clean and grateful for his kindness. He applied stinging ointment to the wound the eun made, then wrapped my forearm with clean gauze.

"Thank you, dear husband."

He stilled. His hands fell from my arm. Wide, hopeful eyes held mine.

The terror and truth of the night had blasted away the carefully constructed barricades around my heart. The attraction I'd been trying to ignore for months exploded through me, and heat and desire licked at my skin. This wasn't gratitude or an *I'll make it up to you* gesture, I wanted his body joined with mine in the way a husband and wife who cared about each other should be.

I wrapped a palm around his neck. His eyes turned into a silvery night sky as I drew him down. I wanted him with every sinew and cell in my body.

Our lips met. Electricity sparked along my spine as his strong arms lifted me off the floor. His hands gripped my thighs, and I wound my legs around his hips as he carried me into the bedroom. I kissed him, heedless of the water dripping off my hot skin and seeping into his shirt.

He set me on the edge of the bed and reached for his buttons. Impatient, I sprang to my feet and gripped the hem, lifting his shirt while he dropped his pants. I wanted to laugh when a button went flinging across the room, but my amusement faded as his hands wrapped around my waist and drew me against his warm front.

A sound between a sob and a moan escaped my throat before his mouth closed over mine. Every nerve in my body came alive as his tongue tangled with mine and his fingers trailed over my ribs.

Still he did not push me to the mattress.

He cradled me close, his hands making slow tracks over every surface of my skin. This was not the man who climbed on top of me when he needed a physical release. This was my husband making love to his wife.

His touch left little fires in their wake. The smell of pine soap and salt curled around me. Torn between consuming him in a mad rush and savoring every tender pleasure, my hands explored the mold and shape of his body, hard and soft. I tilted my head, giving him access to my neck, to the tender place he claimed with his lips instead of his knife.

His warm breath rolled over me, and I shuddered. He looked at me through thick lashes, his gaze hot and melty, before he returned his attention to the skin between breasts. My breasts pressed against the roughness of his jaw.

My body teetered on the edge of exploding as I stepped back, leading him to the bed, *our* bed.

I didn't speak for fear of diluting this storm of want and heat. I let my body say all the things in my heart. My kiss on the base of his throat was an apology. My hand over his pounding heart was a promise for the future. As I lay back and welcomed him to me, I was offering surrender. He seemed delighted to answer my invitation as he kissed his way down my body.

This time I wasn't a removed observer, but an active participant, matching his movement with eagerness and abandon. I wanted to enjoy this riotous pleasure forever.

He didn't close his eyes or turn away. He trained his beautiful gaze, now dark and intoxicating, on me. I thought I might lose myself in those depth, but instead I found my heart intertwined with his. I held him close. Never again would I let even an inch come between me and what was wholly mine.

My hands roamed the flexing muscles of his back, claiming his strength and loyalty. I reveled in the fire that roared through me. He whispered my name against the tender cradle of my neck as he yielded his body fully and completely to me.

I hadn't known love could create a feeling so powerful and exquisite as to render me utterly dazed. I knew it now with every fiber of my glowing body.

Glazed over with satisfaction, I lay in a melty, blissful puddle against his side, my legs intertwined with his. My head rested on his heavy chest, listening to the power of his heartbeat. He kept an arm tight around me as his eyes fluttered closed.

Because of my stubborn pride, I'd missed out on this connection for months. I wouldn't deride myself now, not when this bliss covered us. What was couldn't be undone, but from here on, things would be different between us. Better. Honest. His steadfast honor all these months had protected me like a shield. Now he had my complete devotion.

I inhaled the deep scent of our love and pressed closer to my husband. I was determined to enjoy this feast to the fullest. This was how life was meant to be consumed, with heart wide open and in my man's arms.

He twitched when I pinched his softened nipple. He cracked open one eye in time to see me crawl on top of him. I grinned, my body already yearning for more. Delight glittered in his eyes as I lowered my mouth to his full lips. His hands found my sloping curves, sending a new wave of warmth through my blood. He drew me down, eager to share another dance. We had months to make up for, and we took full advantage of the connection pulsing between us.

As the sky began to lighten, tangled together, I fell into a deep sleep. My lids fluttered as Angus's fingers made soft swirls on my back. I moaned and stretched like a cat before curling into him.

I was never leaving the happy realm of this bed.

Gently, he pressed my head against his chest and kissed the top of my hair. I sighed, reveling that the simple gesture could feel so nice. "Must we get up?"

His mouth moved to my temple, and his lips brushed my skin when he said, "You'd be wise to find my maw before she finds you."

I dragged my fingertips down my husband's muscled stomach, thrilled that I alone got to enjoy this body. I grinned when his abs bunched under my touch.

He rolled on top of me and grinned. "She can wait."

Then he silenced my giggle with his mouth.

CHAPTER 29

Burned

I floated. Birds whooped and warbled. Dawn gilded the velvet leaves on the trees around our house. I skipped down the steep path and emerged at the side of Bear and Naira's home. I rounded the corner to see Naira striding my way, as if headed to my house to drag me out of bed. Her tight jaw brought me crashing to earth.

We stopped an arm's length away. I squinted into the morning sun. "I'm sorry." It came from the heart, but still felt like the weak words they were.

"Ye were wrong to hide Koda's treachery. I was wrong to push you away. A mistake I intend to rectify immediately. You will meet me each morning after breakfast."

I'd wanted this welcome for weeks, even if her tone was cold, but now I felt sick at the cost.

"Today we do burn cleanup." She turned on a polished boot and marched down the hill.

Ash and smoke lingered on the air. I knew what was coming, but still the vision of char and rubble speared my side and lanced my heart.

Hunched Glenns picked through the remains of the stable. Burned grass ringed the site. We approached Siana, who stood by a basket of work gloves.

"How can we help?" Naira asked.

"Rubbish in that pile. Wood that can still be burned over there. Metal and valuables there." Siana handed Naira and me gloves. She looked at me, her brow hard. I stared back. She'd heard my truth. I was sorry, and I wasn't going anywhere.

Siana nodded almost imperceptibly. "Careful of hot spots."

I followed Naira as she stepped into the smoking rubble. We got into an assembly line, and within seconds, a black log landed in my gloves. I passed it along and swung back for another load. And another. And another. When my mouth was dry and my eyes itching, the wood stopped coming. I looked down the line and saw why. They'd uncovered the cooked foal. I gagged in my mouth at the seared flesh and peeling eye sockets.

Ivory had died on top of me. She had been my shield.

"Grab a bevy of water," Naira said, glancing over her shoulder at me.

I bolted, stumbling away from the blackness and into fresher air. Pearl grazed in the field. I tore off my gloves as I ran. I threw my arms around her neck and pressed my face against her living pulsing muscle.

"I'm so sorry." Tears wet her white coat. "I tried to save her. I failed."

Pearl was uncommonly still as I rubbed her neck, her flanks, her shoulders. I tried to comfort her in the only way I knew how. I couldn't imagine what thoughts moved in the fathoms of her deep eyes. I kissed her nose and trudged back to the work site.

After a long gulp of the tart, minty drink Pax brought me and a quick hug, I shoved my gloves back on and joined the group picking through burned bridles and buckles. I smudged a blackened bit with my thumb and tossed it into a pail. That's when I saw him a few strides away, peering at me between swings of his axe.

Despite the death and destruction, I couldn't stop my smile. The axe held over Angus's shoulder lowered a fraction. My cheeks warmed at the thought of his eager hands on my skin. My starved body needed him more than air.

The hunger returned.

I hoped the sunshine hid my blush, but his eyes brightened, as if sharing a secret.

"Lady."

I jerked as if I'd been caught naked. I turned to Scotsbane's round face at my side.

"Hand me that bucket."

I glanced back at Angus, but his gaze was intent on the falling axe and the splitting log.

I did my best to minimize how often I ogled my husband, but it was difficult, especially since every heated glance we shared eased the morning gloom.

Naira motioned me over to where she stood at the edge of the rubble. "We'll grab some lunch and head to the office."

Gladly. I dropped my blackened gloves into the basket. My back was aching and my heart hurt. I stretched my stiff limbs as I walked with her. We followed a trickle of char-smeared faces to the training hall where we cleaned up before we ate.

After lunch, Naira held a heaping plate of chicken and potatoes as she led me to the main office building. Fleming trailed in her wake. We climbed the stairs, and she held the door to Bear's office open for me. I quelled the sudden fear I was being brought to my doom and slipped inside.

Chief Bear's shoulders slumped over the parchments on his desk. He lifted a weary face as Naira set the steaming plate of food at his side.

"Thank you." His gaze flicked to me then he pointed to a peach-colored letter on his desk.

I snagged it and held it close.

"Need sleep," Fleming said to the chief.

Bear leaned back in his chair and looked at me. Unasked questions about Koda itched my tongue, but I wouldn't ask. Naira motioned me out of the chief's office. Glumly I turned to leave.

Bear's voice halted my retreat. "Take a look at this letter." He held out a wrinkled paper.

I read the brief missive from Wolfton, now eager to hear his reports on Campbell. After reading the first paragraph, I looked up in shock. "Red velvet at Cromarty? But how?"

"I was hoping ye could tell me."

"We've all been inoculated. The entire campus."

"Clearly not. Or it didn't work."

I sank into a chair near his desk. "I don't like that thought."

"It's only two people," Naira said. "Both are from the red velvet labs." She sent a pointed look at the folded paper in my hand.

Lanie had been moved out of the lab when Father brought in a new crew. I didn't expect her to know what was going on, but my nerves still throbbed with hope that her letter might contain answers.

I broke the seal and scanned it quickly, not sure why I felt suddenly exposed.

I skipped the bits about Fitz visiting Campbell, and the meals they shared. "She mentions the outbreak. Says one of the assistants died, but the other recovered, never reaching the rash stage. Neither one got the vaccine, which, she said, was a major oversight." I looked up. "That's *not* an oversight."

When no one spoke, I returned to Lanie's sprawling words. I summed up the main points. "The one who died was new to Cromarty. Came from Hogg. No one else was infected, but they've locked down the lab. There will be a delay on the production of any more vaccines." My last few words came out slow and tired. I was past disappointed. Something wasn't right.

Bear's face was grim.

"She's not happy she's not allowed back into the lab. She says Father is avoiding her and spending all his time at Watt's Laboratory." I paused as the name settled like ice. *Watt's.* The laboratory of the weapons inventor housed rebels.

Bear's jaw rippled. "They've developed a new explosive recently."

I breathed a sigh of relief. I wouldn't have to be the one to tell them about the weapons, or explain why I'd failed to share this information before. Or how I knew about it. "What does that mean?" I asked. "Surely those explosives will help against Churry."

His lip quirked up, but his eyes remained hooded. "Surely? No. Not unless we make *sure* of it."

"I'll get more eyes on Watt's Lab," Naira said.

"We need that vaccine." He looked at me, but I had nothing to add. No way to help. We sat in silence a heavy moment. "Thank you for sharing your letter."

I stood.

"We haven't found Koda yet," he said. "One of the euns didn't return. We assume Koda killed it."

I kept my face angled down, not wanting to show my relief. I didn't want him dead.

"He's made impressive time, and he's been smart about his path." Bear slid his lunch closer to him. "I'm not sure whether to be proud of all the wanker's learned in his three months here or not."

I nodded, not trusting myself to speak lest I damage our tenuous newly forged bond.

"He'll become a more dangerous weapon in Hugo's hands."

Of that I was sure, as I was certain Koda would be intent on getting me back, but I'd never say that. I looked up at Bear's warm eyes. How had I ever thought this man evil? I couldn't let Father and Koda—rebels like I had once been—destroy Pinehearth and Alta Glenn.

He waved me off and picked up the fork. With my mind darkened with worry, I followed Naira to her office, an open space tastefully arranged with thick carpets and sleek furniture.

"Today ye'll help me organize the relief and aid efforts for the red velvet outbreak in Arthur."

"Yes, Lady Naira."

"Containment is the number one priority."

The day stretched long, but I put myself to learning. I returned home that evening enjoying the pleasant buzz of a well-used brain. Angus was already home when I arrived. He stood in the kitchen over a pot of my favorite red beans.

"Smells good."

"They need another twenty minutes." He set the spoon down and walked over. He stopped a stride away, waiting to see if I might've reverted to my old ways.

I was never going back there.

"Twenty minutes, huh?" I ran my fingers through the fur blanket on the couch and looked up at him through my lashes.

"You want to rest?" he asked.

"Oh please. I've been waiting all day for this." I closed the gap.

Angus's hands gathered me, and his lips welcomed me. He was air and water and sunlight, and I'd recently discovered I needed him to live.

***

That night I stayed awake long after Angus's breath on my neck had turned low and steady. We were curled together like two fern leaves.

Campbell seemed so far away, and Koda felt like a strange nightmare not of this dimension. I shifted out of Angus's grasp, intent not to wake him while I slipped out. Maybe if I could draw his peaceful repose, I would relax enough to sleep.

As I inched into the cold side of the sheets, a hand snaked around my waist and dragged me back under his wing. I looked at his face in surprise, but he was still asleep, seemingly unaware of his actions. I rolled on my side, and his fingers tightened on my ribs. His body warmed my back and melted my insides.

Don't ever let me go.

A smile bloomed through my body, and I buried my happy squeal in the pillow.

CHAPTER 30

Birth

I looked up from my breakfast in surprise at the sharp knock at the front door. The handle jiggled before Angus had even stood from the table.

The door opened and Naira swept in. "Come with me, Vera." She glanced at my feet. "You don't even have your boots on?"

At least I had clothes on.

"Hurry."

I jumped from my seat and ran to the bedroom. With all my fumbling, I couldn't hear what they were saying in the other room. I stuffed my feet into my boots and tucked in my shirt as I scrambled back out to the dining area. With a wave her of hand, Naira motioned me to follow. Then she was out the door.

"What's going on?" I asked Angus.

He kissed me lightly. "You should be honored."

"For what?"

Naira's voice filtered through the open door. "I won't wait for ye."

With a hand on my rear, Angus gave me a boost out the door. Watching for the sneaky roots and rocks in the now-familiar path, I skipped down after Naira. A chunk of hair had come loose from her braid and her eyes were bright and jittery. I'd never seen her so wild. Fleming seemed equally as agitated. He hovered above her head and cawed. She didn't wait for me. The chieftess actually ran. I caught up when she took the road west toward the hills.

"What is it?"

"We're cutting it too close. We can't miss it."

The road cut through a swath of trees, and the eun houses appeared. A woman stood in the doorway to the largest building. She waved, as if she'd been watching for us.

"Too late?" Naira yelled, her voice high and worried.

"The first one hatched," the woman said.

Naira made a guttural annoyed sound and ran faster. The woman held the door open and Naira tore past. Fleming swooped in after Naira. Curiosity and excitement kept me close behind.

Down the hall, Naira stopped at a door.

"Wait here, Fleming," she said.

"Don't want to," Fleming said.

"Go ask Annie for some fish," Naira said.

Fleming squawked indignantly but obeyed, waddling down the hall. She motioned me to follow her inside a stifling hot room. I choked on the smell of poultry and poop. She knelt next to a wide nest of hay housing five eggs. Another woman sat holding a blob in her hands. Two men waited and watched the eggs. No adult birds.

"Come," Naira said.

I hastened to her side and tried not to breathe. Naira put a warm dirty egg the size of a fist into my hands. Cracks webbed the thick shell. She had another egg in her palm. The two remaining eun tenders picked up an egg each. The smallest one remained in the nest.

The door opened and Bear slipped inside. "Aye. Must it be so hot?"

"There's one for ye," Naira said.

"No, thank you," Bear said with a smile that made me want to put my egg back.

Naira pursed her lips. "Tillson, you handle it."

One of the men picked up the last egg. The egg in my hands jostled. More cracks appeared. A tiny pink beak popped through the outer casing. Shell fragments flaked onto my fingers. The tapping stopped and the beak retreated, as if exhausted. I poked a fingernail against the shell.

"Don't help her," Naira said with a snap.

Bear said, "How can you tell it's a lassie?"

Naira ignored him. Her forehead glistened. "Do you want yer bird to be weak?"

"No," I said. *My* bird? They were giving me an eun? My ribs tightened, and I softened the cradle of my fingers around the precious orb.

"Little chance of that." Bear crouched at my side. "She's got a monster egg."

It was then I noticed my egg was the biggest. "What does that mean?" I wanted it to mean they'd accepted me. I wanted to be one of them.

"An eun fit for a chieftess," Naira said.

Gratification warmed me more than the room.

"She'll imprint on ye. She'll protect you before anyone else."

I'd grown up terrified of the euns. Now, their claws, sinew, and smarts were given to me as a gift. My weapon and shield. I could hardly contain the awe and relish that expanded through my heart. "Thank you."

Naira's face softened at the quiver in my voice.

Bear snorted. "Don't thank her yet. You get to sit through a day of clawing, pecking, and jobbies."

"Why are ye here, dearest?" Naira asked the chief.

"A lad can't spend the morning with his lassies?"

His lassies. I was one of his girls. A smile bloomed over my face. Bear winked at me. The pecking resumed. A large panel of shell popped off. I cupped my hands as a shiny pink glob flopped onto my fingers.

"She's out," Naira said, her voice low, but buzzing with excitement. "She's a wee bonnie."

"She's hideous." Bear said what I was thinking.

The mucus-coated ball wiggled, and a tiny bald head lifted. The black eyes were sealed shut and the poor thing didn't have a single feather or hair.

"She's strong," Naira said with all the pride of a mother. "Hold her close, but be gentle. Keep her warm."

I drew my cupped hands against my chest, but didn't know how I could hold this any tighter without squishing it. I found myself increasingly drawn to this sticky squab. *I will protect you too.* "Can you actually tell she's female?"

"We'll confirm it when she gets her feathers," Naira said.

Bear spoke low. "She gets a feeling about these things."

"I'm often right." Naira's voice was tight and defensive.

"I didn't say otherwise." His eyes danced. "Ye were right about Angus."

"Does it feel the same?" I asked, curious.

Bear laughed so hard he fell out of his squat and landed on his butt.

Naira bristled.

"What did I say?"

The other eun tenders seemed to be suddenly interested in their eggs, but I caught their lips held tight below tilted brows.

"She doesn't like to be teased about being the mother hen," Bear said.

I paled. "I didn't mean to offend. I wasn't teasing."

"I know," Naira said. "It's that big eejit that likes to poke fun. It's because he can hardly control his own imprinted bird. It's thanks to my valuable skills that he's alive to mock me."

I waited, eyes wide, hoping for the story.

Naira's lips curved up. "We were hunting a couple years ago. Bear thought he could take down a mountain cat."

I gasped.

"He'd backed the lion into a lone tree, but his blade missed the creature's heart when it pounced. I had a dozen birds on the cat's back within seconds."

He sat up and kissed Naira's sweaty cheek. "I thank ye for it."

"You were lucky to get away with only a broken nose."

I nearly dropped my baby bird. "That's how you broke your nose?"

He blinked at my tone. "What did ye think happened?"

Father had told me Bear broke it in a fight with Ian and the Wallaces while killing their revolt. I didn't answer. I couldn't bring up rebellions or my father when I was beginning to feel like I belonged. I didn't want to destroy the pleasant company. "I'm surprised, that's all."

"Not everyone gets mauled by a mountain lion." Bear puffed his chest out.

"Most people aren't that stupid," Naira said. He leaned down to kiss her, but she shooed him off, leaning over her hands. "He's coming." The lump of life fell into her waiting grasp.

"Congratulations on a handsome son," Bear said.

"Thank ye, dear," Naira said, ignoring his sarcasm and cradling her newly formed weapon close.

Bear left, leaving the rest of us to nurse our squabs. I fed mine soggy ground-up fish. Her tiny beak sliced my fingers until I got smart enough to get my tender skin out of the way. Naira didn't let me use gloves. She said it impaired the imprinting. Gloves were for cowards.

One of the minder's birds opened its eyes first. She held it close to her face. "Connol." She waited. "Connol. Connol."

The bird spoke with a weak scratchy voice. "Connol."

"Connol." She nestled the bird's head against her cheek and left the room.

The men named their birds next, then left.

My stomach growled.

"What shall ye name her?" Naira asked me. "When she opens her eyes, do as they've done. Say her name first thing."

"Tethra."

Naira paused then nodded. Tethra was the sword of legend for the ancient giant chieftain. Powerful and unstoppable. My eun didn't look like much, but maybe someday she'd grow into her name.

Naira's bird opened his eyes. Naira named him and laid him in the crook of her neck while she waited for me.

"I should name her *Late*." I leaned against the wall, the lazy ball curled up in my scratched hands. Finally, when I thought I'd pass out from hunger, boredom, and stink, she opened her eyes. Miniscule black orbs seemed to see through me.

"Tethra," I said.

"Tethra," the baby eun echoed.

I huffed out a chuckle. She got it on the first try. Her voice was stronger than I expected and sweeter. My chest ballooned with pride. I smiled, and Naira mirrored my joy. She stood and opened the door on a ruffled Fleming.

"You took too long," he said.

"Ye have a little brother," Naira said.

"Now forty-seven," Fleming said. "Put him with the others."

I was reluctant to part with Tethra when we dropped her at the nursery.

"We'll come back tomorrow," Naira said. "The more time you can spend with her, the stronger her connection to you will be."

I nodded.

"If only Bear and Angus would visit theirs once in a while."

I jolted. "Angus has one?" Of course he did.

Naira chuckled. She led me outside and pointed to a silvery bird perched on a log.

"Him?" It was the bird that tested me for truth. Angus's bird had cut my arm. Looking at that sharp beak made the wound itch under the bandage.

"Her," Naira said.

A loud caw drew my attention to an eun in a cage. The bird had missing feathers and gashes down its face.

"What happened?" I asked.

"He won't stop fighting the tenders. He refuses to see that they are here to help him. He killed a squab this morning. He'll have to be put down."

"I'm sorry," I said, surprised to truly mean it.

"Me too. We did our best. We can't make him see if he chooses to be blind."

Was there a lesson there for me?

For Campbell?

CHAPTER 31

Shot

The horse Koda had stolen was found two weeks later in Porto, but there was no sign of Koda. On October twenty-ninth I received a reply from Father. Angus sat in his office chair. I stood at his side and held the letter out where we could both read.

Dearest Vera Girl,

I have good news. We can transport the RV vaccine safely. We've tested it with a shipment to Porto. All laboratories are now working at maximum capacity to produce the vaccine. Tell your husband we will have fifty thousand vaccines for Alta Glenn as promised at the gathering this spring.

Father

I dropped the paper, which suddenly weighed more than gold. That's it? Over five months of silence and that was it? "Great news. You'll have the vaccine soon." My tone betrayed a touch of bitterness. I picked up the next note without looking at Angus.

Tiny Sister,

I'm engaged to Fitz. Fitzgerald and Lanie Marsh. Don't we sound perfect together? We're in love and getting married in Porto after the gathering. You'll be there, right?

Miss you, L

"Fitz and Lanie are getting married." I hated that my voice was sour. Why couldn't I be completely happy for them?

Angus gripped my hips and guided me down to his lap. I leaned into his warmth. "Do you wish to be marrying Fitz this spring?"

A snort broke up my frown.

Gray eyes flushed with pleasure. "So, what's the problem?"

"I feel forgotten." I looked down at his thigh, embarrassed by my frank confession.

His thick fingers caressed my chin, drawing my face up. "No one could forget you." His warm lips drowned my protests.

Angus kissed me long and slow, as if he could clear away all my hurt with his cedar scent and salty tongue. I buried my hands in his thick hair and nestled closer. A sharp cough jerked us apart. He swiveled, his breath rapid. His hand flew off my hip and gripped the edge of his desk.

Framed by the open door, Ana looked as though she'd been struck in the heart by a spear. Her fingers curled around the hilt of her belt knife. I scrambled off Angus's lap as fire licked my face. She shouldn't have seen that.

White-faced, she didn't blink. Her tone came out bland and flat. "A traveler has arrived. He's infected with red velvet. Naira sent me for you." She dragged her attention from Angus and directed her pain at me.

I hopped forward and picked up my heavy coat. "Where?"

She thawed slightly and led me and Angus down the stairs, a bit of color returning to her olive skin. Cold air nipped at my face as we rushed down the street. On the southern road near the harvested cornfield, Naira and four Glenns with guns raised circled a man. We stopped at the row of guards. My eyes nearly popped out of their sockets. I had learned of red velvet at Cromarty, but I was not prepared for this.

The only body part visible was the traveler's head. That was enough to draw vomit up my throat. The rich black hair and square shoulders argued the man was young, but his face spoke only of death. Glistening red sores carpeted his face and neck, as if his skin had been turned inside out. Ooze and puss dribbled freely down his face and into his pus-encrusted coat. Yellow eyes glared at the ring of aimed weapons. How he even had energy to stand, I couldn't guess. The burning pain was supposed to be excruciating.

Naira stepped away from the ring of guards and motioned us to follow her out of earshot of the others. She spoke quietly. "He said he came from Naiby. He was lost and looking for the containment unit."

"That's miles away," I said.

"He's lying," Angus agreed. "Shoot him."

"Wait. I'm immune." I hoped. "I can at least help him die in peace."

"No," Angus said. "I won't risk you, or the disease spreading. We'll be sparing him."

Agony would otherwise usher him to the grave. Angus tromped over to issue the death order. He stood at Ana's side. I stayed well back from the group, not wanting to see more detail. I already knew drawings of this event would pour off me before I'd sleep soundly again. Naira stayed next to me. Whether to support me or because she also wished for space, I didn't know, but I took strength from her presence.

Angus's clear voice sounded. "I'm sorry, lad, but we cannot allow you passage into Pinehearth. We are not set up to give you care, and we have no containment measures."

"Aim true when you shoot," the young man said.

Angus nodded grimly. A fist squeezed my heart, but there was nothing I could do to save him. The four Glenns adjusted their aim.

"I have a message first," the sick man said. His hands trembled as he pulled them free of his gloves. A mix of old and new blood streaked the leather. He stuck a raw hand into his coat pocket.

"We will accept nothing," Angus said. "Tell us what you will."

Alarms rang in my head when the man withdrew a fisted hand.

"Shoot," Angus yelled.

The man's hand flung forward, spraying tiny somethings into the air. "Down with the Grays." Gunshots drowned his cry, and he crumpled to the ground.

Naira and I sprinted forward. Ana turned her face, and cold fear clawed my chest. A bloody thorn embedded in her cheek. She brought a surprised hand up to her face and tugged out the tiny spur, drawing a prick of her own vital red.

No.

She stared at the little thorn in shock. Another Glenn picked a thorn out of his hand. More littered the ground.

"Stop." Fear hardened my command. "Hold perfectly still."

Frozen, Angus turned his face, his horrified expression said it all. He had a thorn on his shirt.

Please. Please don't let it have broken the skin. The little demon cells only needed the smallest opening to get inside a body and kill it.

"I'm going over you one at a time." My voice rang through the silence like a bell. "Do not move an eyelash until I say. Naira, please bring me tweezers, scissors, and antiseptic dressing. Check the soles of your shoes first."

Face stricken, Naira fled. I looked over the group while we waited. All the guards had the sharp burrs in their clothing. How deep they went, I'd soon find out. Anxiety painted their faces. I drew too close to the dead man and nearly fell over from the putrid smell of rotting flesh.

Naira returned with the supplies.

"Please prepare a place for the…" Infected. "Those who need to be cared for."

Naira nodded in understanding and darted off again, her countenance drawn and white.

I used the tweezers to remove the disease-ridden thorn from the folds of Angus's shirt. "This is why you should always wear a coat."

Angus tried to give me a smile, but failed. Robbed of enjoying the process, slowly I unbuttoned his shirt. I wiggled it off, hoping I hadn't missed a hidden barb. I tossed the shirt on the ground. Five Glenns watched as if they were made of ice.

My finger danced over his chest. "I can't find any cuts." My eyes misted in relief. Nothing on his pants. Using tweezers, I pulled a thorn out of the toe of his thick leather boot.

"I think you're clear." The chains suffocating my heart unspooled.

Angus exhaled.

"Go home. Burn your pants and boots. Shower with hot water, and soap up twice."

His gaze shifted to Ana, who stood as still as a stone statue. A stroke of red marred her beautiful face, a dark omen of her future. Despair twisted inside me. I had little hope for her now.

"I'll take care of her," I said with more confidence than I felt.

Eyes stormy and chest bare, Angus trudged toward town. People near the market bustled about and glanced in our direction. I could almost see fear thicken in the air over Pinehearth as word spread.

I worked deliberately and thoroughly. It would be a grave mistake to miss even one thorn. The dead rebel had poisoned an impressive amount of earthly shrapnel. I condemned his actions so thoroughly that it was hard to remember the girl I had been months ago. Eager to overthrow the Grays. Thinking I knew better for this country. What a fool I'd been.

I found a single thorn on the jacket sleeve of the first guard. I took his coat and dismissed him to go help Naira. The next guard followed shortly after. They'd been farthest from the haphazard throw and more protected. I approached Gent next. Gent. My favorite of Angus's friends. Well spoken. Polite. Always kind to me. He could beat Ana at any competition, but that didn't matter now. Gent had a cut on his jaw and another on his chin.

"It wasn't from a thorn, Lady. I promise I got it this morning," Gent said.

I looked at him sidelong.

"It's true," Woods said. Woods was Gent's father and the guard with the thorn in the back of his hand. "He's not so good at shaving his whiskers yet."

Gent's cheeks pinked, verifying the statement. With tweezers, I slowly teased out the thorn tangled in Gent's thick blond hair. His rapid breaths steamed my neck as I worked. I wanted to reassure him, but what could I say? Everything was *not* okay. His hands clenched and unclenched at his side. I removed the two barbs buried in the fabric of his pants, and the seven in his thick jacket. At least he had a bit of padding. I helped him out of his shirt and cut his pants off his legs.

"I think you're clean." I hoped. "But I can't let you go until I'm sure."

Gent stood before me in nothing but his boots and undershorts and the saddest blue eyes I'd ever seen. Chills swept over his skin, not a drop of fat to insulate him.

"I'll get you a blanket as soon as I can."

"I'm fine."

I smiled at his attempt to assuage my terror, and I doubled my efforts to hide my misery and pulsing fear. "Don't step on any thorns. Wait over there." My teeth locked together as I approached Woods and Ana. I didn't have a clue how to do this. I was not equipped to handle this.

Woods had a fatherly arm over Ana's shoulders.

"We already know," he said. "What do ye want us to do?"

My heart broke at their bravery. I picked off the rest of their thorns and cleaned their tiny wounds, but it was more to make us feel better.

It was pointless.

CHAPTER 32

Confined

A group carrying torches and firewood approached as we left the disaster site. Woods lived near the edge of town, and the four of us took over his cabin. His weeping wife and two daughters took refuge with a neighbor, hauling arms full of their belongings as they went. They looked back at us with pale, tear-streaked faces as Woods told them sweet lies about everything being all right.

I confined Gent to his own room. Woods's marital bed would become his deathbed. Ana occupied the daughters' room. I consigned myself to long nights on the couch. They each stood at their respective doors like three planets in orbit around me, but unlike the sun, I would not bring warmth and life.

"So that's it. We're trapped in these rooms until we die?" Ana stood in the doorframe to her new bedroom.

"How long do we have?" Woods's tenderness pricked sharper than her bitterness.

Tears swam behind my eyes. "I'll do everything in my power to help." I wished I had Lanie's medical training. "Let's hope we can stop the disease before it transmutes in your organs." There was no hope after that. "You're all fighters."

"We're fighting for our lives," Ana said.

Silence.

"Leave your clothes by the door. Hottest shower you can handle. I'll see about food."

The house had two lavvies. I made Ana and Woods share one lavvy as they were the two most certainly infected while Gent and I used the other.

Gathered in the kitchen, we ate the soup left on the doorstep by Ana's mother. It was our last meal together, but they didn't need to know that yet.

"Best thing you can do now is sleep," I said as I stacked the dishes.

Three morose figures drifted to their rooms.

Alone in the kitchen, I jerked at the knock on the door. I'd been insistent. No one comes near this house. I set the cup down by the sink and strode to the closed door.

"Hello," I said through the timber.

"Vera." I melted at hearing Angus's voice. "Open the door," he ordered.

I leaned my forehead against the wood. I wanted his arms around me. I needed his strength to get through this. I fretted about how I could do this alone. The handle shook, and I worried he'd force his way in.

"No, Angus. It isn't safe for you. I won't risk it."

"I won't come in. Please let me see you."

"No."

"Are you all right?" His tenderness nearly overcame my resolve.

"I'm fine. Really."

"If I go way back from the house, will you open the door?"

I shouldn't. "Yes." Through the window, I watched until he'd gotten behind the blackberry bramble near the end of the front walk.

When I opened the door, a packet of paper and pencils fell across the threshold at my feet. I picked them up and held them to my chest. He'd known what I needed and brought it for me.

I managed to choke out, "Thank you."

"Do you want anything else?"

I wanted to crawl into our bed and curl up in his arms.

"I need you not to come around here."

He scowled.

"I'm serious. You're a temptation and a distraction. One kiss could kill you."

His face softened into a handsome smile.

"I need you to live." My voice shook with the strength of my plea.

His brow furrowed. "Please don't get sick."

"I won't." If the vaccine didn't work, my death would be the least of his worries.

"Good night, dear wife."

I waved and hurried inside before I ran after him. With the door firmly shut and locked, I leaned against it and brought a hand to my chest above my aching heart. Ana watched me from her bedroom doorway. Feeling like a criminal caught in a vile act, I jerked my hand to my side.

"Can I get you anything?" I said, embarrassed at my reaction and annoyed by her eavesdropping.

"He loves ye. Why?"

I bristled at her callous tone and cruel question. The worst part was he *didn't* love me. "He's a good man." I spoke my new truth. He treated me with honor despite never wanting to marry me.

"He's the well best." Her bronze eyes ignited. "He deserves a lass who can at least hit the stationary target not to mention keep her weasel wee friend from burning down buildings."

I sat down on the couch, suddenly exhausted. *Tell me something I don't already know.*

"How did ye beguile him? He stopped caring for me after he went to Cromarty for schooling."

"He's never stopped caring for you."

Her eyes glazed over. "One kiss. One beautiful kiss is all I ever got from him."

Jealousy seared through my gut.

"Naira interrupted us. He never came back for me. Never tried again. Not after Cromarty." She spat out the last word like a curse.

Clearly, that kiss was the cause of the scar on his back. I looked up at the radiant warrior. "I'm sorry I've caused you pain." Although she was dishing out plenty right now. "I'm sorry if you feel I've wronged you." *I'll never be sorry Angus is mine.*

"I want to hate you."

"You are welcome to."

She slammed her palm into the doorframe in frustration.

"You should really try to sleep." I settled the stack of papers in my lap, trying not to look intimidated by her beauty and ferocity.

She marched forward, and I flinched. "What are you doing?" She folded her arms and peered at the blank pages.

"Drawing calms my nerves." Angus knew that, and had brought me my things. He couldn't be at my side, but still he delivered me comfort.

She stood near me, hovering over my shoulder.

"Shall I draw you?"

"Not me." Her voice trailed off.

I knew who she wanted to see. I took a deep breath and pushed away my petty jealousy. An image came to mind, bright and searing as the day I'd seen them together, dancing as if they were made for each other. I adjusted the lamplight and let my pencil fly. I forgot she was there until I had finished the drawing and shifted it into her waiting hands. Her trembling fingers traced the graceful lines of her body and Angus's arms as he carried her into the air. I could almost hear the drums again.

"It's bonnie perfect." Tears slipped down her face. She drifted away from the couch and silently entered her bedroom, her eyes never lifting from the drawing.

***

Trouble came the next morning. Woods had a fever. I sequestered everyone to their respective rooms. There would be no sharing air or anything else. By evening, Woods was coughing up blood.

I took hope in the fact that Ana and Gent looked good when they went to bed that night.

Unfortunately, the next morning, they both woke with fevers.

I had plenty of food and supplies thanks to the deliveries that piled up outside. Even still, boiling towels and clothing, and serving broth and cooling fevers left me worn and discouraged. When going between rooms, I'd wash my hands twice and switch the scarf I tied around my head to cover my nose and mouth.

Woods stopped eating on the second day when the first velvet spot appeared on his belly. Transmutation. We both stared dumbly at the horrible sore for a while.

Red velvet really was the worst name. There was nothing soft and lovely about the angry boil.

"I'd like to write a letter," he said.

Blinking furiously, I ran for paper. Woods wrote for hours.

"How's Gent?" he asked when he handed me a thick stack to deliver to his wife.

"He's doing fine. No symptoms." It was only a little lie to ease a dying man's burden. Gent was currently in a delirious sleep, but no coughing blood or rashes. I clung to hope.

"Good. He must live."

"Yes, sir."

I hung the papers near the fire, figuring the heat, smoke, and time would cure them of any contaminants. I was doing my best, making up things as I went, hoping it would be enough.

"Help me." The weak voice barely reached my ears.

I wrapped my face and washed my hands and answered Gent's call. I sat at his side and held his clammy hand. His eyes remained closed, even when I wiped a cool towel on his brow, and brushed my fingers through his sweaty blond hair.

"Sing birdie."

"I'm a terrible singer."

Gent frowned as if that wasn't right. Was I part of his dream? His hand tightened on my palm. I sang.

Ma had a little fig tree. It was just my height.
It stayed that way, until I stopped and it did not.
Now it towers o'r me.
I think I hear it laugh, every time it aims true, and drops a
ripened fruit, splitting open on
my shoe.

That night, after my three patients had succumbed to the haggard sleep of the sick, I slipped outside. I dropped on the doorstep and buried my face in my knees. I didn't have to wait long for Angus to appear at the end of the walk.

When I looked up, he gasped. I chuckled, releasing some of the tightness in my chest. His horror turned to confusion.

"I'm not sick, I only look like death."

He dropped to the ground, mirroring my crouched form. He stayed dutifully far away. Much too far to feed the need for his touch. My skin itched with it.

"You need rest, Vera. If you push too hard—"

"Woods is dying."

He blanched.

"He's transmuted. The rash has spread over his chest and up his neck."

"How long does he have?"

I shrugged. "I wish I knew. Days, I'd guess."

He stared at the dirt. "Gent?" His best friend. "Ana Sky?" He said her name with yearning.

I swallowed away my selfishness. "I have hope. They're fighters." Although this was a battle they hadn't trained for, and Gent hadn't opened his eyes since yesterday morning.

"I need to speak to them."

"Gent is asleep."

"Ana?" Wide eyes pleaded.

I hesitated.

"You're all in there together, and I'm shut out."

"Be grateful."

He didn't look grateful. He looked angry and vengeful. Which I appreciated.

"Woods needs something for the pain. He's in agony. He's a brave man, but I can't stand watching the torture." Tears welled behind my eyes. These last few days had turned me into a burbling spring. "See if you can find Rosy."

Angus's brows drew together.

"It's a recreational drug we—Campbell—manufactures."

"I've never heard of it." He didn't seem happy about that.

I was glad he didn't know what it was, but sorry his ignorance meant they probably didn't have any in Pinehearth. "It's really the worst sort of drug. It takes away all pain and inhibition, and it strips the mind of clarity, knowledge, and memories." Not that I'd tried it. "It's lucrative to the sellers. People will pay to leave reality behind. It's popular in the conquered dominions."

Angus spoke through a tight jaw, clearly unhappy about this revelation. "I'll ask my parents."

"It's a pink tablet. If you don't have it, any painkiller would help." I stood and shook out sore legs. "I've got to at least try to sleep while I can."

I left Angus sitting still as stone.

CHAPTER 33

Pain

Ana screamed. I woke with a jolt and shot to her room as I tied the cloth to cover my face. The fire had burned low, and a chill crept through the house and into my heart. I turned on the light and wished I hadn't. She knelt on top of the bed. Blood dripped off her outstretched hands.

No.

"It's happening," she said. "I can't stop it."

"I'll draw you a bath."

"I don't want a bath. I want to live." Her voice cracked, and she coughed, spewing red over the sheets. She doubled over in pain and curled into a fetal ball on the bed.

My heart imploded. I would've traded places with her if I could. Helplessly watching was torture. I perched on the bed at her side and rubbed my hand along her spine. I didn't leave until I heard her rattling breath settle into sleep. I changed my clothes and curled up on the couch. Anguish blanketed me. I didn't think my battered heart could take anymore.

But it did.

In the morning, I checked the outside delivery spot by the blackberries. Angus waited for me. He stood against a tree a little past the yard. Too close.

Hold me. Take me far away.

"We had some." He pointed to a small bag on the ground.

I perked up.

"Father confiscated a haul from his last visit in Porto."

I cradled the small bundle now needed by two patients. My face pinched.

"What is it?" He took a dangerous step forward.

"Ana."

His lip quivered, and his eyes pinked. "Can I see her?"

"I'll ask her."

"I must see her," he insisted.

"I'll go get her." I really didn't want to.

He ran a hand through his thick brown hair, and I shuffled to the door.

"We heard back from Hugo," he said.

I jerked around to face him.

"We're meeting him at Belle Borg in three weeks. He'll bring all the vaccines he can."

"I'm coming."

"I hope you will."

Emotions churned deep inside me. Pinehearth would get the vaccine. I'd see my family again. I was no longer the rebel they thought I had been. I wondered what I'd say to my father or how I could ever trust him again. Which reminded me we were trusting him enough to get the vaccine from him. It didn't seem wise, but there was no alternative.

I ducked inside. Ana lay on her bed, staring at the ceiling. She looked ethereal. Her skin glowed, and her eyes seemed to flicker with live flame.

"Angus wants to see you."

She sat up and wiped blood off unnaturally red lips. "Take me to him."

"You cannot touch him."

She looked down her nose at me. "Isn't that convenient?"

I clamped down on my unkind retort. I guided her out of her room and opened the front door. She walked out back straight and head high, then stopped on the front step.

"Oh, Ana." Angus's anguished voice tore a hole in me.

Her shoulders slumped slightly.

"Can I get you anything?" he asked.

"Talk with me," she said.

He sat on the grass across the yard. She settled against the open door.

They talked. I couldn't stand to listen to their recounting years spent together. I went back inside and sat with Gent, who was still sleeping. I held his hand and rubbed the lean lifeless muscles in his arms and calves. Incessant coughing finally drew me back to Angus and Ana. Her napkin was red with blood, and he'd shifted dangerously close. His hand outstretched.

"Get back," I snapped at him.

Tears dribbled down his scruffy cheeks.

I gripped Ana's elbow and tugged her to her feet. "You need to rest."

"Why?"

Blood splattered on my sleeve as she spat the word at me. I flinched.

"Go," Angus said, his eyes wide as he looked at my red arm. "Listen to Vera. I'll come back. We'll talk tomorrow if you're feeling up to it."

"I will be." Ana glared at me, but was forced to look away when more coughing sent bloody phlegm spurting out.

Woods's wife, Nelly, and his daughters came into view from the street.

"Vera," Nelly called.

"Just a minute," I hollered, my patience paper thin. "I'll be right back." I needed to scrape my entire body clean of Ana's poisonous blood. I hauled her to her bed and closed the door a little too tightly. I stripped, showered, dressed, and went back outside.

"How's my husband?"

"He's a brave man."

The weepy woman smiled. "Is Gent awake yet?"

"Not yet, but I think that's a good sign."

"I wish to see them. Speak with them."

"I'll go in and see."

"I'll be waiting right here."

I believed her.

Inside, I opened the packet of relief. Ten Rosy tablets. I dissolved one in a spoonful of warm nettle tea. It would be hard enough to get him to drink even that much.

Gent slept like the dead. As long as he didn't join them, the sleep might be the healing salvo he needed.

I tiptoed into Woods's room. He lay still on the bed in a state of full alert. Eyes pinched shut, jaw tense, neck strained, hands fisted. He battled silently.

"Good morning, handsome," I said.

Wild eyes peeled open.

"I have a treat for you this morning." I brought the cup near his face.

"No, thank you."

"Drink it."

"No."

Woods hadn't had a drop or crumb since his first red velvet spot appeared on his body. I had my suspicions he was trying to speed up the process by starvation. I didn't blame him.

"Trust me."

"No."

With a gloved hand, I gripped his chin, my fingers pressing against the raw, wounded flesh of his face.

Woods cried out in pain.

I poured the tiny bit of tea in his mouth. "I'm sorry, but I did it for your own good."

"It didn't feel like it."

"You have three beautiful women outside who would like to see you."

"You mock me."

"I would never."

"They can't see me peely wally like this."

"They love you. It doesn't matter to them that your face is a little red."

"A little red." Woods said it with more energy than he'd mustered in days.

Good. The Rosy was working. "Get up and let's get you dressed."

"Bonnie lassies, you say?"

"You'll have to see for yourself."

Woods grinned. "My Nelly is a beauty."

I smiled as the tension in Woods's back dissolved. I gaped as he hopped out of bed.

"You're a pretty one too."

"Thank you."

"'Course you'll look better when you get some sleep and put some effort into it."

"Wouldn't we all."

Wood shrugged off his shirt.

I reeled as the smell of pus and rot washed over me.

"Let's get you in the shower, and then I'll find you some new clothes."

Woods fumbled with his pants.

"You can take those off in the lavvy."

"Why bother?" His pants hit the floor.

Fine.

Woods danced into the lavvy while I scrambled to change the sheets and put the dirty fabrics into the fresh pot of boiling water I'd started that morning.

Washed, but not exactly looking clean, Woods walked back into the bedroom. The blooming red sores covered all but a few patches of un-diseased skin. He dressed in work pants and a plaid shirt.

"We're going to say hello," I said, suddenly worried. "You can't touch them or go to them or leave."

Woods pursed his festering lips.

"You must promise me you will stay at my side."

A seductive grin spread. "Possessive wee thing. Ye don't want to share?"

"No. I don't want to share the disease on your skin with anyone."

Woods balked and seemed to return to himself.

I took his elbow and steered him to the front door. We stood on the doorstep. The November sun glistened on his oozing skin. Nelly and her daughters stood in shocked silence. Angus had thankfully left. This was hard enough already.

"Haw, lassies."

"Oh, Da." A sob shook the girl. The sisters clutched each other.

"How do you feel, my love?" Nelly asked.

"I feel wonderful." He beamed.

Her gaze slipped to me.

"He's drugged," I said. "Otherwise he can't move for the pain."

She nodded, despair hardening her face.

"Why are ye so far away, my love? Come home. Let me kiss you," Woods said.

"She can't." My voice came out a little too sharp. I was exhausted and had little patience left. "You'll get her sick."

"I love you, Woods. You're the most wonderful man I've ever known." Tears poured down Nelly's cheeks and neck as she continued to gush out her love in a heartfelt oration.

"Nel," Woods croaked when she'd finished her lengthy ode.

Disappointment stained her already anguished face.

"I have a long letter he wrote to you," I told her. "Before this."

"Thank you." She said it with so much feeling my heart shook.

"I'm sorry I can't be there to hold your hand and tend to you," Nelly said.

Woods leaned down and kissed my brow. I grimaced. How fast could I get in and scrub that spot?

"Vera is doing a fine job. I'll give you a tip. Always drink her tea."

"Time for bed," I said.

"Good-bye, Father," the girls chimed.

"What about Gent?" Nelly asked.

"Gent?" Woods said. "He's out hunting. He'll be home for supper."

"Gent is still fighting. I have hope," I said.

"My lad's a fighter." Pride brightened Woods's fevered eyes. "The best in the Realm."

"Good-bye, beloved." Nelly placed a hand to her heart.

I ushered Woods into the house, wondering if that had been the worst idea ever. He flung onto his bed and was asleep before I pulled up the blanket. I scrubbed the spot he kissed three times with soap and hot water.

When Ana woke, I gave her some Rosy tea and the letters from her family.

"I want to see Angus."

Heart tight, I nodded. "When he returns, I'll get you."

She closed her eyes again with a blissful smile.

I slumped against the kitchen counter. It'd been six days of brutal work. A six-day death march. The pink pill on the stone beckoned. It would take away this piercing pain.

I rolled the tablet through my fingers. My escape beckoned as temptation grew, egging me to find release.

This was too hard. I couldn't do this anymore.

Yes, I could, and I would.

I shoved the Rosy into the bag and flung it into a cupboard.

CHAPTER 34

Healed

"Hello?" Gent's voice drifted from the bedroom, craggy and dry.

I dropped the bread knife and grabbed a glass of water. Worry lodged in my throat as I flung the bedroom door open.

Gent sat up in bed and looked at me with clear blue eyes. His face was thin and his cheeks hollow, but at that moment he was absolutely beautiful. I sagged against the doorframe. The glass slipped from my fingers and shattered on the floor.

"Lady." Gent jumped up. He swayed and sank back to the bed, clutching his head.

"Don't get up." I stepped carefully over the shards and made my way to his bed. I felt his brow with trembling hands. Cool and dry. "I'll get you food."

Giddiness sent a tremor though my simple words. Frantic with joy, I prepared a quick tray of broth and bread. Gent inhaled the food while I cleaned up the broken glass and water. He asked for more. I gave him as much as he would take.

"How do you feel?" I asked as I hovered like an old grandmama.

"Tired and a bit achy, but fine."

My knees gave out, and I dropped to the floor. Shaking like a storm, I cried. Sobbed. Convulsed.

His warm hand patted my shoulder. "Lady?"

I turned to the boy sitting at my side on the floor. "You're not going to die."

Gent chuckled. "Sorry to disappoint you."

I smacked his leg.

He sobered. "Father and Ana?"

I shook my head. "I'm sorry."

"Me too." He drew me against his side, and I rested my head on his shoulder. I drank up his living warmth and human contact like a starving woman. "I owe you my life. You saved me."

I grunted out disagreement.

"No, you did. I knew you were there, tending me, holding my hand. I kept my focus on you."

Chills ran down my spine. "Thank you for getting better," I said. "You saved me too."

We huddled together for a long time. Thin threads stitched the broken pieces of my heart back together.

"This makes us bonded forever." His hand tightened on my shoulder. "Brother and sister."

"I'd like that." More than I cared to admit, even to myself. I'd had a family once.

"Like it or not, you're stuck with me." His blue eyes danced.

I mirrored his grin. "You have a couple of other sisters aching to see you." We rose to our feet. "Shower first. You can shave later—no cuts right now." I winked. "Clean clothes and don't touch anything when you leave."

I busied myself in the kitchen while Gent was in the lavvy. When he came out looking clean, and on his way to better health, he smiled at me before crossing to the door.

"Wait." I darted forward. "Don't touch the handle."

He froze and put his hands up.

I shrugged. "Just in case." I wasn't too worried about Gent getting sick again, but I didn't want any miniature assassins hitching a ride out with him.

"Thank you, Lady." His voice rang with feeling and sincerity. I hung in the shadows of the open door as he greeted his family. "Maw."

Three giddy girls galloped forward. It took sheer force of will to turn away from the vibrant scene and back to the rotting gloom.

Later that day, Woods died in his sleep. Fury wormed through my veins, lighting my body on fire.

Father had the means to save these people. Woods's death was on his head.

As soon as I got out of here, I would find my father. He owed me some vaccines.

Plus a whole lot of answers.

CHAPTER 35

Dead

"What do you want to do?" I spoke to Bear from our awkward positions across the yard.

"How long does Ana have?"

I hated talking like this. Hated it. "She's younger and stronger. Maybe two days?"

"We're going to burn the house after..." His voice trailed off. I choked on a lump of agony too big for me to swallow. "Can you wrap Woods and leave him until then?" I nodded, unable to look Bear in the face. "I'm incredibly proud of ye, Vera. We all are. What you've done is nothing short of heroic." I caught a glimpse of the kindness radiating out of his eyes. I didn't feel heroic. I felt like a failure. I went inside and tried not to breathe as I tucked blankets around Woods's body. I closed the door to his room and shoved a boiled blanket in the gap under the door.

Ana lingered for nine more days. The Rosy ran out after four. That's when I stopped her family's visits, and I banned Angus from coming over.

"Let me stay with her until the end," he pleaded, inching dangerously close to where I stood by the open door.

"She can't even speak now."

"I can. She'll hear my voice." The pain on his face nearly rent me in two.

"I can't bring her out. She's too weak. Too contagious. Remember her as she would want you to. Strong. Beautiful. Vibrant." My voice broke. I wilted. Sobs wracked my body.

Angus jolted forward.

Frightened, I leapt into the house and slammed the door. "Don't come back," I said through the door. I crumbled against the wood and wept.

The last five days of Ana's life were an eternity of anguish. I left her family and Angus pictures of her on the doorstep. Every morning they were gone. I felt like a piece of my heart went with them. People left letters for me to read to her. I had no trouble with the ones from her family, but the words from Angus burned my throat.

"Remember our archery contest last year?" I read. "I won."

Ana opened swollen eyes. "No, he didn't. I won." Her voice was a wisp.

I kept reading. "I won because you shared your winnings with me. Remember we took the basket of smoked shivites and mulled cider to the lake?" I wondered if they'd eaten together at the same lovely spot I'd found. "Stars, the lake was cold that day."

He'd gone swimming with her. I couldn't even swim. I swallowed and pressed on, distancing myself from the stories. I climbed away from my own heart. Ana smiled as my voice droned on.

Days passed. As I held Ana's hand and read her books and drew her pictures of Angus, I retreated into the dark reaches of my mind. I shriveled to a tiny seed around which I built walls of iron and fire. I blocked out the cries, the putrid blood, the smell of death and decay. I never took off my face scarf, even to sleep. The odor from Woods's decaying body wafted through the cracks. I vacillated between feeling as though the dying girl and I were one being and feeling as though I were disconnected from time and space entirely.

Ana died, holding my hand and clutching pictures of Angus to her chest. I wrapped her and Angus's likenesses in a sheet. I felt bereft and empty. I didn't see how I could join the land of the living as a hollow husk, a ghost for weeks on end.

Methodically I stripped, leaving my clothes where they fell on the floor. With the shower as hot as it would go, I burned away the top layer of my skin. I cranked it to frigid cold, but still I felt nothing.

I dressed in a pair of Gent's pants and shirt from his room, the only clean clothes I could find. I stood at the door and surveyed the wreckage. Stained towels littered the floor. The couch sagged below my worn blanket and crumpled drawings.

"Good-bye." I flicked off the lights and wandered into searing daylight. Sunlight reflected like fiery arrows off the frosted ground. It hurt my eyes, but didn't touch the gathering darkness in my chest.

I didn't expect anyone to be waiting for me. I'd stopped going outside days ago—it was too hard to return to the heavy smell of rotting flesh and Ana's cries. I sucked down clean frozen air, washing my lungs. The winter chill hacked at my numbness. I plodded into town, blinking at the bright spinning world.

"Vera." I tilted my head. My name. I knew that woman from before—before my time with death. "Ye're out."

"Yes." The word fell like a stone. "Ana died, and so did Woods." I spoke as if through glass.

"I know." Isla—it was Isla—put a hand on my arm. "Oh, ye poor hen." She reached up on tiptoes and wrapped an arm around my shoulders. I bent forward stiffly. Isla stepped back with a worried look on her face. "Pax."

The boy darted through the shop's front door. His face split open. "Vera."

Isla halted his approach with an upheld hand and an urgent voice. "Run. Go get Angus. Now."

Yes. Angus. Ana loved Angus.

"Come sit down," Isla said.

"No, thank you. I've been sitting too long." A wall seemed to separate me from my voice, my body, my town.

Isla wrung her hands and scanned the street. Curious faces stopped to gawk. I didn't care...about anything. Angus appeared at the far end of the road. Pax trailed farther and farther behind as Angus sprinted my way.

My, he was handsome. I could see why she loved him. I admired the strong man hurtling my way as if I were an invisible observer. Wavy hair flew back from his angled face. Pale eyes shone above his perfect nose and wide lips. Exactly as I had drawn him.

He skidded to a stop before me. Eager breaths puffed my face. He didn't smell of death or rot. I leaned into the smell of kisses. Too bad he couldn't've breathed life into Ana. "She died."

His bloodshot eyes watered. "Can I touch you?"

"You won't get sick." I hated the chasm dividing me from the world. I hated the sound of my hollow emotionless voice.

"I think she's in shock," Isla said.

Distress darkened Angus's face. "What can I do?"

"Nothing," I said. "She's gone."

"I know, dearest." His voice caught, and he swallowed. Fingers picked up my limp hand. "Come. I'll take you home."

Isla stepped away, and the crowd parted as he angled me up the street. I halted when I heard my name echoing off the houses.

Gent bounded up. "I am so glad to see you."

"She died." I searched brilliant his blue eyes. "You didn't."

Gent frowned at my flat tone. I didn't react when his palms gripped my face. He pressed his forehead to mine. He clouded my vision, but his words got through. "It's okay to grieve. Please know I'm here for you."

"Help me find my way back." I barely whispered the words.

"I'll show you." His wiry hands tightened on my skull. "You didn't kill Ana or Father. You saved me. Remember that." His nose brushed mine before he pulled back. His hopeful gaze searched my face. "Okay, sister?"

My eyes burned with hot tears. "Okay, brother."

Gent gave me a solemn nod before he trotted away.

Angus's hand warmed mine. With a pinched brow, he turned me toward home.

"I don't want to go inside. I want sunshine and life."

"Coat first."

"I'll wait here."

Reluctantly, he let go of my hand and bounded up the street. I hugged Gent's loose shirt to my chest. Sunlight gilded Pinehearth. My town. Pax struggled to carry a heavy bolt of fabric through Isla's shop doors. Scotsbane lumbered up to Peony exiting the fruit shop and gave her something too small to see, but the goofy grin on his face traveled for miles.

Living breathing humans. They didn't die. I'd helped protect them. The comforting thoughts didn't reach their mark. We needed the vaccine. Father was keeping it from these people.

Angus's return tugged me out of my stupor. I realized how cold I'd become when I put on the fur coat and gloves.

"There is someone who'd really like to see you," he said.

"Who?"

He held me close under his wing and marched me to the newly built stables. I sucked down the smell of oats, sweat, and muscle.

"Pearl." I smiled at the happy whinny that echoed in reply.

I jogged to her stall and tore open the door. I flung myself against her neck. Pearl nipped at my hair and slobbered on my brow. "I missed you," I cooed and stroked her long silver nose. My stare stayed on my girl as Angus saddled her.

"Now I'm jealous of a horse," he said.

I sent him a smile that loosened the knot in his brow.

"Get out there. Coal and I will catch up."

"If you can."

He chuckled as I led Pearl out.

The ground was cold and hard when I took Pearl to the barren harvested fields and nudged her into a gallop. The rolling motion and sheer speed sent adrenaline coursing through my veins, waking my petrified heart. Frozen fingers of air fluffed my short hair.

"Faster."

Pearl kicked up the ground and bolted away from town. Welcome wind whipped at my face. My legs protested and my arms buzzed, but I didn't care. After a few more minutes of tearing up the field, I reined in Pearl.

"Thank you, girl."

As my friend ambled back toward home, a black horse and his rider grew bigger. Coal danced to a stop at my side.

"You almost look like you know what you're doing," Angus said.

"Race you to the field's edge." I took off before waiting for an answer.

He howled, and within seconds Coal's head jostled next to Pearl. She huffed and neighed at him, which seemed to encourage the stallion. When I stood in the stirrups, Angus's hand found my rear.

"That's cheating." His touch penetrated to my numb core, and desire awakened.

"I'm giving you a boost." His laughter was a deep beautiful rumble.

"Come on, Pearl." With a burst, we shifted ahead. The finish line was moments away.

Angus almost let me win.

We reined our horses to a stop. I tried to scowl, but I couldn't. Feeling had returned to all my limbs and organs, and life bubbled inside me, pushing out the pain. I let happiness surface. His gaze traveled over my beaming face.

"I missed you, dear wife."

"That doesn't begin to cover it." I turned Pearl toward the stable so Angus couldn't see the tears forming in my eyes.

I'd felt so entirely alone, and had clung to the pictures of Angus as much as Ana had, but I knew he would be waiting for me if I could endure the torture of watching those people die with no hope of helping them.

I lived for the letters he'd left on the door. I dreamed of his arms around me each night. Angus had gotten me through.

I brushed out Pearl's coat and gave her a bucket of oats. Reluctantly, I left the warmth of the stable for the cold call of the death horn.

All the life and joy I'd felt out in the fields evaporated.

Angus and I trudged toward the cabin that had been my prison for two weeks.

CHAPTER 36

Love

"Welcome, kin," Naira said. "It is with great sorrow that we gather tonight."

Angus kept a tight arm around my shuddering shoulders as we stood next to Bear at the front of the assembly.

"We owe a great debt to our future chieftess," Bear said.

Future chieftess. The words hit me like an anvil. My future. I wanted it. I came wanting to destroy, but now I would've given my life to save these people. I'd failed to save Woods and Ana. I would not fail again.

"She has proven herself to be brave, courageous, and selfless. Such a service of love will long be remembered here." Bear's eyes glistened with tear-filled gratitude. "Thank you, Vera."

The crowd howled like wild animals, honoring me.

But Ana and Woods had died. I tucked the tender praise deep inside where I could take comfort and strength from it when I was ready. Ana's mother sang a song of piercing beauty. I hid my tears in the breast of Angus's coat. He cried into my hair. Cried for the woman he should've married when he had the chance.

Gent read a poem, and his sisters danced. Six burly Glenns dropped their torches on the oil-drenched kindling placed around the house.

"Everyone back."

In a flash, flames licked the timbers.

"I'd like to go home now," I said to Angus. I didn't want to talk to people. Fatigue crept over my exhausted body.

I'd had enough.

We plodded home in silence. *Home.* Angus opened the front door and flicked on the lights. I gasped. Flowers weighted down the table. Breads, fruits, and cookies were piled high in the kitchen. Gift packages were stacked on the side table next to a collection of letters.

"There isn't much we can do to show our gratitude, but people still wanted to do something." He peeled the coat off my frozen frame.

"This is all for me?" From the people who nearly killed me as a traitor?

"There's a whole new wardrobe for you in the bedroom."

"Why? They died."

He stepped up close and wrapped his strong, warm fingers around my upper arms. "You saved Gent. How many more of us did you save? You were fast and smart and got the disease contained. You can't stop red velvet. You can only hope to contain it."

"Ana was strong, and she fought as hard as Gent," I said. "I should've been able to save her too."

"Don't do that."

I studied a knot in the wood floor. "She loved you." She deserved him.

"I know. And I loved her."

A blade twisted into my stomach.

His eyes reddened. "I miss her very much. I've lost my friend."

"She didn't want you to see her that way."

"I couldn't give her what she wanted. I tried. Something changed along the way, and I couldn't return her feelings. Maybe we were too much alike." His hands slid down my back. "I never felt for her what I feel for you, Vera."

I leaned closer as hope bloomed in my chest.

His gray eyes searched my face. "I love you."

The words cut straight to my center, breaking open my protective cage and letting loose a tumult of emotion: joy, suffering, love, desire, pain. *Life.* I gasped.

He drew me into his arms and buried his face in my neck.

I shivered with pleasure.

"Oh dearest. I thought I had lost you. I love you. I love you more than I thought possible." His tears wet my skin. His face dipped lower, cradling against my chest as his hands snuck under the hem of my shirt, caressing my back, my sides, my ribs. I basked in his love, like a blossom finding sunlight.

Angus's thick lips found my neck and jaw before settling on my mouth. Unwilling to let go of him, we stumbled to our bedroom. Clothing dotted the floor, marking our passage. Wrapped together, we landed across the bed. His breathing turned deep and heavy as he explored my body as if for the first time.

His touch soothed like a balm as his warm mouth trailed tingling lines over my skin. I was taut as a bowstring ready to snap, but with a look of wicked delight, my husband took his time kissing and caressing me, marking every place on my body his. His tongue spoke a language far stronger than words as he let me knew how deep his love went.

I let out a shivering sigh as we joined not only our bodies, but also our hearts. My very essence mixed with his, and I felt more complete and cherished than I could've imagined.

He was mine, and I was his. I would never waste another moment of our life together.

Later that night, after Angus had made certain I knew how much he loved me, he drifted off to sleep. I didn't. He could've died, as surely as Ana. Tossing and turning more than the leaves outside the window, I dreamed of death and fire, and blood. I woke in the dark to Angus's soothing shushes. Sweat coated my skin, and I gulped down labored breaths.

He lifted me onto his lap. "Do you know why I agreed to your father's proposal?"

The question pulled my mind out of the dark places it had been lurking. "Not his power of persuasion?"

"Well, that helped, but no." His hand drifted up my bare thigh and rested on my hip. "A couple years ago when we visited Campbell, I saw you down by the bakery."

I tilted my head.

"You know the one in McAndrew, by the bookstore?"

"Yes, I know it. I think about their crinkles every day."

He kissed my nose. "You sat on the steps, and were drawing. I crossed the street intending to say hello, but I stopped when a child approached you. She had bright red hair full of tiny curls." His voice softened. "And scars crisscrossing her cheek."

"I remember her."

"She plopped down next to you and pestered you with questions until you could no longer draw."

"You were spying on us the whole time?"

"Hardly spying. I was in plain sight if you'd bothered to look up." He smiled. "Eventually, you offered to draw her a picture. She didn't want one of herself though. You asked her why not and told her she was beautiful. She covered her scars and shook her head; her expression was heartbreaking. Your voice was so kind when you told her that you would show her what you saw." His grip on my ribs tightened. "I was completely transfixed at that moment."

My heart expanded as I pressed closer.

"You drew a beautiful girl, bright eyes, wonderfully wild hair, tiny nose. I thought you would leave out the scars."

"I considered it. I wasn't really sure what to do."

"You didn't. That would have been a lie. You drew them. Soft. Somehow they became lovely lines on her cheek."

A rebellious tear made its way down my cheek.

"That girl changed that day." Angus tilted my chin with gentle fingers. "So did I."

I leaned into kiss him, but he pulled back. "Confident and happy, the girl skipped away with her treasure. I walked up." He chuckled. "I said hello and asked if I could see your drawing."

My face fell as I remembered the rest of the story.

"Your face was so cold, no trace of the goodness I'd seen when you asked me if it was a command."

It had been right after Emilia's death. I had scarcely kept myself from trying to scratch his eyes out.

"I could barely keep from laughing when you told me no. Your tone could have cut granite."

"No," I said. "You laughed at me as I walked away." I had hated him for it at the time. What a fool I was.

"Marched away," Angus corrected. "Head high and sketchbook closed."

I grimaced.

"That's when I think I fell in love with you."

His words smoothed over my rough edges and filled me with a joyful peace. I slid my hands over his neck and into his thick hair.

When I drew him down, he let me kiss him.

Deep and slow, full of belonging and possession.

CHAPTER 37

Storm

We spent the week preparing for the trip to Belle Borg. The night before our planned departure the storm hit. From the warmth of the big house where we'd finished dinner with Bear and Naira, we watched the sky dump its frozen load. Bear cursed our travel delay. I had no desire to ride in that, but hated that Angus and the rest would have to wait longer to get the vaccine.

"Would ye like to sleep here tonight?" Naira asked.

Angus cocked a brow at me. I shook my head. He kissed his mother good-bye. We tightened our coats and ran. White flurries attacked us, and the wind tried to push me off the mountain. Huffing and dripping, we dove into our house and slammed the door on the intruding cold.

"Now that's a winter storm," Angus said as he flung snow off his hair.

"I think I'm going to need you to warm me up."

His seductive smile sent tingles down my spine. We raced to the bed, and he did his level best to create a fire in me that burned for hours.

Later, spent and happy, he fell asleep. Frightened of the howling wind and pelting snow, I cuddled against his side. I rested my head on his ribs and listened to the steady pounding of his heart. If only I could stay cocooned in his arms forever, I wouldn't have to face my family or the threat of red velvet ever again.

The next thing I knew, I woke screaming.

Angus held my shoulders. "Vera. Wake up. It's all right, dearest."

I blinked. His skin was smooth and unmarred by raw red rashes. I choked out a strangled cry of relief and wrapped my arms around him. I squeezed him against my frantic heart while outside white flakes swirled through darkness.

"It's not real." He gathered me onto his lap. "It was another dream."

I kissed him below his ear. "I won't lose you." *I won't.*

"You couldn't be rid of me even if you wanted."

Chills carpeted his skin when I flicked his earlobe with my tongue. "Promise me, Angus."

"With all my heart."

I only wished saying the words made them true.

***

It snowed the next day, and the next. Bear's scowl deepened as the snow built in the mountain passes. I threw myself into training. Bale seemed to understand my need to punch and kick until I couldn't think straight, and welcomed me to his training hall all hours of the day and night. A week after our intended departure date, I woke early from another nightmare. I kissed Angus's unblemished face and headed outside.

Fear clung to me like the cold.

Bale wasn't at the training yard, but a few warriors who'd arrived early had turned on the lights. They worked on sword technique in the corner. I headed straight for the hanging bags near the boxing ring. As I wrapped my wrists and knuckles, tears formed.

No. No more crying.

I grit my teeth and jabbed at the heavy leather bag filled with sand.

Angus was going to be fine.

Punch.

Bear and Naira were going to get the vaccine.

Hit. Hit.

My family was going to be happy to see me.

Kick. Jab.

Koda wasn't going to incite a rebellion against the Grays.

Punch. Punch. Punch. Punch. Punch. Punch.

I didn't stop. If I stopped, I might've had to focus on that last lie, or the one before it. I might've had to focus on how powerless I was to protect Angus. If I stopped, fear would win. I ignored the pain in my arms and shoulders, the screaming in my wrists, and the frantic whine of my thundering heart.

Punch. Punch. Punch. Punch.

"Vera, stop." Strong hands gripped my trembling biceps, pinning my arms.

I thrashed feebly.

"Stop." Gent's voice was a whispered plea.

I crumpled to the floor. He folded next to me. I buried my overheated face in my knees.

"It still hurts."

"I know." Gent's hand rubbed my spine, pushing the darkness back. "I know."

He sat with me for a long, long time.

***

Days bled together in a frozen blur. In some ways, the most pleasant of my life. Hours with Angus. Training with Gent. Visits to Tethra every day. I cradled her. Fed her. She made me feel courage and strength when my monthly bleeding didn't come.

I hesitated to tell Angus, fearing I'd be wrong and bring him disappointment. When I got home that night and smelled Angus's lake trout sizzling in chulip and garlic butter, I knew. I rushed to the lavvy, barely making it before the last bits of my bread-and-bean lunch came out.

"Vera."

I flushed away vomit and washed out my mouth as Angus pushed the lavvy door open the rest of the way.

"The truth is, there's only one man I'd ever want to have a child with."

He halted.

I smiled at his expression, torn between hope and fear. "Yes, I'm still terrified to have a baby. I don't know how to be a good mother. I don't want to bring a child into war."

He softened. "You take superb care of me. At least now that you like me." He winked at my blush. "Why would our child be any different? I promise to protect you, as well as any miniature Vera who might come along, no matter how stubborn she is."

I swooned. "Good, because I'm expecting to hold you to that promise, starting in about seven months."

His face lit up, devastating in his handsomeness and elation. He knelt at my feet. Fingers lifted the hem of my shirt. "Hello, little one," he whispered to my belly. He chuckled. "Wee little one." One of his calloused fingers traced the flat surface.

"That tickles," I said, catching his fingers.

He kissed my stomach.

I squirmed happily. "That tickles even more." His hands gripped my hips, and he looked up at me. Radiant. "I hope she's exactly like you," I said.

"She?"

I shrugged, but my lips curved up into a wide smile.

We took Angus's fish down to Bear and Naira. I wasn't going to eat it. We told them the good news.

Naira kissed me.

Bear cried.

Angus beamed.

I held back vomiting all over their kitchen.

CHAPTER 38

Safe

Tethra had started growing feathers and looked like an awkward teenager. In the warmth of the birdhouse, I approached where she perched on a low tree limb.

"My Vera." She looked me in the eyes. I wasn't sure I'd ever get used to the piercing gaze or intelligent voice.

I picked her up, now the size of a small chicken, and held her close. "Don't poop on me."

"I don't anymore. Unless you deserve."

I smiled. "I'm going down to Belle Borg."

She cocked her head. "South."

"Smart girl."

"When we leave?"

"You can't come. Not yet. Not until your wings grow in. You need to get stronger, and learn more."

"I think poop on you."

I shifted her away from my side, laughing. "No. Don't. It's not my choice."

"Who I poop on?"

I swallowed back my laughter with difficulty. "We'll go together next year."

"I protect you. I watch for liars and enemies. I learn."

"That's excellent." I kissed her fluffy skull. "Good-bye, my Tethra. I'll see you soon."

"Vera stay safe."

***

We left for Belle Borg December tenth. No one was happy about making the trip that late in winter, but red velvet had spread like wildfire through the tent cities near the border of Hogg. Containment had failed. The vaccine was imperative. Speed and a lean traveling party were our allies. Bear planned for a brutal three-day trip consisting of four fighters plus Gent, Angus, and me. Bear asked me if I wanted to stay home. I declined. I wanted to see my blood relations. Father didn't get off that easy.

Three days into the hardest ride imaginable, I regretted my bravado. We'd gotten down from Mount Mary with relative ease. The high snow had been exhausting work for the horses, but the air was dry and sunny. Too sunny. By the time we'd traveled into the flatlands, we were forging slushy mud soup. With each step, Pearl's hooves pulled free with a loud suck. Sweat coated her back despite the chill.

"I'm sorry, girl." I patted her neck with a mittened hand.

She was too tired to respond. She plodded slow as a human walked. I slipped off her back and landed with a squish. Mud coated my boots. How different from the girl who came this way seven months ago. If Lanie could see me now.

She'd see me soon enough, and I didn't think she was going to like what she saw.

"Everything a-rite?" Bear asked from several paces ahead.

I nodded. "I'm going to walk. I won't slow us down."

Bear dismounted his massive gray. "No. It's not ye that's slowing us down." He scowled at the wet road.

I slipped my arm through the reins and strode forward, thinking how nice it felt to walk. The feeling didn't last. Dirt crawled higher up my sore legs. The others walked too, and I distracted myself by chatting with Gent about his favorite books and poems.

"We'll stop here," Bear said, indicating a grassy spot. "Let's hope the temperature drops and this road freezes up."

I had a hard time being genuine in my hope for colder weather. One of the fighters passed around dried rabbit and cold carrots, the best we had under the circumstances. We were supposed to be eating a warm meal at the castle right now. I gave my carrots to a grateful Pearl. The horses munched on dirty grass as the sky darkened. The temperature dropped with the sun. Angus sat on a saddle blanket and leaned against a stump. I snoozed against his chest.

"Let's move," Bear said.

Angus lifted me off his lap, and I stood unsteadily on stiff legs. A rush of cold swirled away Angus's heat. I tightened my coat and adjusted my hood. Silvers and blues shaded the world. An eternity of stars twinkled in the cloudless sky.

"What time is it?"

"You don't want to know," Angus said. He whistled and Coal trotted up, his hooves clacking on the frozen dirt.

When I peed behind the tree, icy wind jolted me fully awake. Pearl had regained a bit of her bounce, and she nipped at my cold nose. Like winter ghosts, we flew across the sleeping lands. As if out of one of Gent's poems, Belle Borg came into view as the sunrise turned the castle a shimmering gold. I swooned with relief. I needed to spend some time indoors.

Angus chuckled. "Was that excitement to see your family?"

Pearl jolted forward, eager for a warm barn and bucket of oats. My mind had been more with my horse. I wanted a shower, clean clothes, and breakfast. My excitement over seeing my family came largely because they brought Angus's protection. Unwelcome memories and feelings filtered in as I remembered how I felt when I'd learned some hard truths.

Father had sold my life for a title. He'd lied to the Grays. He'd lied to me. He'd endangered the stability of the Realm. I didn't think there was anything to say to him that would heal the tear in my heart. He didn't care if people died, and he certainly didn't care about me.

The four euns traveling with us—including Bear's and Angus's imprinted birds—let out shrieks. They tore through the sky to herald our approach and scout for danger.

The head of the castle guard met us at the stable to welcome and inform us that the Wilsons were already here.

CHAPTER 39

Reunion

My family was gathered in the entry hall. I stood stock-still on the threshold, taking them in. The dark circles under Mom's worried eyes. Lanie's hand in Fitz's. The cold set of his jaw. The shock on Lanie's face at my clothing and much-altered appearance. Clearly, she was torn between coming forward and staying in the safety of Fitz's shadow. Interestingly, Father looked the same. Calm and still as a statue. Unchanging. Fake.

Gent bumped into me, nudging me forward, and our wild group dumped into the building. I shifted my furry hood back and unwrapped the scarf stinking of sweat and cold from my nose and mouth.

"Vera." Lanie's too-high squeal cut the air. She took a brave leap forward, away from Fitz, but halted before touching me. Her bright gaze scanned my short hair. Her voice was quiet when she spoke again. "What happened to you?"

"Hi, Lanie. I know I'm disgusting from the ride. I'll shower, and I'll smell better." I forced a smile.

She nodded, but her lips tightened. She looked like she didn't believe me. I wasn't sure whether she'd find a satisfactory sister underneath the grime, but I didn't care. My stomach clenched involuntarily at the tight boning on her bodice and the heavy layers of her skirt, remembering the discomfort.

"Welcome, Chief Bear." Father bowed his head. Had his tone always sounds so smooth and oily? "Daughter. How I have missed you." What a practiced liar.

He held out arms as if to embrace me.

You bastard. My fist, powered by months of training, connected with my father's nose. It buckled with a satisfying crack. Red gushed from both nostrils. He reeled, his hand flying to his bloody face. I tensed, ready to defend myself, but no attack came. I'd shocked the group to such an extent they became immobile. Father blinked in surprise, and his eyes flashed with what I imagined was pride and approval. How could that be? Lanie darted to the protection of Fitz's wing, out of reach of her savage sister.

Bear's hand rested on my posed fist, pressing it down. "Are ye done?"

"Not hardly." I sucked in a ragged breath.

"Well hold off a tick."

Father held a kerchief to his gushing nose.

"Good morning, Hugo," Bear said. "Here's to hoping yer nose turns out half as handsome as mine." Father scowled. "Where's Wolfton?"

"He's too sick to make the trip," Father said.

Bear frowned. "Too sick for messages?"

"Yes."

Mother glided forward and wrapped her arms tightly around my coat. "My baby. I'm glad to see you."

I hugged her back, she felt so thin and frail.

"I've missed you." Her sincerity made Father's unctuous tone all that more apparent.

I wondered if she knew the truth about my marriage and that her life hadn't been in danger.

"You seem to have thrived in Alta Glenn," Father said.

I whirled toward him, and he flinched.

"You lied to me. Forced me away. How could you?" I couldn't keep the pain out of my voice. "Why did you do it?"

"You've grown strong, Vera. Commanding," he said. "I knew you had it in you, waiting to come out. I saw your potential. You're so much more than I could make you." He glowed with pride.

Angus studied Father, his lips drawn down and his brow tight.

My chest heaved up and down. "No." My voice was filled venom. "You betrayed me. Your own daughter."

Father looked me square in the face, blood crusting his lip. "Never. It was for your own good. I knew you'd want this in the end."

I halted, hating that I felt his words twist and writhe inside me. He had an answer for everything, but none of it rang true. He could no more know how I'd feel about living with the Glenns than I did. "I want an eun to test him. Right now."

Angus's eyes widened in surprise.

Bear said, "They don't work on him."

I was shocked that was possible.

Father shrugged innocently. "I always tell the truth."

My nostrils flared as I tried to rein in my frustration. "You could have written more in the seven months since I left."

"I'm sorry, sweet. I've been busy working to make the red velvet vaccine as rapidly as possible. This outbreak must be stopped."

"I know that," I snapped.

"It's a heavy burden on Campbell," Father said.

Fitz spoke for the first time. "There are people who need the vaccine more than others." He sent a meaningful glance in the direction of the Grays.

I balked. Fitz had always been sympathetic to my rebellious dreams. He'd listened to Ian's plans. His loyalties had not changed. He too was a practiced liar. In that moment I saw clearly where I stood. It wasn't on the same side as my family or my old friends. I knew better than to pursue the topic further. I faced Father. "Still you couldn't write?"

"People are dying, Vera," he said.

I choked on grief and rage. "I know that better than you."

"I should've written more than once a month," Father said, his voice apologetic.

"You wrote one letter."

Father looked accusingly at Bear.

Bear didn't look guilty. He and Angus had matching expressions of disapproval. Their heads swiveled back to Father at the same time mine did.

"Not the first time those birds have failed to deliver," Father said.

"*Yer* mail," Bear said.

"You should look into that," Father said.

I was contemplating punching him again when Lanie broke the heavy silence. She never tolerated awkwardness well. "Aren't you going to congratulate us?"

My attention turned to the man at her side who'd watched the exchange with rising interest. I inhaled and smiled. "Congratulations, Fitz. You're a lucky man."

He wrapped an arm around her shoulders and grinned at Lanie. "Yes, I am." For a man who'd professed his attraction to me, he didn't seem at all uncomfortable with having chosen my sister to wed.

"You'll come to the wedding?" Lanie asked.

"Of course. I'm still your little sister." Even if it didn't feel like it anymore.

"There's breakfast in the dining room," Mom said.

"Have the vaccines ready to administer to us after breakfast," Bear ordered.

"Yes, Chief," Father said.

A tiny ripple rolled up Bear's jaw. He knew Father mocked the title.

"Are the remainder packed to travel?" Bear asked.

Father dipped his head. "Five separate pallets, as instructed."

Four would go to the outbreak centers, and one would return to Pinehearth.

"We'll meet in a half hour," Bear said.

It was only after I'd accepted Angus's hand and was entering the hallway leading to the royal suites that I realized I hadn't thought to go with my family. I hadn't seen them for seven months, and it hadn't occurred to me to stay with them. I looked over my shoulder. They stared after me. Mother with longing. Lanie with confusion and disappointment. Fitz with curiosity. Father's face was inscrutable, as always. I forced a shallow smile before turning back in the direction Angus led me. He gave my fingers a little squeeze.

In the short time we had, we showered together and went downstairs clean and smelling like pine soap. My parents and sister stood near the fireplace. I wanted to follow Angus to the table wafting tempting smells my way, but I veered away and embraced Mother and then Lanie. I wore a loose white shirt tucked into worn brown pants and supple leather boots. Lanie's gaze traveled up and down my body like a yo-yo in slow motion. Her fingers tightened on her thick blue bodice.

"You and Fitz," I said.

"I hope you're not mad at me. He was going to be yours before..."

My smile was genuine. "Not at all. I'm happy with my choice."

Mother nodded her approval, as if she could see my contentment. She seemed to relax, and I felt reassured. At least she'd been worried about me.

"It didn't used to be your choice," Lanie said.

"I changed."

"Yes, you have." Lanie nodded as she eyed the length of me again.

I didn't get the impression she was thrilled with the new me. I wanted to tell them about the baby, but the words got stuck in my throat.

"I didn't know about Father," Lanie whispered. She hugged her ribs. "What a horrible thing to do. Cruel. Look at what you've suffered." She glanced at my short hair, tan skin, and riding clothes.

I bit back a retort and looked at Mother.

"He lied to us too," Mother said. "I thought they were going to kill us. I would never have given you up for a title."

"You should've stood up to him. You know he lies to you."

Mother looked abashed. "I know. It's hard for me. I'm sorry. I love him."

Why, I couldn't fathom. "I need your help. Be strong for me. Be strong for yourself." I took off the stone necklace and put it back around Mother's neck. Her eyes filled with tears. "You need this more than I do. It gave me strength, and I thank you for it. Now you need to be like the granite."

She wiped the tears from her eyes. "I will."

I gave her a supportive hug, hoping more than believing she had the backbone necessary to stand up to her husband. This conversation drained me. I wanted to be with Angus. "Have you eaten?" They shook their heads.

We joined the others, and I put my entire focus on cramming as much food as I could down my throat. Lanie looked at me in dismay over her small careful bites.

"Tell us the procedure from here," Bear said.

"Riders are ready to leave now with the pallets," Father said. "I'll show you those first, and we can get them moving this morning. We've set up in the ballroom. Lanie will administer the vaccine to each of you." Father looked at Lanie with pride. "It is best if you then rest today. You should be fine to travel tomorrow, as I'm sure you will wish to get the vaccine back to Pinehearth as quickly as possible."

"Before another blizzard snows us out entirely," Bear said.

"I'm impressed you came when you did. I thought we might not see you until spring."

"Show me the travel pallets." Bear rose. He could destroy Father in a fistfight, but I no longer felt that Bear had all the power. That thought made me nervous.

When I stood to follow, Mother tugged on my sleeve. "Wait a minute."

"I'll catch up," I said to Angus as he and the other Glenns followed my father out.

"I'd like to show you something," Mother whispered. "It'll only take a minute."

Mother fiddled with the stone necklace as she led me through the castle. I ambled at her side, no longer frightened of the stuffed heads or my own shadow.

"What is it?" I asked.

"You'll see." Her eye twitched.

"Where are we going?"

"You'll see." Curiosity kept me following her. She opened a heavy door. "In here."

Something about the quiver in her tone had me looking at her face. She was drawn and pale, her eye sockets deep. Her brown hair had turned nearly completely gray and she'd lost weight. "Are you okay?" When she didn't answer I told her, "I really am happy. Angus is a wonderful man."

Her eyes widened and her face reddened. Her voice was a squeak. "I know what it's like to love your husband in spite of it all."

"What?"

She motioned me into the room. "You'll want to see this."

Still thinking of her odd statement, I ducked into a dimly lit study.

"Wait in here," she said. "I'll be right back." The door shut with a heavy clap, leaving me alone in the office.

"Mother." What in the bloody skies was going on? I leapt to the door, terrified I'd been trapped. Why lock me up? Anxiety ran rampant under my skin. A low voice stopped me cold.

"More beautiful than I remember."

CHAPTER 40

Betrayed

I whirled. Koda stood from his shadowed chair. His full beard failed to hide his impish grin. Shock had me frozen to the spot. He strode over and stopped a hands-width from my face.

"I've missed you."

I tilted back. "You're alive. You're here. How?"

"I came in disguise as your sister's guard. Only your group from Pinehearth would recognize me. The rest of them don't know I'm a fugitive. I'll stay hidden."

Alarm bells went off inside my head. "What are you doing here?"

"I'm finishing what I started and getting what I left behind."

Fear coated my tongue like acid. "What do you have planned?"

"You don't get to help with it this time," he said. "You're a bad liar."

"Thank you."

"You and me, we're Hugo's arrows to kill the Grays."

"What?"

"It seems you've gone a little off course."

Actually, I'd course corrected.

"Hugo is teaching me how to trick the euns. They can never tell he's lying."

"How?"

Koda wagged a finger. I wanted to break it off. "Hugo doesn't want another Ian situation. He learned to be more careful after he lost Ian."

My stomach dropped as realization hit. Ian was Father's man. Father had been hiding a traitor's black heart. How did I not see it earlier?

"Hugo wouldn't have been able to cut from you so easily. We couldn't have you ruining everything."

Father betrayed Ian. He poisoned them. I went numb with horrified shock. He killed our friends. He killed Emilia. I hadn't allowed myself to fully believe it until now.

"Why do you think you didn't get any letters?"

I was so blind.

"I know you're caught in their trap." His fingers caressed my arm. I flinched. "I'll set you free." He licked his lips.

I spoke through clenched teeth. "What do you have planned?"

A horrible grin spread over his bearded face, and I shuddered. He needed to tell me now or I'd punch his teeth out.

"The chief and his runt aren't getting the vaccine. Right about now, they're getting injected with the live red velvet virus. Good as dead."

Fire ignited in my chest and spread through my body. A whine like that of a dying animal came up my throat.

"A large pallet of the disease is headed to Pinehearth to take care of the rest of the chattel. Good thing our next chieftess is here and ready to take control after such a tragedy."

Father had planned this from the beginning. He planted me on the throne for this exact moment. I'd never be *his* chieftess pawn.

I was a Gray.

I inched toward the door as I tried to take in Father's web of lies. He'd skewed my vision so completely, I never saw him for who he really was. He'd even set Ian to filling my head with rebellion before killing him and his whole family.

Koda gripped my arm. "You'll stay here with me. I'm not allowed to let you out for another hour." He licked his lower lip. "I know how we can pass the time."

I wanted to vomit, but I didn't have the time. I had to get to that ballroom. I had to stop that needle. I hit Koda's hand.

He tightened his grip, and his eyes hardened. "Let's not fight, love."

My free fist slammed into this nose.

He reeled back. Blood stained his beard. I chopped his hand off my arm and dove for the door. His arms wrapped my chest from behind. I elbowed him in the ribs.

"I don't want to hurt you," he said.

I responded with a bang of the back of my head into his already bleeding nose.

He let out a strangled cry, loosening his hold. I jerked around and popped his left eye. My boot sank into his stomach. He folded. I kicked him in the lower back, and he dropped against the chair, wheezing.

"You always did underestimate me."

I whirled to the door and sucked in a relieved breath when it opened.

CHAPTER 41

Killer

Angus. Please let there be time. I knocked over a vase and banged against a painting in my frenzy. Which way? I halted for a moment, choosing to go left. Wrong. I stormed back, my heart beating triple time. I would make it. I had to make it. I pushed all visions of my real family's death away. Up ahead, light spilled out of the ballroom. They hadn't even had enough shame to close the door on their murder.

I skidded to a stop and peered inside. Father and the Glenns crowded around a single chair. Facing my direction, Angus sat shirtless in the chair next to Lanie, who perched on a stool by a small table of supplies. Angus looked nervously down at the cleansing cloth she wiped over his muscled arm.

Time slowed as my body shifted into its highest gear. Lanie held the syringe up in her right hand. I charged toward her. Father saw me first, and his mouth fell open in shock. The needle tilted down.

I dove, screaming, "No."

Lanie jerked in surprise and pressed down on the syringe. The needle jolted forward, oozing yellow poison.

My palm shot out.

The needle pierced my skin and dug into the back of my hand. White-hot pain seared along my nerves. I pulled my hand away from Angus's arm. The needle quivered where Lanie had left it deep in my tendons. I cupped my wrist, grit my teeth, and howled.

I'd landed partially on Angus's leg. His hand gripped my hips, lifting me back to my feet. His eyes were wide as silver platters.

"It's the live disease." My voice was a strangled cry.

Confirming my words, Father grabbed a needle and jabbed it into Bear's leg. Bear twisted in terror.

"No." Angus's cry was pure agony.

Not Bear.

The chief whipped out his short sword and sliced it across my traitorous father's neck.

Lanie put her hands up, with a look of bewilderment and surrender. A Glenn jumped to her side. He yanked her from her seat and twisted her hands behind her back.

I tried to discern if she was lying, but the pain blocked out all reason. I plucked the needle out of my hand with a hiss and dropped it on the table. Angus was on his feet and reaching for me.

"Don't touch me." I stepped back, my vision flickering. My hand was an inferno.

A look of sheer agony fixed on Angus's face as his hand dropped to his side.

He was safe. It was all that mattered.

Fighting the roaring pain, I looked into his eyes. "I love you, dear husband." My vision blacked, and my strength failed. I dropped like a stone.

Waves of pain woke me. Angus, wearing his shirt and palming a gun, peered down at me, worry ripe in his expression. I lay cradled in Gent's lap on the ballroom floor.

"You think you're immune now," I said weakly.

"Yes," Gent said. "She already gave me the shot. I'm tougher than you, that's all."

I coughed out a sad little chuckle.

"But, I'll admit it hurts like a hundred hornets." He tilted his chin down and gave me a small smile.

"You and me again," I said. "Fighting death."

"We'll both make it through."

Not Bear.

Gent held me tighter. "Promise me, little sister."

I nodded weakly, glad to call him family. Lanie had nearly killed Angus. Father's lifeless body leaked red onto the parquet floor. "Is Lanie dead?"

"No. She's being held for questioning."

Good. The birds would know. Lanie was not a practiced liar. I needed the truth.

"How did you know?" Angus asked from where he hovered over us, careful not to get too close.

I forced myself to sit up, bumping Gent's chin. "Koda is here. My mother took me to him. He told me their plan, boasting and expecting me to join them. The pallet for Pinehearth has the live disease too."

Angus jerked to action. He called two of the Glenns.

"It needs to be destroyed," I said.

He turned from his march to the door. "It will, Vera. I won't spare Koda either."

"Please don't." He blinked. "But, please don't kill my mother."

His jaw rippled in anger, but he said with a soft voice, "Of course not."

"Be careful."

"Get better."

I nodded.

Angus and two soldiers disappeared into the hall.

Where was Bear?

A woman came through the door. "I've been vaccinated and will be taking care of you. Are you well enough to follow me?"

Gent helped me to my feet. Still dizzy, I leaned heavily on him as we trudged to our second quarantine.

CHAPTER 42

Agony

Bear lay on a large plush bed. I rushed to his side. The pain in my hand had dulled to a low throb.

"I'm so sorry." I knelt on the floor next to the bed where a woman had cut Bear's pant leg enough to reveal the small hole where death had entered his body.

"Thank ye for saving my son. Again." Bear spoke with tenderness. He put a heavy palm on my head, and I leaned into his touch. "He is the world to me, and so are ye, daughter. I would not have wanted you to see yer da die like that."

Tears spilled down my cheeks. Father had tried to kill Angus, and the worst part was he probably thought it was what I wanted. He probably thought he was saving me. "It's my fault."

"Leave the blame with the killers, Vera." His rough hands squeezed my shoulder. "You will make a great chieftess. Yer a strength to the Grays and to the United Realm. You've made me proud, daughter. Take good care of Angus and Naira. Tell my grandchildren about me. I give you permission to embellish."

"You're going to live. You can beat this."

He gave me a warm smile. "Aye, I will fight, but I am an old man now. I know the odds." He unbuckled his belt and put the holstered revolver in my palm, not touching my wound. "Be careful. It's loaded."

My hands shook, but I drew the gun closer. Knowing that I might need it, and hating that fact. I buckled the weapon around my hips.

"Aim true."

"I won't be blinded again."

"I have great faith in you."

Gent knocked on the open doorframe. Sadness darkened his usually bright face. Tears rimmed his eyes. "Can I do anything for you, my chief?"

Bear blinked rapidly. "This is a fight I face alone."

"Not alone," I said. "We're with you." Bear squeezed my arm, but his face remained somber. "I'll have my bed brought in here."

"No, you won't," he said with a growl. "I have a nursemaid. Angus needs ye. I won't have you here. Now kiss me good-bye and remember me as strong, healthy, and painfully handsome." I burst into tears and buried my face in his thick shirt. He patted my back and when he spoke again, it was with tenderness. "I love you, Vera. I wouldn't have given Angus to anyone else."

I lifted my head.

"Your da was crafty, but I'm no fool. I saw the diamond he offered for what she was." He lifted my chin. "A chieftess."

"I love you, Father."

Bear gave me a heartbreaking smile before motioning Gent over for a less tearful good-bye.

I kissed his stubbly cheek. "Fight hard," I whispered.

He nodded and waved us out. Gent put his arm around my shoulders. I leaned heavily on him as we prepared to cross the hall to the rooms set up for us.

If Koda had been in my sights, I wouldn't't've hesitated to pull the trigger.

"Da." Angus's heartbreaking cry shattered the silence.

I jerked up my head to see my husband tearing into his father's room. A guard tried to pull him back, but Angus threw him off with a rough shove.

Bear covered his wounded leg with a cloth, and the woman threw a heavy blanket over Bear's body, smothering the contagions. Still it was too risky.

"Angus, no," I called out.

He didn't acknowledge me as he knelt reverently at Bear's side, his expression full of anguish. The servants and guards retreated, no longer trying to stop him.

Bear held out a palm. His hold on Angus's hand seemed to both push his son away and pull him close. Their fingers blotched red and white as they gripped each other. As if they could hold on tight enough. If they were only strong enough.

Bear let go with a sigh. He rested a palm, nicked with scars and callouses, on Angus's head. Angus bowed low. His forehead pressing into the bed at Bear's side.

Watching was torture.

"Da." He sounded like a frightened little boy. "I need you. You can't leave me. I can't." He swallowed audibly.

Bear chuckled. "Ye've never said those words before." Angus lifted his head. "Don't start now."

"But the Churrys. A war. Red velvet. Campbell."

"Aye, there will always be problems. With Naira and Vera, you'll work through them one at a time, and more will pop up. They always do."

Tears poured down Angus's face.

Bear gripped the side of his son's corded neck. "I love you, son. I am so proud of—" A throaty sob cut off the sentence.

I clung to Gent as pain tore through my heart. The need to go to Angus nearly overwhelmed me. Blood caked my hands. Blood that would kill Angus while I offered him little comfort. Gent and I dragged each other from the room.

A woman waited for us. "You'll be released after two symptom-free days." She motioned me to my plush prison. "I'll have lunch brought up."

"Don't bother." My stomach had turned to acid. I put a hand to my low belly, still too early to swell. *Please be okay, little one.*

The afternoon dragged on. I heard nothing about Lanie, Mother, or Koda. I got a fever that night and woke sweating and afraid. Monsters with bloody fangs and eun's claws appeared in the shadows. I screamed. The visions dissolved as Gent's solid frame filled the door.

"You all right, sister?"

I trembled and managed to croak out, "I'm so sorry I woke you."

He came forward and leaned over me.

"Don't touch me. I'm burning up." He picked up my unhurt hand. "You don't feel cold." I touched his brow. "You're as hot as I am."

Gent lay on the bed. We griped our hands tight, holding on to each other like lifelines.

"The dreams aren't real." He spoke from experience. My brave brother. "Try to sleep." He closed his eyes, and I did the same.

Over and over, I woke with a shout. Each time, Gent's hand tightened on mine, drawing me out of the abyss.

"I'm here, sister. We're safe. We're going to be okay."

The night was eternal. So was the next day. The next night the bleeding started.

It wasn't red velvet.

It was the baby.

I sat up in bed with a painful start. Blood oozed through the blanket, painting me red with my little one's death.

Gent's eyes widened. "Sister?" His voice quivered with fear.

"It's not red velvet."

He nodded in understanding.

"Help me to the lavvy."

His sweaty hand gripped mine. Dizzy and weak, I climbed to my feet. Another painful throb took me, and I doubled over. Gent caught my fall. Together we hobbled into the small lavvy. Blood trickling down my legs as we stood there.

"What can—?"

"Leave me."

"Let me help you."

"No."

Gent set me on the wooden stool next to the tub. "I'll be right outside the door."

"Thank you."

He hesitated a moment longer before dragging his fevered frame out.

I sank to the floor writhing in agony as I descended into a bottomless pit of despair. Throbbing in pain and shaking with fever, life spilled from my body. I cried as I peeled off my pants. I couldn't look at the bloody mass.

Gent's raspy voice carried through the door. "I'm so sorry, Vera."

I tried to rein in my sobs, but the tears kept coming. It took me a long time to shower. Pink water swirled down the drain. I left my old clothes where they were on the floor and put on new ones that had been left by a thoughtful servant.

Feeling like a frail, hollow shell of myself, I opened the door. Gent was slumped in a chair, his chin on his chest, but his eyes alert.

Seeing him, tired and sick but grieving for me, tears filled my eyes again and ran down my cheeks.

He jerked from his seat. His arms were around me as he guided me to the bed he'd stripped of the bloody sheet. We lay down together. I placed my head on his chest, and he put his hand on my shoulder. I cried myself to oblivion.

When I emerged from the painful haze, I found Gent sleeping soundly next to me. I sat up, my body weak, but my mind clear.

The sun peeked over the distant hills. I patted my body and felt my clothing, damp with sweat, sticking to me. I shuffled to the table and gulped water. The cool moisture relieved me. After I showered, I found Gent awake and lucid.

"I'd be happy not to do that a third time," he said.

"Agreed."

The nurse entered and brightened when she saw us. "You look wonderful."

That was a relative term.

"Hungry?" she asked.

"Starving," he said.

"Get as clean as you can and into your new clothes." She pointed to the stack on the dresser. "We'd like to move you."

Dread and suspicion had me ready to use my gun. "Why?"

"Bear's taken a bad turn, and we'd like to have you farther down the hall."

"Have the spots appeared?"

"A few, yes." It didn't matter how many. It was over for the chief. "I'm sorry," she said quietly.

Hugo had killed the ruler of the United Realm. A man dearer to me than the traitor who I'd called Father.

The nurse brought more bad news. Koda had escaped. Again. This time, I would find him. He would pay for Bear's death, and my child's. The eun had determined Lanie was telling the truth. She was innocent. She'd had no knowledge of the murderous schemes. She, like all of us, was no more than an instrument in Father's grand plan.

Thanks to all that is good in the world she was free to go home, and had left already with Fitz to return to Campbell.

Wolfton was dead. Poisoned. A contingent of Glenns had been sent to control Campbell until new leadership could be instituted, and the red velvet labs were cleansed of disease.

What a horrible, wasteful mess.

It seemed the treachery in Campbell ran deeper than I thought. Though our family had ruled there for centuries, I didn't think Lanie was up to the task. She couldn't tell a traitor from a friend, and she certainly could never suss out a liar. We needed to stabilize an important part of our United Realm. *Our.* A lot had changed in seven months.

"What about my mother?" I asked the nurse.

She hesitated. In that moment, I knew. I sucked in a sharp breath. How much loss could a body endure?

"I'm so sorry." The nurse lifted a hand that had been tucked in her apron. She dropped Mother's granite pendant into my hands along with a folded piece of paper.

I unfolded the note. Sitting next to me, Gent read it at the same time I did.

Vera. I'm sorry. Her writing was messy, the ink splattered.

The parchment fluttered from my shaking fingers. "Tell me."

The nurse swallowed. "Poison. They found her body in her suite. The necklace and note were on the table next to the empty vial."

I clutched at my chest as pain spread over my chest. I couldn't breathe. Gent wrapped me in his long arms. I sagged into his embrace, and listened to his steady heartbeat. He held me until the agony dulled.

Gent was alive. Angus was well. All was not lost. I leaned back, rubbing at my face.

"Shall I stay with you?" he asked.

I shook my head.

He kissed my brow before following the nurse to his own room.

I spent the next two days in silent grief, drawing and thinking about the uncertain future for the place I used to call home.

I wanted to be with Angus so much I ached with want. When I was released from my cell, I had a stack of portraits, tributes to the great chief Bear Gray, and a smaller stack of my mother, but none of Hugo.

He was no longer my father.

CHAPTER 43

War

"Angus." I tore down the hall at full speed.

My love picked me up in his arms and twirled me. He pinned me against the wall and nuzzled his face into my neck.

"Stop doing that to me," he whispered roughly, his lips brushing my skin as he spoke, sending heat down my spine. His mouth found mine, and he kissed me until I was dizzy. His hands roamed my body. He seemed to be trying to hold all of me at once.

"I'd do it again for you," I told him through my lips still pressed against his.

He pulled back enough that I could see the joy and relief in his eyes. "I love you." He cupped my head. "Dear wife." He spoke with an intensity I'd never heard from him.

A grin spread over my lips. "I love you, dear husband."

Every question I wanted to ask fell out of my brain when he kissed me again. My body ignited and my focus narrowed to Angus, who was my entire world. My life. My home.

He carried me to our room, and as he started to undress me, I took his hands, stopping him. "My love." My voice was a mere rasp. "Our baby did not survive the trauma."

Color drained from his face. "Oh, Vera." His palm cradled my low belly with tenderness. "I'm so sorry."

A tear escaped out of the corner of my eye. "Me too. I didn't know I cared so much."

His hand lifted from my belly and cupped my face. "I wasn't there for you." Broad shoulders curved forward, and his head hung heavy.

"I thought of you the whole time. Knowing you were healthy and waiting for me gave me strength. I wasn't alone. Poor Gent took the brunt of my tears. I think I've scarred him for life."

Angus's ribs expanded with each ragged breath. "That should've been me." The pain in his voice shredded me.

He gathered me close and we cried together.

When our tears subsided, I pushed back so I could see his handsome face. My husband, a man filled with honor and goodness. "In a couple of weeks, I'll be healed and we'll enjoy trying again." I raked my fingers through his hair and kissed him again for emphasis.

"I look forward it." He made an effort to get me to smile by wiggling his brows.

Despite the ache in my heart and my womb, hope trickled in like sunlight after a storm.

We coiled around one another on the bed and watched soft snow shift through the gray sky as grief pulled at my belly.

"I want to start over," I murmured. He lifted his head and looked down at me, clearly confused. "This marriage. I was terrible to you. I'm so sorry. I feel awful about how we were those first few months."

"I forgave you long ago." His arm wrapped around my waist and he tugged me closer. "I love you."

"I love you too. And I always will." I melted into him as he pressed his lips to my temple.

Closing my eyes, I breathed in the scent of forest and rain.

***

We had barely finished getting dressed for dinner when a knock came at the door.

"Come," Angus called out.

Gent swept in. His brow furrowed and eyes pinched. A chill settled over me.

"News." A tremor ran through Gent's voice. "The Churrys landed in Porto. Thirty-eight warships. They've taken over NewGate and have Chamberlain Marsh, his wife, and Misty hostage. Casualty reports are still coming in, but it doesn't look good."

Angus's face drained of color. "Any word from Maw?"

"We expect her to arrive in three days for Bear's funeral and tribute. We've sent additional messages about the Churrys, but we haven't heard back from the chieftess."

"Gather the team here. We'll meet in the south study in ten minutes." Gent darted out. Angus didn't move, his body rigid. I stepped to his side. "How can I..." he stuttered. "Father would know what to do. How to..." He stumbled under the weight of war.

"Bear has taught you well, my love." I grabbed his hand and squeezed. "He believed in you, and so does Naira. So do I." I put my arms around his waist. "We'll take it one step at a time."

"I need to take an army to Porto."

"I'm coming with you. I'll fight for our lands, same as you."

"Not quite the same." Angus sent me a sly grin, his color returning.

I pursed my lips.

He kissed them lightly. When he pulled away, his eyes were dark and pained. "We're going to war. We need to reinstate a new chamberlain in Campbell, end the rebellion, find Koda, and get the vaccine to stop the disease."

Instead of collapsing under the weight of the overwhelming onslaught of problems, I took his face in my hands and kissed him, long and deep. In a tangle of tongues, I gave him the full ferocity of my feelings for him.

With tingling lips, I pulled away. I wanted to fall into his deep gaze and disappear from every care and pain. Instead, I set my jaw and did all I could to feed him strength.

"One step at a time. We'll figure it out. It's going to be all right." I believed what I told him. I had to believe it in order to keep both of us from surrendering to the enormity of what we faced.

"How do you know?"

"You're strong and smart, and I'll be at your side." I held his handsome face in my hands. "Together we will protect the realm."

The vulnerability in his eyes hardened to determination. His laid his hand over mine and tugged it down between us, lacing our fingers together. "Come, my chieftess."

I nodded. "We have a realm to save."

"Together," he said against my lips.

"Then home." I yearned for our house on the hill. For the town of Pinehearth. For our friends. Our family.

Angus led me forward to face our future, to fight for an inheritance for our children. Together, we would return to our haven nestled in the beauty of the mountains and keep all that was ours safe.

And loved.

ABOUT THE AUTHOR

Mary believes humans are born to create, and promotes creativity in all its beautiful forms. She's learning calligraphy and watercolor. She loves exploring our magnificent planet and finding all the best places to eat around the world. But nothing beats coming home and sharing a pot of slow-simmered spaghetti Bolognese and homemade sourdough with friends and family. If she's not in her writing chair, you'll probably find her hiking in her local Utah mountains with her husband and four children.

Mary loves hearing from her readers.
Website: marybeesley.com
Blog: marybeesley.com/blog
IG: @maryrbeesley
Twitter: @MaryRBeesley
Pinterest: pinterest.com/maryjolley
LinkedIn: linkedin.com/in/maryjolley
FB: facebook.com/MaryBeesleyAuthor

Made in the USA
Las Vegas, NV
03 December 2020

11959430R00144